Gray Sunshine

by G. Joyce Rodstan

To my Best friend
Rose Mary
G. Joyce Rodstan

PITTSBURGH, PENNSYLVANIA 15238

RoseDog Books
585 Alpha Drive, Suite 103
Pittsburgh, PA 15238
Visit our website at www.rosedogbookstore.com

ISBN: 978-1-4809-7870-6
eISBN: 978-1-4809-7892-8

This book is dedicated to
Lonzell Stanton Jr.
and Mr. Clyde D. Rodgers.

Gray Sunshine

This is a story of a young girl that had to grow up too fast. Mary found herself at an early age, being called a "Nigger" by a prejudiced white woman. She asked her parents, "What was a "Nigger"? Because the white lady told her she was one. They told her only stupid and silly people would call her that name.

Mary was allowed to quit school during her second year. Her parents sent her away to live with a white family for two years. She learned how to speak the way they spoke. She was very much afraid, while she was there. Being left along in an unlocked room, she was afraid that she would be attacked by some man during the night, because Mr. Black had his male friends coming in and out of the house.

The Black had two daughters that Mary had to clean up after. Mary had to work outside the home, since the age of nine. She was a mother to her younger brother and sister. She met her husband at the age of nineteen. They were married on his twentieth birthday. This young man was going to be her hero. Until the day he slapped her face, for not having his dinner ready. After this incident, he never laid hands on her again.

They moved from Comb City to Pascagoula, Mississippi, a few months after her father's death. This was a new beginning for her family. No one had to draw water from wells. They had running water and gas in their new home.

You will notice the change in grammar. Mary spoke somewhat different from her husband and the generation before her. You will also find her children's grammar different from her's. The changes can be somewhat confusing to the reader.

The one thing, she and her husband Emerson wanted was for each of their children to have a college education. Mary prayed to God, that she lived to raise her children. She did lived to raised seven children.

Thanks be to God, the older ones were able to help their father rear the younger three.

Chapter One

Mary Lee's Birth

There was a deep blanket of snow covering the small town of Romestown, Mississippi. Snow was everywhere. This has been the coldest winter anyone could remember. Rabbits were hopping about looking for prey. The limbs on the trees were frozen with ice. Some of which had already fallen to the ground. At the bottom, of the hill was a three room shack surrounded by unblossomed rose bushes that was so pretty in the summer, now has the look of death.

Inside the shack, lived a very tall, handsome, bow-legged young man with his beautiful brown-skinned, long-haired fifteen-year-old wife. They were married eighteen months ago, and were now expecting their first child. They had agreed if the baby was a boy, they were going to name him Sam Ginn Jr., and if it was a girl, they would name her Mary Lee. Idana had made gowns out of old sheets and knitted pink booties. She was sure she was going to give birth to a girl..Sam on the other hand, just wanted a healthy baby. When he met Idana, it was love at first sight. He asked her mother, Amy Bridges, if he could marry her thirteen year old daughter. Her answer was NO. Three days later, he returned for a second time, with a twenty-dollar bill, she then said, YES. Amy needed the money. She was raising six children by herself. Her husband, Clyde Bridges, had been sent to prison, before Idana was born for stealing a white man's horse. A week after he was gone, Amy started to keep company with Mr. James, Mr. Robinson, and Mr. Taylor. So she never knew if Idana was her husband's child of one of the other men.

She met Mr. James on Monday nights, Mr. Taylor on Wednesday nights, and Mr. Robinson on Friday nights. Idana could have been her husbands, or one of the other three men. So Idana never knew who her father was.

Today, Sam was out in his old mule-wagon selling wood. The mule-wagon was in poor operative condition. He spent most of his day putting on the front wheel back on the wagon. It kept coming off. Most of his customers did not have money to pay for the wood. Sam's policy was. NO MONEY, NO WOOD. His shoes had holes. The holes had been padded with cardboard. The weather was getting colder. So he decided to return home with his mule named Dan. As he was getting out of the wagon, he heard Idana crying for help. He ran through the doorway, tilting his head, "Wife, what be wrong?" "Sam ize hurtin real bad, I think I be gone have my baby!" "Hurry-up and go git Miss Annie." He picked up his small wife and put her in the bed, covering her with a heavy quilt, which she had wrapped around her body. Her hair had fallen over her face and shoulders. He could no longer see her face. He pulled her hair back and ran out of the door leaving Dan behind.

When he arrived at Miss Annie's house, Mr. Eddie answered the door. "Annie, who that be?" "It be that Ginn." "Come on in boy, you must be freezing." Miss Annie was a very large woman. She was as round as she was tall. She took one look at Sam and broke out in laughter. "Boy, you look like a mule done kicked you in ya behind." "How did you git here?" "Ize run all the way." "Eddie, git that boy some dry shoes." "Miss Annie, its my wife, Idana. "She says she be hurtin." "Ize gitting ma coat." As they pulled into Sam's yard, Big Annie grabbed her bag running as fast as she could. She ran past Sam to Idana's bedside. Idana looked up and saw Miss Annie, "Miss Annie, I think I be gone die." "Do you think I be gone die, I hurt real bad." " Shore, you hurt." "But is I gone die?" Idana asked her again. "Hush that pretty little mouth of yourn." "Big Annie ain't lose no mama or baby in thirty years." "And I don't think ize gone lose you." Within fifteen minutes, her baby girl was born. She was a healthy eight pound, two ounce baby. After Miss Annie cleaned Idana and te baby, she called Sam and Mr. Eddie. Sam held his baby girl and said to Miss Annie, "why she be so white?" "Don't you know all babies look like that when they born?" said Miss Annie Idana looked at Sam. "The baby is the same color as your pa, he look like he be white."

A few months later seeing the baby was still light, he became very jealous of Idana thinking of the history concerning her mother. He began plowing around the house everytime he went into town, to see if any man's footprints was there when he returned. Idana became afraid of her husband. One day she confronted him. "Sam, you think ize be like my mama?" Ize love you wit all my heart. You beez good to me." "And Ize love you too, wife." "But I kill any man who puts his hands on YOU." "Sam you got to trust me or me and the baby will leave YOU." "Wife you know I be done had lots of women in the past, but you be the only one I ask to mer me." "Please don't be talkin that crazy talk." "Wife I reckoned I hush my mouth." "Don't worry yourself, I ain't gone git myself in no trouble." "You just stay here with me." "Well, I guess I be wit you, until the day one of us die." There wasn't any conversation concerning her leaving him again.

Sam's wood selling business had gotten slow. he hardly had enough money to buy milk for the baby. He came home early one afternoon, and told Idana he had heard of a man by the name of Jerry Holcome, who had a large farm and cotton field, and he needed cotton pickers. He told her that he was going to see Mr. Jerry the next day to see if he would hire him and pay him well. "Sam, she said,"What is we gone do with our land?" "We gone keep it, wife." "White folks don't have to know we own our land. All I want to do is work.fer Mr. Holcome, make the money, come back here, and plant my own cotton field and have people work fer me."

Chapter Two

The Move to the Holcome's

On the day of the move to the Holcom's plantation, Sam and Idana loaded the wagon with their belongings along with little Mary Lee and her white dog and black cat. Mary Lee called the dog, Dog and the cat, Cat. The sun was high in the sky and the tall trees shaded the road for almost twnty miles. As they were driving along, Mary Lee began to sing, "Yes Jesus Loves Me". Idana joined in, "Hush mama you can't sing that song." "Why not Mary Lee?" "You said jesus loves me, not you." "Mary Lee, Jesus loves everybody." "Even my daddy, mama?"

"What about my daddy?' 'Yes, him too." "Okay, mama you can sing wit me." Sam was laughing to himself. Without warning, Idana was falling out of the wagon. Mary Lee started to cry verv loudly. "Daddy, daddy" He caught her just in time. "What's wrong wit you, wife?" Idana was out like a light. Poor Sam didn't know what to do. His baby was crying and his wife had fainted. He pulled to the side of the road and began to pray. A few minutes later, Idana was back. She was still very weak. They was only a few blocks away from Mr. Holcome's place.

Mr. Holcome and his father was standing in the front yard. As Sam drove speedily into the yard, Idana was on the floor of the wagon. Mr. Holcome and his father walked closer to the wagon and saw Idana lying on the floor of the wagon. Old Mr. Holcome said, "Jerry, who are these people? "Paw, this is the boy I told you about." "Boy, what's wrong with that gal?' "She be sick?' 'Jerry, look like we got a sick nigger on our hands." The field workers came out of the cotton field to see what the commotion was about, Zeb, Mr. Holcome's flunkie told the field workers to get back to work. He said he will take care of everything and let them know the outcome. They all returned to work as told. Mr. Holcome told Zeb, "Go fetch Dr. Owens and see what he has to say about this girl." "Thankyou, Mr. Holcome. I pay the bill." "Keep your money, Boy," "You owe me nothin." "As much whiskey I buy for him, he will be glad to come." Zeb rode one of the horse into town and brought back Dr. Owens. Mr. Jerry and his wife, Nancy had taken Sam and Idana into the house they were going to rent. This was one of the most nicest places they had ever lived in. After the doctor examined Idana, he told them she had been overcomed by heat. "Just give her plenty of water and let her rest for a few days."

Betty, the Holcomes cook, had taken Mary Lee into the kitchen, as she was told by Mrs. Nancy Holcome, who loved everyone. Betty was holding Mary Lee's hand. "Stop crying." "Your mama got you dress just like a little white girl. "Well, I ain't white!" Betty ain't say you be white, but you shore is pretty. Mary Lee stopped crying. "Where is my daddy?" "He say he is gone come get me." "He is child, just wait here wit Betty.' Sam came for Mary Lee within an hour after the doctor had left. Miss Nancy asked Sam if Mary Lee could play with her daughter, Sally for a little while, and if he could bring her back tomorrow, that would be fine.

The next day was Tuesday, Sam took Mary Lee to play with Sally. Idana stayed in the bed as the doctor ordered. She dranked plenty of water and ate a small amount of food. As she began to feel better, Sally and Mary Lee was becoming friends. Cat and Dog had made the move with them and was running about freely. Mary Lee called out for Cat and Dog to play with them Sally thought that was funny." Mary, why don't you call Cat, Kitty?" "Okay", said Mary Lee. "Can my dog still be Dog?" "Yes, he can.', said Sally. "Mary, why is your hair red?" "Cause it is." "Why is your hair yellow?'Cause it is.' The girls had lots of fun that day.

When Sam came home from the cotton fields each day, he brought Mary Lee with him. Idana was now up and about. Mr. Holcome came over and told Sam he was doing a good job. When Sam picked cotton, he was being watched by Mr. Holcome. Mr. Holcome said to Sam, "Boy, you pick cotton like that John Henry." "Who he be, Mr. Holcome?" "Don't tell me you have never heard the story? "Well, he was the nigger man who out ran the choo-choo train and died at the end of the race." "Of course, you know that is a tall tale."

"How long have you been picking cotton, Boy? "Well, Sir, Mr. Jerry, since I was knee-high to a duck. "Boy, you got a way of saying things." "I like that about you and that is the truth." Zeb was picking cotton a few rows over and could hear everything being said. As soon as Mr Holcome left, he called to Sam. "Hey Sam, he ain't mean what he say." "I have to watch all us folks and let him know whats going on." "He said if I don't, he'll have Long Tall Joe and Big Steve beat me. "Man, I believe you is lyin." But Zeb was telling the truth. Even Betty's husband, Roy told him how he treated some of the Negroes. Roy did not have any problems with him, because he was his half-brother. Some of the Negroes said he had been there all his life.and other Negroes before him. "If this is the truth, I tell you ain't no Negro or no White man gone put his hands on Sam Ginn, or his wife or baby." "I kill him and nobody will find his body." Roy looked at Sam eye to eye. "Boy, I know you mean what you say." "But don't you say that ever again!" "Them whitefolks will hang you!" "I say that to you." "I be hopin you ain't gone be tellin nobody, cause I do mean it!

Sam never had any trouble with Mr. Holcome or anyone else. Idana loved his wife, Miss Nancy. She never worked the fields. Miss Nancy asked Idana if she knew how to cook. "Yes, ma'am, I do." "Can you come over during the day with that pretty little girl for a few hours and help Betty cook?' Idana came with Mary Lee each day. One day, Betty caught Idana spitting in a pot of beans. "What you doin, gal?" "You see me, don't let them white people see you!" "Cause I done did if before myself. The only thing is I feel bad when I see Miss Nancy, Sally, and the boys eat it. But, I don't care if Mr. Jerry or his daddy eat it." "Sam said he be nice to him, Betty. He be nice to Roy and Long Tall Joe." "I tell you what Idana, he shore do like Negro women, like his daddy did." "Hush, Betty, Miss Nancy is a comin in the front door." Miss Nancy came in pushing her long-blonde hair out of her face. "What is it you girls are talking about?" "Look like y'all is having a good time." "Idana would you mind helping the boys with their school lessons today?" "My friend Edna is coning for lunch with her little boy, George. I need Mary with me, if you don't mind?" "Yes, ma'am."

Mary Lee and Sally were playing in the front yard, when her friend Edna drove up in her pretty black car. The girls ran over to see the tall, thin lady with her black curly hair. "Nancy, who nigger child is that?" "You girls go back to where you were playing." "Edna, please don't call that child a nigger. Mary

Lee didn't know what the word "nigger'meant. George asked his mother if he could play with the girls. "No, George, you cant play with that nigger." "What's a nigger, mama?" He pulled away and ran where the girls were playing. He never seen long braids before, so he pulled Mary Lee's hair. Mary Lee Smacked his hand. "Nancy, did you see that nigger hit my boy?" "Edna, I told you, she is a child!" "Nancy you a nigger lover. "Everyone says that you are "I'm taking my boy home and giving him a bath!" "Make sure you take one too, Edna Edna drove away so fast, all you could see was a big cloud of dust. This incident ended their friendship. Betty and Idana saw the whole thing from the side of the kitchen window.

That night, Mary Lee asked her parents, "What a nigga was?" They had to tell their little girl the truth, that white people sometimes called Negro people, niggers, and that it was considered a bad name. But Negro people, was not really niggers and the ones that called them that name was stupid and silly. Mary Lee knew the meaning of those two words, silly and stupid."Miss Nancy told me that I was not a nigger, that I was just a Sweet baby girl." "Miss Nancy is right, you is our sweet baby girl."

After a year of working for the Holcomes, Sam decided that he did not want to work for anyone again and that he was going to leave the Holcomes. He secretely sold his land. He told Roy, Zeb, and Long Tall Joe that he was going to move to Comb City, and they told Big Steve. But first, he had to write his papa, Benny Ginn a letter to ask him if he and the others could come. A few weeks later, his papa wrote him back and told him to come and bring the others. Benny Ginn, Sam's father lived alone. Sam's mother passed away when he was eighteen. His father never married again.

Sam had to tell Mr. Holcome that he was leaving. That same night, Roy told Mr. Holcome that he was leaving also... "Boy, ain't I been good to you?" "Yes sir, said Roy. "Roy, I promised your mama I would never work you hard and that you would always have your own land." "Mr. Jerry, can I sell my land to you?" "Yes, Boy you can." Sam said to Roy, "But we only got one wagon?" "No, Sam I got my own wagon. I just never used it and Mr. Jerry be done gave me two horses." Miss Nancy heard them talking and begged them to stay another week. So they did. Zeb was not crazy about the idea of Long Tall Joe and Big Steve Coming along. Zeb asked Sam if he was sure he wanted someone like long Tall Joe and Big Steve to come along. "Zeb don't worry about that they only did the bad things of beating up the Negroes, that Mr. Holcome told them to do, and if they didn't they would've been killed." While the men were still talking, Roy Said, "Sam I know you be done heard what people say about me and Mr. Holcome." "My mama told me that he be my half-brother." "Don't tell nobody." "I ain't". "Roy why you be wantin to leave?" "I ain't never been out of Romestown my whole life." "Betty needs to be my wife and cook my supper."

Miss Nancy Comes out again, "I know you boys thinking about leaving tomorrow?" "Roy, you know how much we and our children loves you and Betty." "I'll miss little Mary Lee and Idana." "WHY!" "Sally won't know what to do with herself." Sam said, "I'm Sorry Miss Nancy." She went away crying. No one told Mr. Holcome that Zeb, Long Tall Joe, Fat Sam and Big Steve were also leaving. This would have been too much for Mr. Holcome to take. That night, before the morning of, Big Steve asked Sam if he could help get his wife into the wagon, "She shore is a load of woman." "I think she's too fat to ride wit us." "Sam, I just won't go, cause I can't leave her." "Hey Steve, how big is her dress size?" "It be fittem, just as big as you can gittem." The two of them had a big laugh. "Sam, what size do Idana be?" "Man, my wife is so little, I be thinkin maybe we can put her on Mary Lee's little dress." "All her kinfolks calls her stick.'

"Sam, I glad we be friends, cause them there be fightin words, and if we wives heard us, it would be a fight anyway, cause they won't give us none." "Man, we got to have some help to git her into the wagon."

Chapter Three

Moving to Comb City

Now its time to move to Comb City. Everyone was packed and ready to go. Mary Lee, Cat and Dog were on the floor of the wagon with Big Steve and Fat Helen, along with Sam and Idana. In the other wagon, were Roy, Betty, Zeb. Long Tall Joe and Fat Sam. It was a rough ride as they left the Holcome's place. They traveled for six hours. Finally, they arrived at Sam's father's house. Grandpa was sitting on his front porch in his old rocking chair, smoking his pipe. When he saw Sam, he was so happy that he did't notice the others including Mary Lee and Idana. "Boy, is that you!' "Yessir." "You is jus as tall and black as you ever was, but you is good-lookin like me." He hugged his son. "Pa, said Idana, as she stood behind her husband holding Mary Lee's hand. "Oh gal, I glad to see you too, and this must be my grandcoon." Grandpa called all his grandchildren "grandcoons". Mary Lee held on to her father's legs crying. "Don't cry Mary Lee, "said Sam. "This be my daddy." "Don't cry pretty gal, I ain't gone hurt you." "Don't worry pa, she cries a lot." "She's just a crybaby." "Mama, I ain't a crybaby." "I is a big girl," "Yes, you is." "Y'all come on in this house." "Wait a minute, pa we brung other folks." Pa looked at Big Sam and Long Tall Joe, and said, "Them is the ugliest niggas I ever seen!" "Hush pa, they might hear you." "I don't care if they do." "Boy, don't you be tellin me to hush!" "Pa, said Idana in her little soft voice, "you don't want to hurt anyone's feelings." "Now Sam, you ought to learn how to talk to me like your wife." "Where's we gone put all them people, and that big fat gal?" "I ain't gone let her break my bed down." "Pa, you and Sam just let me handle this." Idana somehow had a place for everybody,

The next morning, Grandpa Benny was up, in the kitchen drinking coffee, when Betty walked in. "Good morning, Mr. Benny." "Gal, you scare the doo-doo out of me!" "I sorry, Mr. Benny." "Well, old man don't mind a pretty fine looking gal like you." "You want a cup of coffee?" "Not right now." "I just wanted to know if you want me to cook breakfast fer you?" "I guess you better feed them other ugly folks Sam brung wit him, too?" "Betty, that Long Tall Joe is the tallest man I ever seen and the ugliest too!" "Mr. Benny, I ain't gone say another word about nobody to you." Betty went and got Idana to help cook breakfast. Everyone enjoyed their breakfast and was ready to work. Grandpa has pigs to feed. People often gave the pigs all of their leftover food called slop. So someone had to slop the pigs, feed the chickens, and milked the cows. Big Steve loved plowing and planting vegetables. Long Tall Joe, Sam and Fat Sam used grass blades to cut the tall grass. When Grandpa saw all the good work they had done, Grandpa called Sam. "Who did you say y'all work fer?" "Mr. Holcome." "Boy, that man is too rich." "I used to know his pappy, he was real rich too." "How he treat you?" "He treat me nice, I think he had eyes for Idana." "Well, Ize glad you had sense enough to leave there." "Pa, I don't want to work fer nobody but myself." "I knows you good wit your hands and knows you be gone take really good care of yo' wife and baby." "Yeah, pa I is."

It was clear to Sam that all the folks he brought with him to his father's house could not stay forever. So Sam began to build houses. Grandpa had already given his other six children money. Not only did Grandpa had a farm, he had a still which he made corn liquor, and sold it to Whitefolks and Negroes who could pay. They say Grandpa made the best whiskey ever! Within six months, everyone had jobs and were living on their own. Grandpa had taken a-liking to Zeb and asked him to stay. Zeb, Long Tall Joe, and Big Steve had become friends. They wanted to live as close as possible to each other. So they stayed in two of the houses they had helped Sam to build.

Chapter Four

Grandpa Benny Leaves Comb City

Grandpa had decided to go back to Romestown for a while. Just before Grandpa left, Sam said, "Pa, think I'm gonnna buy one of those automobiles after I save enough money." Boy, you is crazy!" "Ain't no Negro in all Comb City got one of them things." "Pa, when you come back, I let you ride in it." "I ain't never gonnna ride in one of them things. God made horses to pull my wagon and I ain't gonna ride in no machine." "Pa, it ain't no machine, it a car." "Boy, you too smart fer your own britches." "Well, pa ain't no use talkin to you about this." "It sure ain't." "Yo' cousin Billy is gonna pick me up." "When I git back, and if I git back, I don't wanna see ne'er one of them machines in my front yard." Sam Called Idana and Mary Lee to say goodbye to Grandpa, as Cousin Billy drove up in his wagon. "Cousin Billy, don't you want to eat somethin'?" "Idana done made supper." As Pa climbed into the wagon, Cousin Billy jumped out. "Where's you goin' Billy?" "I'm gonna git me some of Idana's food." An hour later, Grandpa Benny was still sitting in that old wagon waiting for Billy. Billy said goodbye, as they drove away in that old rusty wagon.

Idana and Mary Lee loved and missed Grandpa, but having the house to themselves was nice. Mary Lee was playing outside with Cat and Dog, when Mr. and Mrs. Johnson and their daughter, AnnieMae, were passing by. All of a sudden, Dog attacked AnnieMae. AnnieMae's father, Doc picked her up. "Mister, please don't hurt my dog!" Idana heard Dog barking and ran to AnnieMae. "Mister, Ize Sorry about the dog attackin y'alls little girl, as she pushed the dog back into the yard. Idana introduced herself to the Johnsons, and said, "This is my only child, Mary Lee." Mary Lee looked at AnnieMae, "what is your name?" "My name is AnnieMae." "Mama, can I stay and play wit that little girl?" asked AnnieMae. "Not today, but you can come back tomorrow." The Johnsons and the Ginns became friends right away.

Doc, Amy and AnnieMae lived down the dusty road a block from the Ginns. AnnieMae had a pretty little ragdoll. Mary Lee asked AnnieMae, "Can I take the doll home and let my mama see her?" "No, said AnnieMae. She took her doll and pushed Mary Lee down to the ground. Mary Lee got up and pushed her back. Amy saw the girls, she became angry. She then spanked Mary Lee, but she didn't spank AnnieMae. Mary ran home crying and told Idana what had happened. Idana ran down the road in her barefeet and asked Amy, if she had spanked Mary Lee. Amy said, "Yes." "That little woman, Idana threw her down and gave her a Boss Beating!!! Doc heard the commotion, came out of the house and pulled Idana off his wife. "What is wrong wit you, girl?" "She beat my child and didn't beat her own" Idana was still coming after Amy. Doc told Mary to run home and get her daddy, Sam ran his bow-legged self down the road, and picked up his wife and put her over his shoulder. 'Why you be fightin' yo' friend?" "She beat Mary Lee for pushin' AnnieMae, but didn't beat AnnieMae for pushin' Mary Lee!" "Wife, I gone pray fer you." "You gone pray fer me?' "Wit all that whiskey you got in the barn?" "That's pa's whiskey, I ain't touch it." "Ize a changed man."

True friends don't stay angry long. They were soon friends again, with the understanding that Amy would never lay hands on Mary Lee. Within the next four months, Mary noticed her mother had a big stomach. "Mama, why your stomach so big?" "I ate too many beans." "I ain't never gonna eat too many beans." When AnnieMae came to play, Mary told AnnieMae that her mama had a big stomach. AnnieMae said, "Everytime my Aunt Pearl had a big stomach a baby comes." "AnnieMae, where do babies come from?" "My mama said that babies comes from cabbage patches and under tree stumps." "Come on, Mary and lets go a-lookin in your daddy's garden." They looked at every cabbage and the root of every tree that they could. "AnnieMae, let us be gone home, we ain't gone find no babies today." They look for babies most of the summer. Baby Cleve arrived a few weeks later, when Mary Lee told AnnieMae about the new baby. AnnieMae said, "Mary, I told you when a mama get a big stomach a baby comes." Mary loved her baby brother and tried to take care of him as well as a five-year-old could.

Mary Lee told Idana that AnnieMae told her that everytime her Aunt Pearl had a big stomach, a baby comes. "That girl be too grown, you ain't gone play wit her no more!" Mary turned to Sam, "Daddy, mama ain't gone let me play with AnnieMae no more." "Don't worry, you can play wit her tomorrow." The next day, they were happy playing again. "What did your mama name your baby brother?" "My daddy said his name is Cleve." Two years later, came baby Ellen, and she was the apple of Sam's eye and Mary had to help Idana with both babies,

It is now September, Mary is in the first grade. She could recite her ABC's forward and backward. Mary grew taller than most children here age. The children would tease her and told her that she was too tall and her feet was too big. Everyday she came home crying. AnnieMae fought all of Mary's battles. The children would pull her hair, because they didn't like the color. The very next year, when she went back to school in the second grade, she was a fair reader and a fair speller. Sam could not read at all or write. He asked Idana to please help Mary with her schoolwork. But Idana never took the time to help poor Mary. AnnieMae was a good reader and writer, she was willing to help Mary learn to read on a second grade level. Mary came home one day, disgusted with the children, and asked Idana and Sam if she could quit school. They allowed her to quit at the age of nine, in the Second grade, because of the bullying. What is a Negroe girl going to do with her time? Sam was not happy with the idea of Mary staying home. But Idana, said, "All I did was merry you. My mama and my Grandmammy jus cook and clean fer the white folks.

Chapter Five

Mary Lee Goes to Live with the Blacks

To Mary's surprise, Mrs. Black, a woman who Idana had cooked for sometimes, wanted Mary Lee to come and stay with her family five days a week and help her around the house. No one asked if she wanted to go. Mary was very much afraid to say no to her parents. This little nine-year-old Negroe girl found herself in a strange place with strange people. She had a very nice, small bedroom off from the kitchen. For weeks, she was afraid to sleep in a place she now calls home. For the first week, she cried for fear that some old nasty man would try to hurt her. She could not understand why her parents sent her there in the first place. The Blacks had two daughters, Susan and Ruby. Now Mary's job was to make their beds, clean their rooms, and mopped the floors. Then she had to help Mrs. Black wash the filthy clothes, and cleaned the two bathrooms. Mary had never flushed a toilet before. She was ashamed to ask. So she watched the girls as they flushed by pulling the String down. Mary kept the toilet bowls clean. There were no toilet brushes, so the nine year old used a rag to clean the toilets, The girls took baths in the big white tub insde the bathroom. Mary was given a foottub to wash herself. Each day after breakfast and supper, Mary washed the dishes and put them away. She also had to clean the yard. The Blacks' daughters played outside with their friends, while Mary watched. Mary wished she could play. Mrs. Black was not Mrs. Holcome, not at all! Mary learned to talk like White people. She was only home on Saturdays and Sundays. She stayed with them for two years.

When she came home, things have changed around the Ginn's house. Not only were they going to church on Sundays, they were going every night of the week. One Sunday after church, Mary was in the kitchen washing dishes, when suddenly, they heard a pots falling. When they came into the kitchen, Mary was also on the floor. She was unconscious, lying there with a large black-pot near her head. Sam first thought was, the pot had fallen and knocked her out. They were not able to revive her. Sam and Idana along with the children, took Mary to Dr. Evan's house. In those days, it was not uncommon for the doctor to come to you, or for you to go to him. By the time they arrived at Dr. Evan's house, Mary was burning with a high fever. Dr. Evans told them, she might have malaria. "How did she git it?' Idana, asked. There was no explanation. "There seems to be an epidemic of it in this town." The doctor took Mary to the hospital in his car.

When Sam got to the hospital with the family, Dr. Evans told them that Mary was awake, but don't take the children near her. Sam walked into Mary's room. "Daddy, don't you and mama worry about me, I'm gonna be alright, but I can't walk." Idana was afraid that she and Sam was going to lose their child. Dr. Evans returned to the room and saw they had taken their two babies in the room with Mary. "You people must be crazy!" "I've told you, people are dying from this fever." "Do you want to lose your babies too?" "What do you mean, Doctor", asked Sam? "Let us go outside." Dr. Evans explained how Serious this disease was.

Two weeks later, Mary was much better and they were able to bring her home. Some of the old church folks told them to shave her head, because her hair was going to fall out. Idana could't stand the thought of Mary losing her hair, So they never shaved her hair. A month later, she was still unable to walk. On Sunday morning, they was going to take Mary Lee to church. Reverend Lindsey, was the pastor of The Church of God in Christ, which was started by Elder Charles Harrison Mason, a few years earlier. Sam walked into the church, carrying Mary Lee in his arms and sat on the last row. "Brother Ginn, bring that child to the front of the church." "Bring that child to the Lord." The Pastor ordered him to lay her on the offering table. "Brother Ginn, do you have faith in the Lord God?" "Yessir, do." "Child do you believe that God can heal your body?" "Yessir, daddy said God can do everything." He then took her by the hand and asked the church to pray. All the people began to pray with him. Before the prayer was over, Mary let go of his hand and began to walk. Sam stood there, crying and thanking God for His Goodness. Mary never stopped walking from that day on. Mary Lee loved God with all her heart and soul. She knew that her parents had received the Holy Ghost, according to Acts 2:4, when the Holy Ghost came from Heaven as a rushing mighty wind, and the Disciples began to speak in other tongues. Mary wanted to receive the Holy Ghost. It just so happened, that she and her friends were playing church, acting out everything they saw the grown-ups do. All of a Sudden, Mary wasn't playing anymore. Suddenly, she was speaking in tongues. God has baptized her with the Holy Ghost.

It was a few weeks later, God had called Sam to preach. Although, Sam had never learned to read or write, after his calling. He was able to read and write little by little. Soon he was able to read completely on his own. How could this be that a man can read the Bible, if he could not read any other book? Only God knows "Wife, he said to Idana, I feel that God want me to start my own church." He began his church in a Brush Harbor in 1927. A Brush Harbor is an opening in a wooded area where people gathered. Inside those woods they used candles to see. No white man knew they were there. This was Negroe's land. Sam had a deacon by the name of Jeff, that told everything he knew to the white man. But he never told Mr. Nelson, the man he worked for about them having church in the woods. White people did not believe in loud noises and they certainly would not have approve of the Negroes dancing around in the dirt. If they had known, they might have been hunged high. Jeff loved Sam and Idana and would have given his life for them and their children.

Soon after that he had built a small church. People were coming, standing and listening to the Bible. Sam wanted to teach the Bible, the way Bishop Charles Harrison Mason taught, when he first started The Church of God in Christ. Sam wanted people to understand every word as it was written. Many people were very angry, concerning this teaching of the Bible. Many wanted to harm him. This did not stop him from preaching The Word. Sam and Charles Harrison Mason became friends. He would later appoint him superintendent of several churches in Mississippi.

Sam often walked through a very dark path on Tuesday, Wednesday, and Friday nights, to get to the small church he had built. One night, as he was walking, he noticed a tall man dressed in black, with a wide black hat, walking beside him. He spoke to the man, but the man never said a word. When Sam was safely out of the woods, the man was not there anymore. Sometimes Sam rode his mule-wagon, the same man sat beside him, until he was safely out of the woods. This continued until Idana and the children was able to go to church with him. Sam had never told anyone about the man. Until one night, Idana saw him looking around, as if he was looking for someone. "What's wrong wit you, Sam?" "Wife, I tell you later." After church when they returned home, he said, "Wife, I have something to tell you." "Remember when you asked me what was I looking fer?" "Well, for weeks a man dressed in black have been walking and riding wit me through the woods." "When I was safely through the woods, he disappeared." "What, what, Sam, what do you mean?" "I mean what I say !" Idana said, "Sam I think that be a angel God had sent you," Mary understood what her mother meant, because she believed according to the Bible they were angels. "Daddy, I think mama is right."

Chapter Six

Mary Lee is Lonely

Mary thought about the angels almost everyday and wondered to herself, if God had an angel for her. Mary had been helping Idana with the children everyday. Idana had had her fourth child. Mary took charge of the new baby. Idana was having bad headaches. The two doctors in town, could not find anything wrong with her. Mary said, "Daddy do you think mama's lazy or sick?" Sam could not answer that question and certainly no one was going to ask Idana. "Mary Lee jus help yo mama." "Yessir daddy, I do all I can." As soon as one sickness was over with, Idana would get sick again. One day, Mary was feeding Baby Joe. Idana was lying across the bed crying, "My side, my side, call your daddy." Cleve ran out and got Sam. "My side, Sam, my side." Sam laid his hand on Idana's side where the pain was and began to pray. The pain was gone and the three of them began to praise the Lord, as the younger children looked on. They could not understand what had happened. When he removed his hand from her side, water was coming through her skin. After taking her to the doctors, they later found out that her appendix had burst and drained. There was a small hole in her side. "Reverend Ginn, said the doctor, I can't understand how this can be. I have never seen anything like this in my life." "Doctor, God done this." "God can work miracles." "Reverend, the next time you pray, pray for me and my family." "Yessir, I do that right now." Idana never had that pain again.

Now Mary is thirteen and starting a new job with the Martin family. She works three days a week for fifty cents a day. It wasn't very long before she had a seizure at work. Mr. and Mrs. Martin got her parents and they all went to Dr. Evans. This time he told them, that she had a bad heart, and would not live to see her eighteenth birthday. "This child works too hard, she needs rest!" Sam told the doctor, "That she was not going to die, she will live." "Reverend, seeing how you pray, I need to believe that." "Doctor, you jus watch and see, she be fine." Another miracle had been worked by God.

This Church of God and Christ preacher, Sam Ginn, believed in God so much and prayed so hard, it seem to people around him, that he was in another world. I guess, Mary was in the same world. She believed as hard and as much as her father did. By the time Mary was fifteen, Idana had had two more babies, James and Sam Jr. Idana is now a mother of six and still a child. Mary was the mother and the children knew and looked up to her for everything. James even called her "mama".

Chapter Seven
The Three Gunmen

It was a Sunday night, Reverend Sam Ginn and his family had driven to Magnolia, Mississippi, where he had built his second church. Sam was preaching from the pulpit, when three white men rushed through the door with shotguns in their hands. One said, "Boy, pointing the gun at Sam, we heard you been telling white folks. as well as niggers, that it was wrong to drink and smoke, and God don't want people to do no kind of sin." "You know everybody got to sin a little, and we all tell little white lies." All the people in the church gathered around Sam to protect him, "Ain't you never read the Bible?" "It don't matter", they said. "If you don't stop preaching that stuff, we gonna have to kill you." Sam looked them in the eyes and said, "If you make one step, God is gone kill you." They tried to pull their triggers, but they were frozen in their tracks for at least five minutes. "What have you done to us?" "As you kin see, I ain't raise my hand." When they could move, they ran out of the church, telling everyone they saw, not to bother that nigger preacher. "Just leave him alone, he's a strange man, and if you get too close to him, you'll be sorry."

Sam kept on preaching The Word of God, without any threats. Many more people were joining the church and many just stood outside the church, listening to Mary Lee singing. Idana and Ellen also sang. But no one could sing like Mary Lee. Idana and Ellen were Sopranos. Mary Lee was an Alto.

The following Monday, Mary Lee went back to work for the Blacks again. Mr. Black watched her as she worked. He offered her money. "I don't want your money, I only want what I work for." Mrs. Black saw Mr. Black trying to pass her a five dollar bill. She just pushed pass him and continued to work. Mrs. Black came into the room and told Mary that her husband is just a "Dog", and told him to get away from Mary Lee. "Mary, you a good girl, and if he ever put hands on you, Call on me and I would knock him down. Mary, I don't want to put you in this position again, I just give you ten dollars, and send you home." Please don't tell your mama and daddy what happened." "Yes, ma'am."

Mary was home for a few days, before Idana asked her "why she was not going to work anymore?" "Mama, Mrs. Black gave me a ten dollar bill and said I could stay home for a while." "But, I still be working for the Martins." Mary was afraid to tell Idana the truth of matter." "Mary Lee, don't tell your daddy about that money," said Idana. "Why not, mama?" "Don't be askin me why, just do what I say!" "Sam never asked Mary why she was not working those two days. All he wanted to know, if she was alright. But he did ask her if she had a boyfriend that he had not heard about, "No, daddy." "I know that James Clark has got eyes for you, but do you got eyes for him?" "Daddy, that James is crazy, he ain't got a teaspoon full of sense." "Nobody want him." James was a country boy from Magnolia, Mississippi. He wore his pants too high, and too much grease in his hair. James came to see Mary twice a month on Sunday afternoons. He never has too much to say, only a few words, and all he did was laugh. "Daddy, please don't talk about him again."

Chapter Eight

The Ginns Mees Bud

It was the end of summer, Sam was in the field when a young boy about Mary's age, walked up and asked him for work. Sam asked the young boy, "where did he come from and where was his folks?' "I ain't got no mama and daddy." My daddy was hanged when I was seven, my mama, she died a month ago, and I had to bury her myself, and I ain't got no sister or brother, it's only me. "Son, where is it that you live?" "No where." "What is your name?" "It be Bud." "Come on, come wit me and we gone talk to my wife." "Wife, this here boy ain't got nobody. His mama and daddy is dead, and he ain't got no brother or sister. He want to work for us and Ize can shore use the help." "Where is he gone stay, Elder Ginn?" Idana now call her husband, Elder Ginn. "Well, can he stay with us, wife?" "You know, I can't say no." After they had talked it over, they decided to allow the young man to stay. Idana asked him, "What is your name?" "It be Bud, ma'am."

The children loved having an older brother. Mary was happy for the first time in her life she had help, Bud was very good with his hands. He built a small wagon for the children to play in. Bud could cook and clean as well as any woman. Mary Lee wanted to learn more about her new found brother, but Bud never answered any questions about his past. He stayed with them for six months. When it was time to go to church, he was the first one, to get dressed. Cleve and Joe taught him how to read and write. But no one taught Mary. Mary was still the mother, not Idana. Although Idana was still there lying around. Sam had taken her to both doctors in town. They could not find anything wrong with her. But the truth was Idana had severe migraines. But when she felt good, she kept the house clean as a pen, and she loved washing and ironing. She taught all her children how to clean and iron their own clothes and cook when they were very young. But the duties of the mother was all on Mary Lee.

One Sunday morning, as they was getting ready for church, no one saw Bud. Sam thought, maybe he was still in the small enclosed porch where he slept. He wasn't there. Mary Lee said, "Daddy, he must have a girlfriend." She said it, because she did not want her her daddy to worry. But she felt in her spirit, that he has gone away and they would never find him. Ellen, James, and Sam could not understand why? Cleve and Joe were crying. They were late for church that Sunday. Sam knew he had to go preach The Word of God. He told Idana they had to fast and pray for Bud and just leave it in God's hands. They fasted and prayed, eating only after five o'clock for a week. Bud had vanished and was never seen again.

Mary and Ellen grew closer and closer after Bud's disappearance. Mary took Ellen to work with her everyday. She kept her eyes on her younger sister every step she made Ellen was right there. Mary had gone through awful things. It has been very hard for Mary working in white people's houses, spending most of her early years away from home, cleaning, washing and ironing since the age of nine. Mary did not want her baby sister to experience that kind of life, having to clean and wash the dirt of old, smelly clothes, nor sleep in their beds crying and watching all night for her safety, to see if some ugly, old nasty man would come out to rape her. Mary Lee and Ellen often walked home together singing Gospel songs. They're were not only sisters, but best friends. Ellen asked Mary, what kind of boys does she like? "Ellen, you too young to be talkin this kind of talk, but I like tall, dark, slim men." "Ellen, what kind men do you like?" "Mary, please don't get mad with me. But like all kinds of men." "What do you mean, Ellen?" "I mean Black, White, short, tall, fat, slim. I just like them all." "Enough, young lady!" "Mary, also like them bald-headed, bow-legged, cock-eyed and crazy." They both laughed. Ellen could always make her older sister laugh. Ellen also uses as many curse words, when her parents were not around. When they were home, most of the time, Idana was still having headaches and waiting for Mary to cook dinner.

Ellen was learning to cook also. Joe and Cleve helped their father cut wood and grass. They were learning a few things about farming and going to school everyday. Sam made sure that the children go to church almost every night and on Sunday mornings. On Sunday mornings, Sam always called Mary to sing. Brother Washington was the piano player. He could play that old piano, as well as Mary could sing. Today, Mary sang, "Just A Little More Faith and Grace Is All I Need." The church was clapping for Mary to sing another song. Sam's uncle from his dad's side, was attending church that day. Uncle Art came up drunk and singing LOUD, staggering all over the floor. "I want to sing, Mary Lee. Help me, please help me sing." Mary pushed him away. One push did not stop Uncle Art. Sam came down from the pulpit and took him by the hand. But Uncle Art kept clapping his hands. "Come on, Mary Lee, and help me sing." No one could control Uncle Art.

A tall, dark curly hair, young man had been outside peeping through the window, came in and put Uncle Art over his shoulders and carried him outside. Sam folloved him to the door to see what the young man was doing with his uncle. Mary came out to help her father. The young man told Sam, "You look like you could use a hand." Sam returned to his pulpit. When church was over, the young man stood up. He had been sitting on the ground beside Uncle Art, to keep him from going back into the church. "My name is Emerson Hodges." "That name is familiar", said Sam. "Is you related to Sister and Brother Hodges?" "Yessir, they is my parents." Sam and Idana thanked the young man for his help. Mary was just standing there looking at the young man. "What's your name?"asked Emerson. "My name is Mary Lee Ginn." "You shore is pretty. Do you want some ice Cream?" Sister Washington sold homemade ice cream in the church yard, every Sunday under the old oak tree. Mary said, "Yes, I would like some ice cream." "My mama told me the pastor had pretty girls, but you take the cake." "Thank you, sir." "I told you the name is Emerson and nothing else." "Okay." "I like that pretty yellow dress you wearin." Mary was wearing a light yellow dress that seems to blend in with her complexion. "Can I come see you sometime?" "I guess so." Idana heard them talking and invited the whole family for supper.

Mary and Emerson sat in the yard under the shed that Sam had built. It placed chairs and a table. Today, Idana had cooked all kinds of food. The Hodges children and Mary's little sister and brothers were getting to know each other. While Mary and Emerson drank lemonade under the shed,

Emerson asked, "Do you got a boyfriend?" "No, but there is a silly man, James Clark, he is So stupid, and don't have a teaspoon full of sense. All he want to do is eat mama's food and laugh," "When do you see him?" "Every now and then. Once or twice a month, he comes with his brother and his brother's wife. He said he's gone to merry me." "ls you gonna merry him?" "No, I don't want him." "Well, how's he's gonna merry you?" "He ain't." Emerson put a big smile on his face and kissed her hand.

Emerson and his younger brother, Benny came to see the Ginn's house after church almost every night. He brought Benny along to walk with him through the woods. Sometimes they stayed too long, Idana and Sam let them sleep in the empty room next to them. Sam kept his eyes open and made sure Emerson stayed in his room. Mary had fallen in love with this sweet young man. Ellen liked his curly hair. Her brothers did not want any man to get close to their sister.

Emerson came home with the Ginns, on a cold Sunday evening in January. He and Mary sat on the front porch in the cold. He told Mary he was in love with her. "I love you, too." He wanted to ask her to marry him, but he didn't know how. Mary looked at him and said, "I think you want to merry me.' "I sure do." "Well, she said, "What are you gonna do about it?" "I guess we get married." "Well, I guess I got to tell my mama and daddy." "Why", said Mary. "You and me is already nineteen years old". "I shore wish I went to school," Mary said. "You mean a pretty girl like you didn't go to school?" "No, I can't read or write, guess you don't want to merry me now?" "I don't care about that, said Emerson. "I is nineteen and still in the eleven grade." "Well, I did finish the second grade", said Mary. "At nineteen, I am too old to go back to school and be with little children." "I can teach you what you need to know, Mary." Emerson went home to tell his parents. Grandma Tilly was visiting. She was white as any white woman. Mama Tilly would never use the out house. She would push her butt outside the window and have bowell movements and urinate. "Mama, I asked you to stop doing that", Said, Luella. All Mama Tilly would say, "Let them little black nigger children clean it up!" She was referring to her own grandchildren Grandma Tilly was a bit senile. After Grandma Tilly was taken back to her own house by her son, Willie, Emerson told his parents he wanted to marry Mary Lee. "Papa, do you like her?" "Boy, that's a good gal and ize love her." "Mama, what about you?" "Boy, I jus want you to finish school." "I told Mary Lee you was gonna say that. Mama, ize gonna be twenty next month, and it is too late and I'm too old to be in the eleven grade again." "I guess you is right."

That Monday night, Emerson asked Sam for Mary's hand in marriage. All Sam said is, "I already know you gone be her husband." Idana did not want Mary to leave home and neither did Ellen. Idana knew that Ellen was not going to do much around the house. She wasn't at all like Mary. Ellen stepped out at night and went dancing. Mary was afraid for her sister and thought that someone might harm her. Cleve and his brothers were happy for their sister,

Emerson and Mary were holding hands, when five year old Sam Jr. said, "Can't you or is you suppose to kiss her in the face?" James said, "No, he suppose to kiss her mouth." Joe was crying. "Why you crying?" said Mary. "I love you Mary. I want you to get married, but I'll miss you taking care of us. I promised Joe I still be very close to you. We will find a house close by." Emerson gave her a hug. "Mary, when you and Emerson gonna get married?"asked Joe. "As soon as possible." Mary looked at him and said, "I want a wedding and that takes a while." "Okay, but not too long, I jus want you to be my wife?"

Sam, Idana and the children, left them alone so they could talk in private. "Wife, did you hear what that boy said? He want to merry that gal as soon as possible." "Elder Ginn, look who's talkin. You want to merry me in three days." "That cause I was gettin too old." "Well, you know I was too young, but we made it." Sam said, " So far, so good."

When Mary got home from work, the next day, she made dinner. After dinner, Idana washed the dishes. "Mary, I really don't want you to get merried, I was jus puttin on a front for your daddy. If you get merried, who's gone help me?" Ellen came into the kitchen just in time to hear what was being said. "Mama, let Marry Lee get merried, I'll get a job and help you around the house and help you cook supper". As she winked at Mary Lee, "Thank you, Ellen, said Mary." "Emerson and me is gone to get us a house close by." "Hush, Mary Lee is time for Ellen to go to work." "Please, mama don't let my little sister go to work for them white folks." "I don't want her to be nobody's slave like me!" Idana did not say another word. She knew Mary was angry,

Before Mary went to bed, she asked Idana if she could make her wedding dress. Idana was an excellent seamstress. It seems as well as she could sew, she would have made her daughter's dress. Idana said, "No, I won't. Make it yourself." "Mama, please." Sam spoke up and said, "I buy the material. What material do you wont Mary?" "Daddy, I want white satin and a Chantily lace veil."

"I still ain't gone make no dress." "Well, I guess I get Sister Spriggs "Sister Spriggs was a member of Sam's church. She was also a good seamstress, who had a daughter, that didn't have a name until she was seven, before that they called her "Girl". She named herself, Roberta.

Chapter Nine

Mary Lee and Emerson's Wedding

Mary went to Sister Sprigg's house and told her that she was getting married and needed her to make her wedding dress. "Mary, yo mama sews better than I do, why is it she ain't makin you no dress?" "I begged her to make it for me." "But she won't do it." "Mary, you such a good girl and So pretty, I just can't understand this!!" "Don't worry, I make it fer you. What kind of material do you wont it made out of and when do you wont this dress?" "I want a white satin dress and a Chantilly lace veil. My daddy would buy the material. I'm getting merried February 16th, that's Emerson's birthday." "Mary, is he that good lookin boy of Sister Hodges?" "Yes, ma'am."

Emerson was a good-looking man, and he knew it. "Mary, he got good manners. hope he make you a good husband." "Yeah, he better, said Brother Spriggs." "Or, I have to do Somethin to him." Sister Spriggs made the wedding dress and it fitted Mary's body to a "T". Emerson, on the other hand, did not have a suit, and was too poor to buy one. So he borrowed his cousin Roscoe's suit. Emerson was at least four inches taller than Roscoe. He wanted to borrow his brother Buddy's suit, but Buddy had misplaced it. Buddy was already married and so was his sister Lou. His sister Lou was a very short little woman who married an older man that owned his own farm, and a very large one at that. When she heard her brother was getting married, she and her husband came to town for a week. In the meantime, Mary was preparing for her Wedding day. In three days, it would be February 16", which will also be Emerson's twentieth birthday. Mary had turned twenty, two weeks prior. On the day of the wedding, people had brought many gifts to Idana's house. Idana asked Mary, "Mary can I have half of your gifts?' "No, mama. You have a lot of things already." Idana became very upset and slapped Mary's face and said, "I ain't gone to yo' weddin." Mary was sitting on the floor, in her wedding dress crying. Sam had pulled the car in front of the house for Mary to get in. "Why is you cryin Mary Lee?" "Mama said she ain't comin to my wedding." "Don't cry, he said, as he took her hand and pulled her off the floor. "We gone pray for yo' mama." "She said she want half of my weddings gifts." "Why she say that?" "Daddy, do I have to give them to her?" "No, you don't. Today is yo' wedding day and Emerson's birthday." Ellen was Mary's Maid of Honor, Buddy was Emerson's Best Man. Sam no longer rode around town in a wagon, he had a new car. He, the children, and Mary was already in the car. Idana was still in the house. Sam picked her up and placed her in the backseat of the car with the other children.

When they got to the church, the church was packed with people. Even the church yard was full. The weather was cold, but it did not keep people from the wedding. They knew it was going to be plenty of good food to eat, and it was, Mary was a beautiful bride. Emerson's suit was fitting his six foot one, one hundred and sixty pound body to a "T". Mary was wearing a long-sleeved, white satin dress with a lace veil that covered her pretty lemon face. After the wedding, everyone had a place to sit and eat at Sam and Idana's house, even the uninvited guests outside the church came to eat. Idana loved giving food away. Sometimes, Sam had to say, "That's enough!"

Chapter Ten
The Newlyweds

After the reception, Mary and Emerson moved into their own place and began their life together.

Emerson's job paid him three dollars a week, Mary was earning five dollars a week. They were able to pay the rent and buy food, but Emerson did not like his wife earning more money than him. He was not good with his hands, as far as helping Sam fix the house where they were living. The house needed repairs. What Emerson and Mary did not know, that Sam had brought the house they now called home. When Emerson found out his father-in-law had brought the house, he was grateful and thanked God. Sam did not want any rent from them anymore. "Elder Gen, I ain't got much money, can pay you at least six dollars a month?" "No, Boy, the three dollars you payin is enough." "Man, I love you, this place is lookin good!" "Nobody ever showed me how to use a hammer or a mail." "All my papa know how to do is farm." "But my mama said, papa's daddy ain't showed him nothin either." "Son, don't worry about this here, jus you be a good husband to my girl." "Yessir, I'm gonna do that." Emerson found out later that day from Mr. Jim, Sam's friend, that his father-in-law had brought the house for them. When Mary came home from the hairdresser's that day, he asked her if she knew anything concerning her father buying the house they were living in. She laughed, and said, "That sounds like something my daddy would do," "But I didn't know he own our house." "When we pay our rent, we pay our rent to Mr. Jim." "Mr. Jim owns houses too."

"Ever since I was nine and had my own job, my daddy took half of the money. He said we had to pay him rent." But I know that he was saving every penny." "What do you mean, Mary, about your own job at nine?" "When I quit school, my mama said that I could go live with the Black family." "Were they whitefolks or colored folks?" "Emerson, you know they were white." "Ain't no Colored folks ain't gonna pay nobody no money, except my daddy." "He didn't have much money, I don't thank back then." "I ain't never heard nobody lettin they nine year old little girl, work in no white folks house." "Mary, did them old diry white men try to hurt you?" "Ain't nobody try to hurt me!' "I mean, did they put their hands on you in the wrong way?" They tried well jus one." "But I kept my eyes on them." "Sometimes, I was scared to go to sleep, cause he be watching me while I was workin." "What happened, what did you do at their house?"

"Emerson, do we have to talk about this?" "Yeah, I want to know." "I clean their two girl room. The girls were really pretty." "Most white people don't let their children clean." "They like to pay us colored people to do everything for them." "When the girls came home from school, they got their lesson and then they go outside and play with their friends up and down the street." "After supper, I wash the dishes, Sweep the floors, and sometimes their mama would tell me to mop the floor." "Why in the world, you have to sleep there?" He pulled her close to him and held her in his arms, as the tears ran down their faces. "You is my wife now, wish I had money like them white folks." "We could let them clean our house" Emerson, you is crazy!" "Someday, we gonna have children, and we is gone send them to school." "My girls won't spend their lives workin in Somebody's house." "My boys would have gpod jobs." "How's we gone do all that?"

"My mama and daddy always told us, where there is a will, there's a way." Emerson always has a way of letting Mary feel good about herself. He learned a lot from his mother. She was a strong woman and knew how to take charge. His father let his wife have her way, and did everything to please her. They got along very well. "Mary, when we was children, we walked in the dark woods after a hard day of sharecropping." "Mama was afraid of the dark." "Papa would carry her on his back and we walk behind them." "Brother Hodges, shore do love yo' mama." "Wife, I love you more." "What did you call me?" "I said, wife." "That is what yo' daddy call yo' mama." From that day on he called her wife. She loved that name and felt being called a wife, meant she was really grown up and ready to be a wife.

The next day Emerson came home from work, all hot, sweaty, and hungry. But there was no Mary. He had a bath and took a nap. Thinking that his wife would soon be home. When he awaken at 8 p.m., Mary still wasn't there. "Something is wrong," he said to himself. He walked to her folks' house to see if she was there. When he got there, they were no lights. He knocked at the door, but no one came. The doors was locked. He thought someone must be sick or dead. He was afraid of what bad news must be waiting for him. He began to run as fast as he could to his parents' house. Mother Hodges saw him running toward her house. She said to her husband, Will, "Here comes Emerson runnin." His father got up and ran toward him. "Papa, I can't find my wife!" By that time he had entered his parents' house. His mother, Sister Hodges, put her hand on his shoulders. "Mama, I can't find my wife, and no one is at Elder Ginn's house!" "Boy, they all is fine." "They went to the Delta to pick strawberries." "You jus stay here with us." "Mama, I can't do that." "What is you gonna do?" "She is my wife, I'm gone git her and bring her back home!"

The next day, Emerson caught the bus to the Delta. Got his wife and brought her home. "Wife, why did you leave and didn't tell me, is you mad about something?" "No, you ain't do nothing to me." "I had to go." "Mama and daddy told me they needed me to come with them." "Wife, you don't have to be treated like a child or a slave." "I'm gonna take care of you." "Don't you ever do that again!" "I'm gonna tell your mama and daddy myself." Mary looked at her husband with tears in her eyes. "Please, don't say nothin." He held her hand and said, "I got to do this."

Emerson went to the Ginn's house. "Elder Ginn, I want a word with you and yo' wife!" "I don't mean you know harm, but Mary Lee is my wife and her place is with me!!" "I thank you for the house, but my mama told me to pay you back every penny you paid for it." "Boy, you is a real man." "I love you fer that." Idana agreed. So Mary Lee never went any place without telling her husband after that incident. Emerson borrowed the money from a businessman in town, Mr. Westbrook and paid Sam off.

Emerson and Mary Lee visited their parents often. Late one evening, Mary was sitting in Granpa's rocker on the front porch, and had a dream. In the dream, she saw someone running and being shot in the back. When she awaken, she was in shock. "is somethin wrong wit you Mary," Sam asked? "Why is you lookin like that wife," Emerson said? She told her dream to her husband and her parents. "I know somethin bad is gonna happened." Sam said, "Let's pray." Mary could always see things before they happened. Emerson understood, because he was the same way and was amazed. But he never told anyone.

Chapter Eleven

Chance's Death

A few days later, a policeman came to the house, and told Idana that her brother Chance was shot in the back by a policeman who told him to "Halt!" The policeman did not know that Chance could not hear or talk. Chance was always running. The police thought he had stoled something. Idana fainted. Sam picked her up and laid her on the bed. She looked at Mary, and they all knew this what Mary had seen. Her mother, Amy died soon after Chance was buried. They all knew if something happened to Chance, that Amy would not make it. She was close to all her children, but she felt she had to always be there for Chance. He was just a year older than Idana .

After the deaths of Chance and Amy, the family was sad for a long time. Everyone loved Chance. Sam Jr. was only five years old, and love girls already. The other brother, James stayed with Emerson and Mary. Emerson also had a young brothers and sisters, Rose, Nora, and Laura. In which they all stayed with Emerson and Mary at times. Three years had gone by. Mary was afraid that she was never going to have babies. She felt since, she had raised her sister and younger brothers, that God was not going to give her children of her own. Emerson was not worried at all. He knew that when the time was right, and if it was God's will, they will have children. Sam Jr. is now eight and James ten. All they want to talk about was getting girlfriends and getting married. "You boys are too manish, "Emerson said. "Junior, your daddy said you is gonna be a preacher, don't you remember that?" Mary said," He was only five, when my daddy put him on the pulpit, and told everybody that he is gonna be the next pastor." James and Sam Jr. laughed so hard, they fell backwards on Mary's clean floor. "Yeah, Mary Lee, Sam is gonna be a pastor," said James. "No, we gonna get us a wife!" Mary and Emerson laughed and took them home.

Early January, Mary started to look pale and throwing up. Mother Hodges, Enerson's mother, saw her throwing up. "Daughter, I think you is gonna have a baby?" "No, Mother Hodges, think I have a cold." "Watch, what I tell you." "Emerson, your wife is gonna have a baby." "Mama, I think you is right." They were right!! That September the ninth, Emerson Jr. was born. Emerson was a happy man. He rode the bus everyday to work. One day as he got on the bus, three men were laughing. They said to Emerson, "I heard you married one of them Ginn girls?" "I did." So What! "We heard things about them?" "What you hear?" "Can't tell you that." Emerson waited until they got off the bus, and beat all three of them, they tried to fight back. When they saw how strong and angry he was, they ran away.

Emerson came home and sat on the porch, Mary came out and sat beside him. "Where is my baby?" "He's with Mama." "Wife, the baby is too young, to always be with yo' mama." Emerson Jr. was such a good-looking boy, his grandparents loved showing him off. "Wife, you always took care of yo' younger brothers and sister, what is wrong with you?" "My goodness, yo' hand is bleeding, why is that? "Mary, I know I was first with you. "You not only first, but you was the only one." "I know that wife." "But them three nigga men on the bus, was making fun of me and laughing at you." "They must be talkin about your sister, Ellen." "Yo' sister is a flirt and a tease." "She jus like havin fun". Said Mary. "Too much fun, if you ask me. Slippin out of the house at night, gone to Juke Joints, dancing wit everybody, and havin men fightin over her."That is my sister, you is talkin about. Let me take care of that hand, all I can do for my sister is pray for her. Maybe one day she'll change."

Mary washed her husband's hand, and wrapped it in a clean white rag. "Do it hurt?" "I'm airight, but you outta see the three who backs I beat." "You is too strong." "You betta watch out for them." "They don't wont more than what I gave them." The next day, Emerson walked to work. Mary felt it was best for his safety. When he came home that afternoon, she told him she wanted to go back to work, because they needed the money, "My mama say she will keep the baby." "Seems to me, wife, she is keepin the baby more than we do." "Well, I guess you can go back if you really want to." "You know he already ready to suck the bottle." "He is a good baby and good-looking like his daddy." Emerson looked at his wife and said, "He almost as pretty as you. "Yes, he is a beautiful boy." "Mary, boys ain't beautiful they is good-lookin and handsome."

As the time went by, the baby became closer to Idana than he was to Mary. This did not please Mary, but what could she do about it. She felt she needed to work, after all she was used to earning money. So, she had to let Idana continued keep the baby while she was at work. Her brother, Cleve had married a young lady by the name of Marge. He also joined the Navy the same week of his marriage to Marge. Within three months, Marge was expecting her first child. While Cleve was away, Marge had the baby and moved in with her mother and father. Marge was so small, that she slept in the Crib with the baby. Sam and Idana would have loved to babysit Cleve Jr, but Marge would not let anyone keep him, not even her own mother. Marge did not have to work, as Mary did, nor did her older sister Millie, Millie died while giving birth to a baby girl, who also died. Her husband, Earl and her two sons were left alone.

Marge became bitter after Millie's death, and could not get along with any family member, except Mary and Emerson. Emerson was no longer just a church member. But now he has given his life to God and received the baptism of the Holy Ghost. When he come home from work each day, he has prayer with his wife and child. Marge's parents, Brother and Sister Gardner, was also members of Sam's church. They were all good people. Everybody knew everybody, and if someone needed food or clothing, they were ready and willing to give to each other, and did not talk about each other. At least, most of them didn't. Emerson Jr. and Cleve Jr. were baby boys playing together, as Marge and Mary looked on.

Chapter Twelve

Emerson Rejected by the Army

Emerson had been drafted into the Army. As he was going through Basic Training, his Sargeant was glad he passed every test he was given. He was one of the few men drafted that could read and write. After his training, while playing around one day with the other men, he fell out of the tree. He was not hurt. During a routine checkup, his Sargeant was told he would have to release him because of his bloodwork. His blood was very low, but he was not sick. He just felt dizzy at times, and that was all. Emerson was sent home right away.

He did not tell Mary what had happened. All she knew, her husband was home and he would not be killed during the war. Junior was beginning to talk. The only words he could say was, "Mama" and "Shit." "Shit" was the only word Idana would say when she was angry. Mary knew this word came from her mother. She had heard this word her whole life from her mother. To church folk, this was a cuss word, and Emerson didn't like it at all. "Wife, you know no baby should say such a word!" "I know daddy." Mary had gotten into the habit of saying "daddy", while trying to teach Junior to say it. This was pleasing to Emerson. It made him feel like a "King". Although, he was not happy with his mother-in-law, and he sure didn't like the nickname she has given the baby. The nickname she had given the baby was "Boonie." "What kind of name is this for a baby boy?"

Mary was happy just being with her husband and baby. Until her brother Joe, came by and told her he was getting married. "Joe, you too young to get married." "May Lee, I want you to meet my girlfriend, bring her by tomorrow. There's somethin else forgot to tell you, I join the Marines." "You mean you gittin married and leavin your wife at the same time?" "May Lee, I can't make much money around here." She hugged Joe and cried. "Can you please, stop crying." "Mama and daddy already signed for me to go." You know I love you, but you cry too much." Joe brought Kitty by the next day. Kitty looked just like a white girl. Both her parents and all of her brothers and sisters looked the same way. Mary and Kitty soon became close friends. After Joe and Kitty was married, they moved across the street in a big yellow house. Mary soon became pregnant with her second child. Kitty was there for Mary.

While Joe was away in the Marines, Kitty found out she was also pregnant. She was not going to tell Mary, before she could tell her husband. Mary and Kitty was washing clothes, in Kitty's backyard, because Kitty and Joe had a well in which to draw water, Mary said to Kitty, "Ain't you gonna have a baby?" "Don't say that, May Lee." "Why, I know you is." "Yes, I is, please don't tell anybody until I write to Joe and tell him first." "Can tell my husband?" "May Lee, said nobody, not even my mama." "Okay, I won't tell I just keep it to myself." Anything you ask Mary Lee not to tell, she would not tell. Kitty told Mary Lee she was different from anyone she has ever known, because she had never heard her say anything bad about anyone. That's the way Mary was. If She hadn't anything good to say, she would say nothing at all.

Months later, Mary had a baby girl. Three months later, Kitty had a baby girl. The girls were beautiful. Mary and Emerson named their baby Ruthshelle. Kitty and Joe's baby girl was named JoAnne. Now there was four grandchildren for Idana to spoil. Really, there was five, but she was not allowed to be in Cleve Jr.'s life. Marge kept him away from everybody.

Emerson's brother Bud and his wife Val, had two boys older than Boonie, and a girl one year older than Ruthshelle. Mary got along well with Val as she did Kitty. Although, Marge kept to herself most of the time, to Mary everyone was family. Mary would not let anyone say anything bad about Marge. All Mary would say, "We all is who we is and God love us all." That's what my mother-in-law told me." Mary loved her in laws, and boy, did she love Brother Will, her father-in-law. He loved her as well, he said she was an angel. He told Emerson, "Don't never put your hands on her." "No sir, papa, I never do that."

There came a day, when Mary wasn't feeling very well. Trying to take care two small children. She was unable to make dinner. Emerson came home early,

"What's wrong with you wife, you ain't cook my supper?" "I ain't been feeling well today and the babies got colds." Emerson became angry. "My mama always have supper ready, when papa came home from the fields." He slapped her face. Mary began to cry. She didn't say a word to him, she just turned and walked away. "Wife, I'm sorry," as tears rolled down his face. "I don't know what made me hit you." "Please don't tell your mama and papa, or my mama and papa." "I know you gonna tell Ellen." "Yes, I'm gonna tell her and she's gonna cuss you out until the day you die." He tried to put his arms around her, but she pushed him away. "You just try to take care of two sick babies yourself, clean, washing and ironing all on the same day." "Your food is gonna be cooked later today." All you said to me was, where was my food." "I ain't never not cooked you and my children food!" "YOU JUST SLAPPED ME!! He tried to hug her again, she pushed him away and made dinner for her family.

Cleve was home on furlough and came by a few hours later. He knew she had been crying and saw her face was red. "Emerson, did you hit my sister?" "May Lee, did he hit you?" "I know you ain't crazy, nigger?" "You say, you is saved?" "Well, you gonna die tonight!" Joe was also home. "Please, Cleve, don't tell Joe!" "Shut up, May Lee." Joe was in his front yard and could hear them talking loudly. Joe came running. "You betta run, Emerson, Joe's got a knife."

So Emerson ran to his brother Bud's house. He told Bud what had happened. Bud said, "You know if them Ginn boys they gonna harm you, THEY IS GONNA HARM YOU!! Idana and Sam got wind of the matter, and went to Emerson's parents house to talk to Emerson. They told them, that he was not there. He was at Bud and Val's house. They all went to Bud's house along with Cleve and Joe. Emerson's father asked him, what had happened. Emerson told the truth about him slapping Mary. "Did you ever saw me hit yo' mama?" Joe and Cleve rushed through with their knives to cut him. Sam said, "Stop, this now!!" "Devil git outta here!" "I demand you to go now, in THE NAME OF JESUS." Sam told them to go home to their wives and put the knives away, after he had prayed with them. He said, to his son-in-law, "Go home to my daughter and grandchildren." "I'm so sorry, Elder Ginn. I'll never as long as I live put my hands on yo' daughter again." " Well, you betta keep yo' promise, or God will git you." Joe and Cleve always obeyed their father. But, Mary was special. She never harmed anyone.

All she ever did was take care of her brothers and sister, as well as her parents. She had worked hard at long hours, as long as she could remember. God only knows what she had gone through living away from home so early in life. Cleaning, washing, ironing, and not being sent to school, like so many other Negro girls had also done.

Chapter Thirteen

Young and Stupid

Emerson went home, but was ashamed to go in. Mary heard something in the yard, and opened her back door. "What is you doing here?" "My brothers is going kill you!" "Not no more, Elder Ginn told them to leave me alone." "You know they going to mind they daddy." Mary let her husband in the house. He was happy to be home. But when it was time for bed, Mary said, "I let you in, but you ain't going to sleep with me." "Where's I'm going to sleep?" "I don't know, and don't care." Emerson slept on the hard floor for three weeks. He was in the doghouse. Finally, she told him that he can get in bed. As soon as his head hit the pillow, he must have slept for at least twelve hours. She allowed him to be late for work.

When he got home from work, he said, "Wife, I almost lost my job." "You did?" "I guess you look at the clock next time." "Wife, I've been asking you everyday to forgive me." "You said, you did, but you didn't." "Daddy, I thought you was going to protect me and keep me safe from everybody, but you slapped my face." "And you hurt me to my heart." "Wife, what else can I do." "Can we just pray?" He held her hand and they prayed together. After the prayer, she forgave him. "Daddy, God forgave me for many things." "Nobody's perfect." "We all might fall short." "Wife, is you sure you can't read?" "What you just said is in the Bible."

Life went on as usual. Mary took Junior and Ruthshel to her mother-in-law's house. Buddy, Val and the children were there. The children played outside in Mother Hodges' garden. Ruthshel was afraid to really play, because she did not want to get dirty. Junior was just happy to be out playing and cared less about his clothes. When Ruthshel was ready to go home, she would just say, "Well, then." Mary knew it was time to take her home. "Mary, you raisin them children like white children." "Well, that who raise me mostly." "Did Emerson ever tell you that I live with white folks for two years, and learned their ways, and I guess it's still in me." "Daughter, I'm Sorry, I didn't mean to hurt your feelings." Mary was not angry with her mother-in-law at all. She knew she might have been somewhat over protective. But this is the way Mary was.

Early spring, Mary began to have flu Symptoms. Her arms and legs were sore and her body was very weak. After a visit to the doctor, she found out she was pregnant. Mary thought to herself, I had two babies and I've never felt like this. She was not having morning sickness nor feeling faint. She was just sick. Another visit to the doctor's office, revealed that she had had rheumatic fever as a child and didn't know it. As months passed, she became weaker and could not walk. Mary had to crawl and take care of her children. Idana came often to clean and cook for her daughter. Sam was a great help also.

When Mary's mother and father could not come, Emerson's parents were there. Mother Hodges' didn't do any cleaning, she just cooked. Brother Hodges helped Mary washed clothes. He carried tubs of water on his head. No one understood how a man this small could be so strong. He was only 5'8 and weighed only 170 pounds. Mary was so amazed at the strength he had. She told Emerson when he came home, how strong his father was. "Daddy, I know you is strong as an ox, but your papa is stronger than you, I think." "That ain't nothing," he said. "One time a big tree fell in our front yard and mama was scared to go out of the house, because she might fall over it." "Papa jus pick up the tree and threw it in the other side of the yard." "Daddy, what happened to the tree?" "We jus chop it up for firewood." "You go wash up, Daddy and I fix you somethin to eat." "Wife, you can't even walk." "I fix you and my children food." Ruthshell was only two and a half and was very careful not to waste food on her clothes. After supper, Emerson washed the dishes, gave his children a bath and put them to bed.

Chapter Fourteen

The Large Baby

On November 26th, Jim was born with a layer of skin over his eyes. Which country people called a "veil". Miss Robbie, the midwife, pulled the skin from his face. He weighted 11 pounds and 3 ounces. This was the largest baby Mary ever had, so far. Miss Pearla, who lived across the street from Emerson's mother came to see the baby. She was a very superstitious woman, she said, "Sister Mary Lee and Brother Emerson, I think this baby would be able to see ghosts." "I heard he was born with a veil over his face." "It was jus a piece of loose skin," said Emerson. "Brother Emerson, I know I got money buried in my backyard, sometimes I hear change rattling in my backyard, and I don't want nobody to dig for that money, but you, and when you dig and we find it I give you some of it." When Miss Pearla left, Mary told her husband," I hope she don't come back anymore."

Mary gained her strength within a couple of months and was back to her old self. With three little children to care for, Emerson told Mary he had been praying that they won't have anymore children. Mary said, "If its God's will, they won't have any more children, and if it's not his will, they would have more. " And if I do, your papa will help me..." "Wife, my papa is sufferin from a very bad tooth infection and he went to the doctor to late." Within six months Brother Hodges was dead and Mother Hodges had to find a way to raise her little children on her own. Living in Comb City, the children were able to go to school without any problems. Although she missed her hero, who had protected her from danger, loved her, his children and grandchildren was gone forever. Little six month old Jim, will never know the strong man that took care of his mother and loved him. He would never be able to know his grandfather and that was sad. Emerson also knew, he and Bud would have to help their mother. His younger brother Robert, joined the Army to pay for their family home. Mary had given her time and money to take care of her own family, and now she had to help her husband's mother and younger brother Chuck, who was only eight years old, three sisters, Rose, Nora and Laura, ages ten thru fourteen.

Mary loved her father-in-law as much as she did her own father and Sam knew this and was not jealous at all. He and Idana loved the Hodges as well. They had been friends as well as family. Will Hodges had one regret in life, and that was, when he was a young boy he had frightened his little sister to death by slipping up behind her and making the sounds of a bear. He had told Mary, "If he died, he would never come back from the dead and frighten anybody." He also told her, "To never let his grandchildren play those silly games frightenin each other." Mary promised to do what he asked. Everybody knows that Mary keeps her promise. Mary wondered to herself, why this sweet man did not take better care of himself and why he never told her that he was not feeling well? She prayed that somehow that he would make it into Heaven. She believed, if he was living according to the Ten Commandments, which God had given Moses in the Old Testament in the Bible, and did all the things in the New Testament God had commanded, she will see him in Heaven.

Chapter Fifteen

Kitty's Premature Baby

Jim is now a year old. Kitty has had two other children. This time Kitty's third child is premature. He is so small that he fit inside a large matchbox. They were afraid the baby would die. No one knew what to do, except Mary. God had given her so much wisdom, that she knew how to keep this little baby boy alive. She built her own incubator. She took a washpan and filled it with warm water and placed the baby inside the matchbox and another small pan and used a dropper to feed the baby every two hours, until the baby began to grow. Kitty took care of Mary's children as well as her own two girls, They named the baby, Silas. Silas gained five pounds in one month. Kitty was now able to take care of her own baby. She was very thankful to God that he had given Mary the knowledge and wisdom to keep Silas alive.

For two months, Mary had been so involved with the care of Silas, that she forgot to take care of herself. Emerson came home from work, and found Mary sitting in a large chair. "Wife, your skin look pale, you feel alright?" She looked into the large mirror on the wall, "When was you last time?" "I don't know." "I think you need to see a doctor." "Daddy, I go tomorrow." The next day, she went as she promised her husband. Yes, Mary IS PREGNANT AGAIN Mary carried the little baby girl, eight months. The baby girl lived three days and they named her Glotus Jean. Emerson had to bury his own little baby girl in his backyard. "Wife, that it the hardest thing I ever had to do." He a placed her in a shoebox. Mary said, "All I have done for others, this is God's will and to God BE THE GLORY. She began to cry. "Please, don't cry wife. This here is God's will." Mary returned to work again, Idana was taking care all the children. Within a year, Sam Jr. had married Nora, Emerson's younger sister. Laura and her husband had a son. His brother, Benny had moved to Chicago and married Ruth. Chuck and Rose was still in high school and Mary's brother, James had been drafted into the Army. In the meantime, Mary was pregnant again! She had another small baby girl. Althought, the baby was underweight, she was healthy. They named her Gladys Joyce. She was named by a white lady Mary had worked for, who brought all the baby's clothes. Which was a blessing for Mary.

Everybody was having babies, except Ellen. Ellen married Carl. Carl was very jealous of Ellen. Mary, Emerson and the children was visiting her parents this night, when Ellen came running through the door crying from next door, Carl came in behind her. As she fought back, Ellen could fight as well as any man. But Carl was stronger. Sam got between them. Carl hit Sam. Mary was crying, "Daddy, don't let him kill my daddy." When Emerson heard Mary crying, he gave Carl a push, knocked him to the floor, picked him up and proceeded to throw him out the backdoor. "Please, Emerson, don't kill me!" "Son, don't kill him," cried Sam "Well, betta not put yo' hands on Ellen again "Leave Ellen alone." "Come on, Ellen you going home with me and Mary." "Ellen do he always put his hands on you?" "No, Mary Lee I fight back." "But tonight, he beat my ass!" "He ain't gonna beat you no more, you ain't going stay with him."

Carl had to leave, because the house they were living was on Sam's land and one of Sam's houses. They were divorced. Ellen moved back into her house. Carl never came back. Ellen started going to church. As you know, this didn't last long. She was soon back to being Ellen. Staying out late, until she met Mose. They were married. Mose loved her family and the family loved Mose. They kept all kinds of booze in the house. Mary's children became very close to Mose. Ellen didn't want to be bother very much with the children, so she said. When Mose was at work, she would lock the door, to keep the children out. But when Mose came home, he would let them in. Ellen was a very good cook and so was Idana and Mary. Mose told Ellen, she had to be good to her sister's children. "I love them, but they get on my nerves." "I don't care if they do, you just be nice to them." "Mose, they don't listen to me." "They come anyway"

"Mary Lee don't do nothing but have babies." When seven year old Emerson Jr. heard these words from Ellen, he went home that night, and said, "Madea, when are you going stop having them babies and having them babies?" Mary looked at him and said, "When God gets ready." Well, if she only knew David was on the way. Joy was walking and talking. David was born November 7th, that same year, Emerson was called to preach and so was Mary's younger brother, Sam Jr. Sam Sr.'s health began to fail. But the women were still after him. Yes, Sam had made some mistakes. The women had taken him down. He had prayed for God's forgiveness. God and him knew what the mistakes were. Mary never lost faith in her father, She stood beside him no matter what. The members of the church began to fast and pray for their pastor. All of his sons were out of the Armed Forces. Cleve was out of the Navy. Joe was out of the Marines, James was shell-shocked and was sent home from the Army, during his second term.

Chapter Sixteen

The New Pastors

Sam was growing weaker. He had a nervous breakdown. Sam Jr. was the pastor for now. Emerson was pastoring the other church. He, Mary and the children was going to Mount Kingdom and Summit, Mississippi. Not having a car of his own, he paid Mr. Penn to drive them. Mr. Penn had a truck with benches in the back nailed to the floor of the truck and a cover over it to keep out of the rain. In Mount Kingdom, the people did not have electricity. The had oil lamps in the church and in their houses. Some of the houses had dirt floors, They were not ashamed to have guests.

Mary took food for her children to eat. The people were always glad to see Elder Hodges and his family. Every first and third Sunday they were in Summit. Every second and fourth Sunday they were at Mount Kingdom. Most of the people did not have money to put in the offering, they brought him chickens, meat, from their hogs and cows. Some brought eggs and cheese. Only a few had money. Emerson wasn't worried about the money, as much as he was concerned about their dirt floors.

Meanwhile, Sam was sent to Whitfield to an institution. When he returned home, he told his family, "Ize ain't crazy, where you sent me, they is crazy. They drink out of toilets, jump out of windows. The doctor said, "I did not belong there." " He said the swelling in my legs is because my kidneys is bad." "He said sometimes, this condition can make people talk out of they head." "Please, don't send me back there. I was under more pressure there than you would ever know, I saw things I can tell nobody but God." "People be done did terrible things to me, told nobody. I jus wanna keep my family safe." "God's gonna take care of everythin." "I will always trust him." Mary said, "Daddy, as long as I live you won't go back there again." "You hear that wife," he said to Idana. All of their children agreed to take care of their father. Idana was somewhat afraid. The children could not understand why, because he had never laid hands on her. Being afraid, did not stop her from giving him the best care possible.

A few days later, Sam decided to take a walk to Mary's house. Idana was afraid he was out of his head again. He was not. He just wanted to visit his daughter and his grandchildren. The children saw him coming down the hill and cried out to their mother, "Here comes grandpa." Mary was so glad to see him. "Daddy, is everything alright, where is mama?" "Mary, she is runnin around in her barefeet callin for someone to bring me back." "I tell her I'm alright." "She ain't believe me." "Just, sit here daddy." "Junior go tell mama, daddy is alright, and I'll bring him home later." Sam began to feel better each day and was able to return to his church to preach and sing.

Emerson and Mary now have five children. It was Sunday, David's second birthday. Mary was having labor pains during church service. It was Sunday night, Reverend J.B. Hayes, one of the elders in Sam's church, had to take her, Emerson and the five children to Idana and Sam's house to have the baby. Although, she lived one-half block from the church. Reverend J.B. Hayes, wife and daughter was renting part of their house until their own house was built. He and his wife were very tall people and had a daughter, Minnie, who was a good-looking fat girl, who loved to sing. When Reverend J. B. had dropped the family off at Idana and Sam's house, he went to pick up the mid-wife, who had delivered Mary's last three children. Miss Roberts, was a small dark-skinned woman, who always wore a white uniform. The baby boy was named Hue, who looked just like Emerson. They now have six children. Mary wanted to stay at her parent's house for a week. Emerson wanted to take her home within three days, but he did what ever she wanted within reason.

Emerson had to leave for work each morning, Monday thru Friday at 4 a.m. Junior, (Boonie) as he was called by most of his kindredth, had to go across the street to his uncle and aunt's house to draw water before he went to school and again when he came home from school. Ruthshel had to stay home for a week, each time Mary had a baby. Emerson and Mary did not see anything wrong with this. Mary began to change. She became very nervous. She and her husband would leave the children alone on Saturdays to go food shopping. Boonie was not nice to his younger brothers and sisters. He would beat Ruthshel and Jim. Joy was not having this. She would hit him with sticks, bottles, and whatever she got her hands on. When Mary came home, and Emerson would go to his mother's house, the children told how their oldest brother treated them when she was away. When Mary tried to discipline him, he would get in her face and say, "Who do dash in my face!" She didn't tell Emerson, because he would give him a well-deserved whipping. Although, she could trust Ruthshel with the children, she knew she could not trust her older son Junior to stop beating them up. So she had to send them to Idana'shouse. She always send enough food for them to eat. .

Idana gave most of the food to her youngest son's children. There was not enough food to feed them all. Jim, Joy and David would slipped over to Ellen's house, when Mose, Ellen's husband came home for lunch, and Ellen was not there. Mose gave them food and let them come in and eat and told them the rest of the food was not to be given to anyone, except their sisters and brothers. Ruthshel and little Mildred, Sam and Nora's oldest daughter did not play outside very much. Ruthshel had to help Idana clean and little Mildred always had a baby on her hip and a headache. The rest of the children played all day. Jim, Joy and the Dilliard children, sometimes slipped into the woods to pick berries. The Dilliard children were, Sam's nieces' children, who loved to fight.

Sometimes, Jim, Joy and David went down the hill to Emerson's mother's house, to play with Laura's oldest son, who lived with his grandmother. Laura's husband had build a nice house on the corner next to Grandma Hodges. Rob and Bo, Laura's youngest, at that time, was kept in Laura's yard. Laura always had food for her children. "She was the best sister and sister-in-law anyone could ask for," said Mary. Laura's husband, Evan loved his wife and children to death. Mary's children loved being down there. I don't think Grandma Ginn knew they were missing. Mother Hodges told Emerson, they came there during the day, so no one would worry. Because Mary was a worrier.

One night, Mary had a dream, in that dream all she could see was a hospital bed with a child in it. This worried Mary. She began to pray and thought to herself, I share this dream with Nora. She decided to go up the hill, to Nora and Sam's house. When she was halfway down the hill, she saw Nora walking toward her. They both were crying, because Nora had a dream similar to

Mary's. When Mary told Nora her dream, Nora said, "Mary Lee we need to fast and pray, because something is going to happened."

Within days of the dream, Mary got up after Emerson had gone to work, and called the children in for breakfast. Everyone got up, except Joy, Mary called to Joy, she could hardly hear her answer. When Mary walked into the room, she screamed. The other children came in behind her crying. Joy's body was twisted. Her feet and hands were curved. She could not move her neck. Ruthshel and Boonie ran to their Uncle Cleve's house and told him that something was wrong with Joy. Cleve came running with the children back to the house. The only person who had a telephone was a lady, down the street called Miss Cele and her husband Hambone. Miss Ceele called the doctor. The doctor came. After examining Joy, the doctor placed a quarantine sign on each door. Cleve took the children to Idana and Sam's house. Sam drove up to Mary's house. Dr. Moore was still there. He told Sam, "This child has polio." Someone got in touch with Emerson, who met them at the hospital.

Chapter Seventeen

Joy is Stricken with Polio

Emerson then took charge, with tears in his eyes, he held his small child and in a soft, weak voice she said to her father, "Daddy, I don't know why you are crying, I'm not going to die." Emerson wiped his tears and began to pray along with Sam. Mary could not pray or talk. She just sat in the chair with her head back. After the prayer, Sam tried to comfort her, but it was no use. Emerson put Joy back into the bed, and held his wife. "Wife, you got to have faith." She said nothing. Dr. Moore told them, "They didn't have the equipment there to treat her. They would have to send her to Vicksburg, Mississippi. There was other children who had been sent there with the same disease.

She was sent to Vickburg. There she was placed in an iron Lung. Mary refused to leave her there. After being told she could not stay. The doctor then agreed to let her stay. She sat in a chair day and night beside her child. Finally, she began to pray. Joy's condition had improved. She was able to be placed in a regular room, which Mary slept in the bed with her. Each morning, Mary gave her a bath. One day, Mary forgot to put her panties back on her. When the doctors came in to check on her, she told them, "To go away," because she did not have her panties on. They said, "We wait pretty girl, until your mother put them back on you." "Turn your back." They did as she asked.

The doctors told Mary that Joy was getting better each day. Emerson, Sam and Idana along with Mother Hodges came to visit and pray. Mother Hodges told them, "I believe my grandbaby is gonna come back home to us soon." They were only allowed to stay for an hour. Emerson wanted Mary to come home, but she refused. She was not going to leave her child until she was well enough to come with her. After two months, Mary was told that she could take her child home the next week, and that her blood was very low and that they would have to give her two tablespoons of Red Wine, twice a day, and set her in the Sun each day.

When Joy was discharged, Emerson came by bus to take them home. Her body was now straight, but she could not walk. Mary was glad to be home and sleep in her own bed. The other children could return home. Boonie cried everyday, seeing that his baby sister could not walk. Rushshel, Jim and David did all they could to help their sister. David just rubbed her feet and Hue would just laid beside her. When Mary gave Hue his bottle, Joy was able to help him hold it. She was able to use her hands more. Boonie told Mary, "She's using her hands." When Mary came into the room and saw Joy using her hands, this made her very happy. Daddy said, "my baby is healed, but she still can't walk." Emerson was at the table eating supper. "Wife, sometimes a person is healed, and we ain't going to understand somethings. Believe what your daddy said, we just have to wait and see and keep the faith." "Yes, daddy, I know, but this is my child." "Wife, there's a song that says, "What He Do For Others, He Will Do For You." "Now, do you understand what I been trying to say?" "I reckon, I do."

They prayed with their children as usual each morning, and if Emerson left early, they prayed while the children slept. Prayer was always in the home. Mary remembered when she lived with the Blacks family, how she taught those two little girls to pray. When Mrs. Black asked her what she was doing, she told her about her love for God and God always have time to listen to prayer. She was not sure Mrs. Black understood her, but she came into her daughter's bedroom each night and prayed with them. "Daddy, you is right." "God do heal before you see the results." "Wife, you just got what I been saying." "I been praying in my heart all day." "Daddy, been doing the same thing." "I going help you more." "I'll come home at lunch time, and work with Joy's arms and legs." "That's what the doctor said we need to do, daddy." Emerson came home on his lunch break for weeks. Mary's brother, Joe also came to help his older sister,

People who came to visit Joy, gave her money, but when Joe wanted to get drunk he would borrow five dollars. Each time he got drunk, he would pay her twice. Mary's cousin Lovett also came. Lovett gave her money and prayed everytime she came. On this Sunday, Lovett prayed, suddenly Joy began to walk. Soon after that, she was well. Emerson said to his wife later, "Now wife, you know Lovett ain't saved." "It had to be God, daddy, and you don't know if Lovett got saved or not." "I just know my child is walking."

Chapter Eighteen
After Polio

That September, Joy was able to start school. Mary watched her closely for a while. Boonie, Ruthshel and Jim was careful not to hurt her while playing. Joy became stronger and stronger each day. She could do anything the other children did. She did not like pity and would not let anybody help her do anything at all, including her parents. She always said, "1 can do it myself." Joy played football, baseball and basketball with the boys. She also learned how to box, as well as her brother Boonie. Matter of fact, she was so good at boxing, that Boonie used her to teach other little boys how to box, as he collected twenty-five cents.

When Mary found out what Boonie was doing, she immediately put a stop to it! She wanted Joy to act more like a little girl. Ruthshel was a' perfect little lady" and wanted to teach joy to be more "girly", by playing with her cousin, Barbara, and not the boys. This was not pleasing to Joy. But she knew Ruthshel knew what was best for her. In the meantime, Ruthshel and Joanne became very close, and younger sister Myrt felt left out and alone. Joanne was hard to talk to, so she asked Ruthshel if she could go to the Front with them. The Front, was a place where all the teenagers met and ate ice cream. It was owned by Mr. and Mrs. Gates, who had a daughter about Ruthshel and Joanne's age.

When Joanne told Myrt, "she was too young to be with them, Myrt said, "I have the biggest feet and I'm taller than you." Ruthshel took Myrt's side and she became as close to Myrt as she was to Joanne. In the meantime, Joy and Barbara were happy outside braiding the tail grasshair and putting bows on them. They were pretending that the tall grass was doll's hair. Joy was not nice to Barbara, because she wanted to be taller than Barbara. Barbara felt right at home at her Aunt Mary Lee's house. Of course, Mary Lee didn't know how Joy was treating Barbara. She would have put a stop to it!! All of Mary's nieces and nephews loved her dearly.

Joe's oldest sons, Jim and Silas were always in trouble. Mary Lee and Kitty were always looking for them. Sometimes they were no where to be found, and when they where found, they were either fighting someone else or running around with a wagon that Boonie built, selling green plums for peanuts. They often sold them to Miss Martha and Mr. John. Miss Martha was not fooled by them. Matter of fact, she loved those boys, but felt it was her duty to tell their parents. One day, while playing, they had a fight. Jim got the best of Silas and Silas chased Jim with an axe. Laura's oldest son, Earl, a year younger than the two of them, happened to be there. Being larger and stronger than Silas, took the axe and beat Silas' behind. Silas was still trying to fight. Mary came out, pulled him up from the ground and took him home.

She told Kitty what had happened. Kitty told Mary she was going to punish him. Not knowing what Kitty was going to do, Mary left. Kitty placed Silas in a sack and hung it to a bed pole, and held fire under him and smoked him. "Madea, please let me down!!" "I won't do that anymore." "You want me to tell your daddy?" "Your aunt ain't going let you come to her house anymore." "Because you tried to kill her child." "Don't nobody want to play with you." "Please, Madea let me down!" When she took him down, she did not allow him to go outside to play for a week. When he was able to go out, he slipped out that night. No one could find him. Emerson was coming from his mother's house, when someone jumped on his back. It was Silas. "Save, me Uncle!" "I saw a ghost!" "Boy, you can't get in my clothes." Emerson took him by the hand and said, "you mean somebody's bad as you, is afraid of a ghost?" "Please, Uncle Emerson take me home." Emerson laughed and walked him to his front door. Joe wanted to know what happened. "He said he saw a ghost." "It should have gotten his bad behind!" "Come in here, boy and go to bed."

The next day the children was playing as usual, Mary left them home alone. David and Lawrence, two five year olds were playing together. When Lawrence, said to David, "We're gonna get gas in our house." "No you ain't," said David. "Yes, we is." Lawrence said, "If ye don't git no gas, you shore ain't." Lawrence said, "Let's play Grandpa Ginn and Grandma Ginn." "You be Grandpa Ginn, and I be Grandma Ginn." "I'm gonna cook my husband a chicken for supper." "Me don't won't no chicken." "Me wont pork chops and ham." "Me don't like chicken that much." "Don't you know that we don't got no hogs?" "Aunt Ellen got hogs." David said, "She's stingy" "She won't give ye none."

"Aunt Ellen is a artificial woman.' 'What is a artificial", said Lawrence? "That means she ain't real." "She is too." "Well, she ain't got no children." "She might get some." "How is she gonna git some." Joy and Barbara was playing nearby. Joy said, "She need to see Miss Roberts." "Babies fly from the sky and Miss Roberts catch them in her black bag and bring them to you." "Joy, she is artificial and she don't want no babies." "Cause she always says bad words." Joy said, "When she say bad words to me, say bad words too." Barb interrupted, "Oh, Aunt Mary Lee gonna beat you!"

"Nobody gonna beat me, they think I'll get sick again." Joy did get sick again. This time it was rheumatic fever. She was not able to walk. Mary wasn't afraid this time. But her nerves had the best of her. She was not patient with her children, nor her husband. lt seems like everyday, Mary was upset about something. She fussed, if the children did not wash the dishes clean, they only had a little cold water to wash the dishes in. Sometimes, Mary heated the water on the wooden stove. One night, while removing the water from the stove, Ruthshel accidently scalded David. Boy did he cry!! Ruthshel did not know what to do. She had spilled hot water on her little brother. She was very sorry. Mary Lee knew exactly what to do. She used cold water and Vaseline on his skin. It was not a third degree burn, David's wound healed quickly,

Mary was afraid to leave them home alone, because of David's wound. She did not want the skin to reopen and get infected. She did not trust children to take care of children while she worked. The children went back into the woods, while Idana was on the porch with her friends. Sam's nieces children, who was being watched by their older sister, Frances, who was also in the woods with Jim and Joy. Jim told Joy to stay in the wagon, while they picked berries. While Joy was sitting in the wagon, a big snake wrapped himself around her leg. Joy screamed out for help. Her older brother, Jim came to her rescue and pulled the snake from her sister's leg. All the children ran home, Jim pulled the wagon as fast as he could. They spilled all the berries. When they got to Idana's house, and told her what had happened; Idana was angry with the children for slipping off. She did not say anything to them. She called her husband, "Elder Ginn,

Elder Ginn," Sam came from the back room, where he spent most of his time praying and reading the Bible. He prayed for his granddaughter's leg. The right leg was twice the size of the left leg. "What, happened, to her, wife?" "A snake bit her." "Wife, wait until Mary Lee Come home and we will take her uptown to a doctor.

When Mary Lee came home, Sam asked Mr. Parks, the young man from across the street, to drive his daughter in his new car into town. Sam did not let anyone drive his car, but he was not feeling well. He trusted Henry Parks to drive the car. When they arrived at Dr. Moore's office, there was very little swelling on the leg. He gave her a shot of Penicillin and told them don't worry and to continue to give her Penicillin tablets for seven days. Sam told Mary not to worry that his precious grandchild will be alright. Mary asked, "Why do so much happen to this child?" Sam said, "God has somethin for her to do." "She might be small, but she's strong." It did not take Joy's leg long to heal. Soon she was up running and playing with the other children.

Mary took the children home and had a late supper. Emerson had gotten home early that day, and was not worried about Mary and the children, because sometimes they were late coming home. All Emerson wanted to do was eat. He was very much like his mother in that way. Grandma Hodges loved food and would eat anytime of the night Mary told Emerson what had happened after supper. "Wife, can you just stay home and take care of my children?" "Yo' mama didn't work." "Daddy, you don't have that kind of money, and besides that you is always giving money to your mama." "Wife, Bud is trying to help me get a job at the Rail Road Shop." The next day, Emerson stayed home with the children.

Emerson heard a knock at the front door, he opened the door. There was this big, white man, as large as Emerson standing there smiling. Joy was holding Emerson's leg smiling. "That little gal has some pretty white teeth." "Thank you, sir." "Now, who is you?" "Just call me Big Bill." "I've heard a lot of good things about you." "Yessir, from who?" "Your brother Bud." "Do you want to work at the shop?" "Yessir." "When can you start?" "Rite now." "Boy, why don't we just wait til Monday morning?" "Bud told me you can read and write." "Yessir, I can." "I think I'll all work out," "Just be there Monday at seven o'clock and ask for Big Bill." "My office is the first one you come to."

Chapter Nineteen
The Railroad Shop

That Monday morning, Emerson was hired on the spot. No Negro had ever had a job as easy and paying forty dollars a week. All he had to do was ride a bicycle and carry documents from office to office each day. The Negro men began to spread lies, saying he was spying on them and that he was a white folk's nigger. The rumors unnerved and upset him. He told his wife, Mary Lee about it. "Daddy, don't let them niggas run you away from a good job." "I don't know, wife." "Your brother been trying to get you this job for years." "Now, you got it." "You know they is jealous of you, because most of them is like me." "They can't read they own name." "Wife, why you say that?" "You can read yo' name and other little words." "I can only read as good as a second grade child." "Wife, they can't read nothin." "And I do mean, nothin."

Emerson went back to work at the Railroad Shop. He tried to make the best of it to ignore them as much as he could. But as he rode his bicycle from shop to shop, someone would call out, "white man's nigger." The old Emerson would have beat someone's butt, but the new Emerson, who has became a Christian was not up for a fight. He talked to his brother, Bud concerning the matter. Bud said, "You got to be strong, because you have a family to feed and nothin they say to you is worth losing your job." Emerson stuck it out as long as he could. Finally, he just gave up.

Now Emerson doesn't have a job. But there was a pipeline going through Comb City. They were hiring at that time. Again, Emerson was hired on the spot. This was very hard work. He had to leave for work at 4 a.m. and did not return home until dark. Mary and the children were alone, and Mary was about to give birth to her seventh child. The labor pains had begun. What was Mary to do? Boonie and Jim were young boys, but Boonie was afraid of the dark. Jim wasn't afraid of anything. "Madea, do you want us to go get Miss Roberts?" "I guess, you will have to." So Boonie woke Jim up and they walked along the highway to Miss Robert's house. Mary had Ruthshel to take the younger children to the other side of the house. Joy and David asked Ruthshel, "What is wrong with Madea?" "Boonie and Jim is going to get Miss Roberts and we goin to have another baby in the house." "How do you know that," said Joy. "I just know it. I even know where babies come from." "Where do they come from, Joy?" "They fly from the sky, and Miss Robert's would catch it and bring it to Madea." "Joy, you are a stupid little girl."

There was a crack in the wall, Joy could see between the wall planks. "Why is Madea in the bed?" "Don't no baby come from no sky." "That baby is comin from Madea." Joy thought to herself, "Ruthshel must be crazy!" "I know babies fly from the sky." Boonie and Jim returned with Miss Roberts and joined Ruthshel and the other children in the large livingroom. Soon they heard a baby cry. David was so happy. Hue asked David, "What is that noise?" "That's Madea's baby crying." "You mean Madea got a baby?" The two of them ran to the other side of the house to see the baby. But Miss Roberts did not allow them to come into the room. "You have to go back now, and I call you later." "You have a little brother.'

Later, Miss Roberts called all the children to the room and told them that the baby was a boy. Boonie wanted to know, what was Mary Lee going to name the baby. She told him, "We're goin to name the baby tomorrow, not today." They would name the baby the next day. The next day, Bud's oldest daughter, Dot came to see the baby. "Aunt Mary, came we name the baby, Darnel?" "It sound's good to me, ask the other children." The oldest four, thought that was a good name. So the baby was named Darnell. As you know, Ruthshel had to stay home everytime Mary had a baby. This was early January, Ruthshel had to stay home for two weeks. Grandma Hodges came every day to sit with Mary Lee and take care of the baby. Grandma Hodges was not going to do any housework. This is because she didn't clean her own house, and she wasn't going to clean anyone else's. Ruthshel cleaned and cooked the best she could. If she needed help, Grandma would help her. Idana was not able to come, because Sam needed her more, and besides she was taking care of Sam Jr. and Nora's children.

Two weeks later, Ruthshel returned to school. Being behind in her classes, was not a problem, because her teachers understood that she had to help her mother. In those days, it was not uncommon for the oldest daughter or son to be out of school, when a parent was sick or having a baby. It was unfortunate, that little Negro boys and girls had to go through this. But Negro people did not have money to hire help. They did the best they could.

Mary began to feel guilty about have to keep Ruthshel out of school. But she didn't know what to do about it. She thought, "if I had another baby, I would have to get up and take care of things on my own." Joy and David helped Mary take care of the new baby. They could hold the baby and help feed him. Barbara came to help Joy hold the baby sometimes, Barbara Ann loved baby Darnell. Joy was jealous and told her to go home, she said, "Michael is your baby brother, and I don't want you to hold mine." Barbara Cried and went home. David told Mary Lee what Joy had done. "Joy, you can't treat your Cousin like that." "Don't you ever do that again, young lady."

Chapter Twenty
Challenges

Mary Lee goes back to work again. The children now are able to stay home alone. Ruthshel is twelve and very responsible. Emerson Jr. is in Louisiana with Aunt Valma. Aunt Valma was Idana's younger sister and loved Boonie more than the other kids. He never had to worry about clothing or shoes. She sent him home after his visit with a new wardrobe every year. She even brought him a new watch. He would not let his brothers or sisters touch his watch, nor see his new clothes. He kept them in a suitcase under his bed.

When they went to play Tin Can Ball, they did not have a baseball nor softball. Mary and Joe's children played together all day. But when it was time for Joe and Kitty to come home, Joanne would take her sisters and brothers home and cook dinner. One day they got carried away playing "Tin Can Ball", David and Hue was watching their little brother, Darnell. So they thought. All of a sudden, they heard people screaming. Darnell had crawled in front of the bus across the street. The driver stopped just in time. A nice lady got off the bus and got the baby, while the driver waited for her to return. She asked Joanne, "Who did the baby belong to?" Joanne told her that," it was her little cousin and that someone was supposed to be watching Darnell." Ruthshel took Darnel into the house, gave him a bath. No one told Mary or Emerson what had happened that day, except Hue. All he knew how to say was, "A lady on the bus got Darnell." "What is he talkin about, " Mary asked. David tried to tell the truth, but Jim pulled him back. Mary Lee got the belt and said, "I'm going to beat all of you, if somebody don't tell me the truth!" David was not a liar. He explained, "Madea, Darnell crawled in front of the bus." "Everybody was playin "Tin Can Ball". "I wanted to play too, So I from forgot about him." Mary was so angry. "Ruthshel, I left you in charge "Madea, Boonie is older than me." "Why can't he be in charge?" "Yeah, Madea, I am older than that cat-eyed girl." "Emerson Jr., you know I can not trust you." He stood in Mary's face again and said, "Who do?" Before he could say the words, "Dash in my face," she hit him with the belt again and again. He caught the belt in his hand and held it. "Now, I have to tell your daddy about this"

Mary knew how hard her husband can be. She could not stand how rough Emerson could be with Junior. So, she did not tell him. But Joy, climbed into her father's lap wanting to tell him the truth. Mary looked at her and said, "Get out of my husband's lap." "He's not your husband." I guess it must have been a joke, but Mary held a straight face, and said to her again, "Get out of my husband's lap." "He is not your husband, he is my husband!" "Wife, why you say somethin like that?" "You don't mean that." Mary didn't answer him. She just walked away and gave the children their supper.

After supper, it was Jim's turn to wash the dishes. Jim went across the street and drew two buckets of water from Joe and Kitty's well. He had enough water to wash dishes and for everyone to take baths in the big wash tub. Mary always bathed the youngest children first and the older children had their bath later in the same water. After they was in bed, she would mopped her floors with the same bath water. If Jim had a bowel movement at night, he would not go outside to the "Outhouse". He was afraid, because he remembered the story his father had told him, about a man named, Nolan who was bitten by a spider and could never walk straight again. So, Jim used old newspaper at night, and rolled it up and set it by the backdoor. When this happened, it made the house smell awful. The next morning, Mary used bleach-water to freshen the house.

Jim was teased by his other brothers and sisters. All he could do was cry. Emerson ordered the other children not to tease him, because it was his fault in the first place. Mary asked him "How was his day?" He said, "It was good, but he was still being teased and called names by the men who had no schooling. "I told you, daddy don't pay them any attention. "But, wife they is so dumb." "You mean they is dumber than me." "Wife, you ain't dumb." "You was smart enough to merry me." "A good-lookin black boy like me, you know um in there." "You is always bragging about yourself." "You is a good-looking dark-skin man, I guess you want me to say how pretty you is?" "Wife, you know ain't nobody as pretty as you." "Hush, daddy the children is in the back-room waiting for us to walk them down to daddy and mama's house, so daddy can learn all the preachers in our church more about the Bible."

Chapter Twenty-one

Teaching the Word

Elder Sam Ginn, would sit in his rocking chair in the backroom of his house, as the four preachers sit in from of him so he could explain the Bible to them. One of the four preachers was his son Sam Jr. Mary's children sometimes sit on the floor behind the preacher's chairs and listen to their grandfather also. As he answered questions the preachers would ask. Most of the time, they went next door to Nora and Sam Jr.'s house. Nora stayed home because there was always a new baby that needed her attention. Nora was a very playful aunt. She played games with her children as well as Mary's children. Their favorite game was "hide and seek." Nora along with Emerson Jr, hid the small children under the beds, in the closet, anywhere they would fit. Emerson Jr. felt that he was as grown as Nora and Sam. On his thirteenth birthday, he told his younger sister and brothers, that he was a grown man. They thought he was a man. He said, "I got a girlfriend, and her name is Doris." "How do she look, Boonie," asked Joy. "She is cute." "But her hair is so short, you can smell her brain."

One day Doris came by the house after school. She looked like she had put a whole can of grease in her hair. Hue, who always spoke his mind, asked, "Girl, why do you have so much grease in your hair.?" Doris was embarrassed, and did not answer. David said, "Girl, my brother said why you have so much grease in your hair?" Emerson Jr. told them to go outside and play. Ruthshel told Doris she had to go and could not come back, unless their parents were home. Junior said he was a man and that Doris could stay. Doris left and got on the bus that ran in front of their house. He looked at his sister, "I wish your cat eyes would stay out of my business!"

David could not wait for his mother to come home. As soon as Mary walked into the door, David said, "Boonie had a girl in the house." "What did you say, David?" Whenever anyone misbehaves, slipped off, or had a fight, they would say, "Don't tell Madea and daddy." David said, "I won't tell, but if they asked, I have to tell them the truth." Jim said, "Boy, can't you lie sometimes?" "Just, leave him alone, Jim." "You know he's too stupid to lie," said Joy, Boonie punched David in the chest. Of course, Joy and Jim jumped Boonie. Joy broke his new watch, Aunt Valma had brought him that summer. He said, "You broke my new watch." "I don't care and you better stay away from me." "I hit you upside your head with this baseball bat!" Cousin Billy had left his bat at Mary's house.

Cousin Billy Ginn was Sam's first cousin, who came to town with a suitcase full of money. One, five and ten dollar bills. He came from New Orleans, where he played his harmonica and sang on the street pretending to be blind. He liked "to feel on women". So he ran his hands over their bodies, trying to say, "thank you for the money", they dropped in his basket. All that the women would say, "That poor blind Billy, don't mean no harm, he jus tryin to feel us to see who we are." When men dropped money in the basket, he shook their hands. Every three months he came to town to visit his cousin Sam and give him money. Sam never told anyone how much money Billy gave him.

Emerson Jr. didn't want to be hit upside the head with a baseball bat. Jim took the bat from Joy and held it, then a tallman took the bat from Jim. It was Mary's uncle Hillery, Sam's baby brother. Hillery was a drunk and he would drank anything with alcohol. Mary brought vanilla flavor in large bottles, Hillery would drank all the flavor, he even drank shoe polish!! When Mary got home, and found Hillery there, she went straight to her kitchen cabinets, to see if she had any flavor left. it was all gone! Hillery laid drunk on Mary's livingroom floor. "Get up, Hillery, get out of my house before my husband come home." "Mary Lee, you know Emerson like me." "He don't want you lyin here drunk in front of his children." "just let me spend the night. sleep right here on the floor." "Hillery, you smell like alcohol and pee." "I got fresh clothes in my sack." "I go over to Joe's house and wash my dirty clothes."

When Joe saw Hillery, he told him to come inside. "Hillery, you don't have to drink that bad stuff." "Drink some good whiskey with me." The two of them sat on Joe's back steps and got sloppy drunk. Hillery, somehow, found his way back to Mary's house. Emerson looked up at him, and said, "Man, what am I gonna do with you." "I don't know Emerson, jus let me sleep on the floor." "Hey, Emerson, you know them bad children of yours, was tryin to kill each others." "Man, I save they life." "You oughtta thank me." "Wife told me everything." "You can sleep on the couch and sober yourself up." "Tomorra, get up and go to your brother's house." "You know you got to be sober to be there." "My father-in-law ain't gonna take no stuff." "I know you right, Emerson." "My brother ain't never took no stuff." "Did I ever tell you about his women, before he merried Idana?" "I don't wanna here it." "That was before the Lord saved him.'

The next morning, Hillery left, Mary was not sad. She was glad to see him go. Although, she loved her uncle, she did not like his drunken ways. "Daddy, it wouldn't bother me at all, if he would just stay away." "He drank all of my flavorin." "Now, I have to wait until the man come and bring more." "I guess, I won't get no cake this Sunday." "I guess, you will." "This Sunday, we will go to Mount Kingdom." "You know all those fast women want to fed you." "Wife, you know they give you and my children food too." "Daddy, you know I cook my children food before we leave this house." "But I don't want to hurt anyone's feelings." It didn't matter which church they were at, Mary always brought food from home.

On this particular Sunday, Sister Ross looked at Joy and said, "She is such a cute little girl." "Can I give her a slice of cake?" "Please, honey, don't give her any cake." "But she is so cute." "Please let me give her a slice." "Well, okay." Joy took the cake and looked at Sister Ross, after she had tasted the cake. Joy said, "This cake is nasty!" Mary placed her hand over Joy's mouth. "Madea, this nasty cake ain't got no sugar in it." "Sister Ross, I'm so sorry." "She's spoil, because she's a sickly child." "Eveybody just let her say what she want to." "Madea, you eat some." "You see." The cake was nasty.

After church service was over, Sister Ross asked Mary, if they could drive her home. Mr. Penn took most of the church people home with Emerson, while Mary and the children stayed behind. After church one night, while they were driving home, Mary, Mr. Penn and Hue rode in the front of the truck, and the other children rode in the back. Emerson Jr. told his brothers and sisters, that he was not going to fight them anymore. He was going to be good, read his Bible and become a preacher. He did changed and became a preacher, while he was still thirteen. He said that God had filled him with the Holy Ghost and God had told him to preach. His father allowed him to preach one Sunday night at his church. He did really well. Ruthshel knew he wasn't real and so did Jim. He returned to his old ways soon after.

Monday morning, Emerson went to the Pipeline, where he wrote down the hours the men worked. After work, several men wanted to fight him. He told them, "I can't take no more of this, I prayed." "I'm not gonna fight you." "You won't see me here again." He had to tell Mary that he had quit the job. Mary began to cry, "You let people run you away from a good job." "You oughtta had stay there." "You can outlive a lie." "You know they was lying." "Wife, I want to stay save." "So it was best for me to leave." Emerson stayed home for a few days. Later that week, he went to New Orleans to work. He was away from home for two weeks, before he sent money in a letter home to Mary. He told her that it was his first paycheck and that he loved New Orleans. Mary could not read the letter. Ruthshel had to read it for her. Whenever Mary received mail, she let Ruthshel read it for her, because Junior thought she should be able to read it herself.

The next week, Emerson sent sixteen dollars. While Ruthshel was reading, Mary threw the money on the floor, and said, "What am to do with sixteen dollars and seven children." "Madea, don't you cry," said Jim as he hugged her around her waist. She rubbed Jim's head. "Madea ain't going to cry, but I got to go back to work." "Madea, all you do is work." "When I grow up and become a man, I'll give you all the money you need, won't we David?" "Jim, it going to be a long time before we grow up, but you will." The following week, Emerson sent fifty dollars and in the letter it said, "Wife, I want you to come and visit me this weekend." "I will not be able to pastor the churches anymore." "Please tell your daddy, I love him, but I need to make money to feed my children." "I will never forget God and thank Him for the trust He's got in me." Mary told Idana she was going to visit her husband and that Ruthshel will be going on a school trip. She had given Ruthshel five dollars for the school trip and food. Mary, Hue and Darnell went to New Orleans to visit her husband. They went to Lake Ponchartrain. Mary loved the beach. She did not have a swimsuit. She pinned her sundress between her legs to go into the water. They spent most of the day on the beach. Later that day, they returned to Miss Bee's rooming house, where Emerson was living with other men, they each had their own bedroom. Mary asked Miss Bee, if she could cook supper for everyone.

Miss Bee was glad to have Mary there. She did not cook as well as Mary. Mary wanted to stay longer and Emerson wanted her there. She called her mother and asked her, if it was alright for the children to stay with her for the next week, Idana agreed. Before the week was over, Idana had to call Mary and Emerson to come home. Sam's condition had worsened. Sam had been in bed for days, unable to stand or sit. When Mary and Emerson arrived, all of his children were there. Sam could hardly speak, but when he saw Mary his eyes lit up. His whole family was in the house. Mary's younger children were sleeping in the room, where Grandpa Benny had died two years before.

Sam pulled himself up in bed and began to preach to them. He said, "In the book of Job," Job said, "All my appointed time I'm gonna wait until my change come." "Now, family my change is come." He gave a big smile and died, with a smile on his face. Idana laid in the bed beside him, trying to arouse him. "Mama," Sam Jr. said, "Get out of bed, Daddy's gone." "But he still smilin," said Ellen. James held Ellen's hand. "Ellen, Daddy is gone." "Cleve is the oldest now," "And we have to let him handle everything." Cleve turned around to Emerson. Cleve said, "Emerson, you know Daddy loved you like a son." "Now you got to lead us." Emerson said to Mary's family, "I have always loved you as I loved my own sisters and brothers." "But, Elder Ginn said, your younger brother, Sam would be the next leader.' And Sam was.

They all sat around with their wives and children. Early that morning, the undertaker came for the body. Little Hue looked at Sam's bed and asked Mary, "Where's the Grandpa?" "He is gone." "Where is he gone?" "When will he be back?" "He's never comin back." "Where's the gas he had?" When Sam broke wind, Mary told Hue, her Daddy had gas. He was afraid to get close to him, because he was told gas was dangerous. "Madea, where did Grandpa go?" "He went to Heaven to be with God." "And when you go be with God, that means you have been very good." "And maybe, one day, when you is a old man, you can be with God." "Madea, don't cry." Mary could not stop weeping. This made everyone weep. Even the little children. Ellen seemed to be the strong one. "We gotta stop cryin, and let Uncle Jim, Aunt Mindy, Aunt Fannie, and Aunt Letha know." "Nobody know where Hillery is."

Chapter Twenty-two

A Powerful Preacher Dies

After everyone was notified, they came to town. Idana's family also came. Uncle Jack, Uncle Wilmar, Uncle Esco and Aunt Valma. They stayed with family members, except for his three sisters that stayed with Idana. Idana called them all "sister" and they treated her as a sister. The night befor the funeral, Sam's body was brought back to the house. The house was filled with people, relatives and church members, preachers from everywhere in Mississippi were there. The morning after the wake, before they took the body away, Idana held Joy in her arms and told her to kiss her Grandpa goodbye. When Joy touched him, she said, "Grandma, Grandpa is laughin at us." "I don't think he's really dead." "Yes, he is dead." "He will never open his eyes again."

All his children and their families went home to get dressed for the funeral. Marge loved her father-in-law more than anyone realized. She did not take his death very well. To Cleve's surprise, she stayed with Idana and rode in the family car with the others. It was a very sad funeral. Mother Hodges and Sister Washington served everyone after the funeral at Sam and Idana's house. Some of the family ate at Mary's house along with the preachers. Mary was about to serve the preacher, Elder Belt. He sat in his chair along with the others. "Daughter, where is your children?" "They outside playing." "I would not eat a bite, until the children come to the table." "Daughter, don't ever feed anyone before your children.' "And don't give them any leftovers," "Always give them the best." He did not know that Mary had always given her children the best.

Three months later, Mary went back to New Orleans with Hue and Darnell to be with her husband. This time while she was away, one of Idana's hogs got out of the pen. Everyone was running around trying to catch the hog. Boonie slipped and fell on a glass bottle. He had a deep gash on his upper right thigh. Idana wrapped the leg with a white sheet to stop the bleeding. Emerson's brother, Uncle A.P. was visiting Nora. When he saw what had happened, he drove to the drugstore and got everything Idana needed to clean and take care of Emerson Jr.'s leg. The bleeding stopped. Uncle A.P. washed his nephew and put him to bed. As he sat in Idana's livingroom, he asked Idana, "How long has your husband been dead?" (Idana replied, "Three months." "You fine, you fine, swear you fine." Idana just smiled and walked away.

He followed her into the kitchen, smiling. "is you ready to date?" "No, my husband jus died." "All I want to do is be wit my children and grandchildren." "A.P. you can leave now." "Anyway, heard you brought your girlfriend wit you." "I did." "I only brought her because she beg me to come." "And she's half crazy." "I left her down at my sister's house." "Well, where is you stayin?" "Ain't nobody at Emerson's house." "I know him and Mary Lee won't mind if stay I there, while they is in New Orleans." He stayed there while they were away and left twenty dollars behind on Mary and Emerson's bed.

Mary found the twenty dollars on the bed. Twenty dollars was a lot of money in those days. Uncle A.P. was a good man. He loved all his nieces and nephews, but he said Emerson's and Mary's children were special, because they never asked him for money. Mary did not allowed them to beg or eat at anyone's house, except their own. If they were visiting their friends, and was asked if they wanted to eat, they had to say, "No thanks." If they felt hungry, they had to go home and eat. There was rules to follow in their home, and if they didn't follow them they were punished. Emerson was very much like his father. Whatever Mary wanted, Mary got it. The main purpose was to teach the children to live free from sin and always have faith in God. She thanked God for the money that she was not. expecting and used it wisely. She filled the house with food and brought ice from the iceman.

They had an icebox that was not electric. So she brought a big block of ice from the iceman, five times a week to keep the food fresh. She always had a bottle of Kool-Aid and if she did not have Kool-Aid, she had sweet water. The children was just as happy. Sometimes the other children, who was not fortunate enough to have the KoolAid or sweet water with ice, came to her backdoor and begged her for something sweet to drink. She gladly gave the other children whatever they were drinking or eating. Often food was low, but she could always make a meal. They had chicken feet soup, baked sweet potatoes that she threw into the fireplace and baked. They never went to bed hungry. She often worked late. Sometimes, the people she work for did not have enough money to pay her full salary. They gave her leftover food and worn clothes.

Mary did not complain. She just took the old clothing and food. But if the food was old, she threw it away and the raggedy clothes also. Mary was not going to dress her children in rags or feed them bad food. She always knew how to have credit in a clothing store to buy the children's clothes, that she was unable to pay cash for. So, she paid a little on her account every week. When she felt that Emerson did not send her enough money, she began to wonder, what is he doing with the money. "Was there another woman?" Or. "Is he loaning the money?" "What could he be doing?" She might not be able to read, but she was not stupid.

Chapter Twenty-three
Mary's Suspicions

Ruthshell had to write letters for her mother to her father, letting him know she could not survive with such a small amount of money for that week. The next week he sent twice the amount. Emerson was the type of person that would give money to anyone with a sad story. He was too generous. Although, Mary knew he was generous, she felt something was wrong. So, she went to her mother-in-law's house to tell her what was going on with the money. Mother Hodges said, "Daughter, he is a preacher and I don't want him to be a "shambally" preacher." "I would rather see him dead than to cheat on God." "Mother Hodges, don't say that." "Daughter, right is right." "He is my son and I love him, but I don't believe in no crooked preacher." "Wait until he come home." "We gonna have a talk." "And we gonna talk!" Emerson came home that same weekend. Mother Hodges told him, "Your wife came to see me." "Is you foolin around on her?" "Mama, you know I ain't gonna do that." "If you ain't gonna do right, Emerson, I rather God take you." "Mama, um still saved." "And, I ain't cheated on Mary." "But, I was sick and I didn't want her to know it, that's why I didn't send her as much money as I should." "Mama, sometimes I get so dizzy, but I don't tell nobody." "I know I have to keep goin." "I ain't did nothin wrong."

"Emerson, you know how your daddy died." "You need to see a doctor." "Mama, I been prayin."

"Keep prayin, but you got to see a doctor" After having a physical, he found out that his blood pressure was very high and that his white blood counts were also low. The doctor said, "Lots of Negro people have high blood pressure and low white count." "All I have to do is take medicine and rest for a few days." Emerson knew what high blood pressure was, but he never understood about low white blood counts. His mother and Mary talked. Mary now understood what was going on. He decided not to go back to New Orleans, but to stay home and try to find something there. Times were very hard for them.

Laura's husband, Evan stopped by to see Emerson. The Brooklyn Dodgers and the New York Yankees were playing on the radio. Evan liked the Yankees and Roy Campanella, Emerson liked the Brooklyn Dodges and Jackie Robinson. "Evan, the Dodges is the best team." Evan said, "No, the Yankees is the best." They went on and on. They were getting on Mary's nerves. "Don't the two of you have nothing to do better than that." "Them folks making a lot of money." "And we ain't got much money." Evan said, "Mary, don't you like baseball?" "I don't know." "I don't have time to listen to the radio."

Evan almost forgot the real reason for stopping by. He came to give Emerson ten dollars, while he was recuperating. After Mary saw the money, they didn't get on her nerves anymore! Evan told Emerson that he was also moving to Pascagoula. He had a job offer at the paper mill and that they would be moving very soon. He wanted him to be the first to know. They were close brother-in-laws. Emerson was not happy at all. He was losing his little sister and his favorite brother-in-law.

They waited two months before the move because, his youngest sister, Rose was coming home from Dillard University in New Orleans, where she became a Registered Nurse, to marry her fiancé, Thomas Wells. She and Thomas were married in Nora's house. Sam Jr. performed the ceremony. After which, they moved to Chicago. Thomas was a singer and a barber. He was half-Cherokee. Rose would never forget Laura, because she had been very generous to her younger sister, as well as her other sisters.

Chapter Twenty-four

Supporting the Mother

Now there is no reason for Emerson to feel that he has to give money to his mother, brothers, or sisters. Buddy is still in Comb City working at the Railroad Shop. Everything seems to be going well. Until, his wife Val lost her only brother. Mary remembered what Val had told her earlier, how she could not live without her brother. Mary became overly concerned, so she thoughVal can't mean that. Within a few months, Val became very ill and died. Buddy was left with four small children. Mary had so much love for Val. She didn't know what to do. She went to Buddy and told him the conversation she and Val had. "Mary, why didn't you tell me?" "I thought, maybe, she was just talking." "I didn't know she was gonna grieve herself to death." Mary didn't know the real reason Val died, nor did she asked Buddy. All she knew, was that the children needed to be taken care of.

Soon after Val's death, someone introduced Buddy to the District Missionary's daughter, whose name was Pearl. Pearl was the largest lady Mary had ever seen. When Buddy brought her to see Mary, Joy was very much afraid of her. When she tried to shake Joy's hand, Joy hid behind her mother until the lady left. Soon, she and Buddy were married. His children fell in love with her, because of her kindness toward them. His youngest daughter, Chrissy, was a year older than Joy. They both were in the same grade.

One day while in school, Chrissy and Joy had an argument. Joy told Chrissy, "I don't like your big, fat mama." "And your hair is too short." Barbara, who is also in the first grade, and Joy's first cousin, on Mary's side, told Joy to, "Shut your mouth." Chrissy said to Joy, "Your hair is so nappy it looks like ants on a meatskin." Barbara did not like that. She pulled Joy away, so there wouldn't be a fight. "We all are cousins." "Chrissy is our cousin too." "And cousins don't fight." After recess, they went back to class, and there were no more words between them.

Joy, Chrissy, and Barbara were given assignments. Chrissy and Barbara had a parent to help them with their assignments. Joy did not ask for help. She decided to do it herself. The next day, when they went back to school, and passed their assignments to their teacher, Miss Palm. Miss Palm called Joy to her desk, and asked her, "Who helped you with your assignment?" "My mother helped me." "I think, you did it yourself, little girl." After that day, Joy studied hard and became one of the brightest students in the class, along with Barbara and Chrissy.

When Mary got wind of what happened at school, she told Joy, that, cousins love each other, she had to treat Chrissy as well as she did Barbara. The truth is, Joy wasn't nice to Barbara either. Chrissy stood up to her. She was not going to let Joy put her down. They started to get along. She really had no choice, because her behavior was not acceptable to Mary and Emerson.

It seems that Mary and Emerson was having problems with the children. Jim left home every morning for school with Ruthshel, Boonie, Joy, and David. But somehow, Jim would not make it there. He and his friend, Eugene, one of their neighbor's boy, hid behind the school and would not come in for days at a time. The other children thought he was in school, until report card time. Only then, did his parents knew he wasn't in school. Mary gave Emerson Jim's report card. After reading it, Emerson took his belt off and whipped his behind: Jim failed that year. He promised he would go to school every day.

Each morning before breakfast, Mary prayed with her children and sent them off to school. After which, she took the youngest ones to Idana's house, which was Hue and Darnell. Then she went to work. Thinking that Jim was doing better, he brought home homework that he never finished and just left it there on the kitchen table. The next morning, Jim did not report to school. It was lunchtime, when Cleve brought his and Mary's children's lunches to the end of the schoolyard, Jim was not there. Cleve brought hot biscuits with sausages, that Marge had cooked on his lunch break. They all sat together and ate. When some of the children saw them eating biscuits, they made fun of them. But would not dare try to pick a fight. They were too many cousins in the same school. There were at least eighteen cousins, who will always stand together and would never backdown. If you mess with one, you mess with ALL.

After that day, no one teased them again. But there was a fight. Ruthshel and Boonie, as well as Will, J, and Dot, Buddy's oldest children, were coming home from school. Maxine was an older and larger girl, from school who had stuck Joy with a pencil, and the lead was still in her leg. The cousins offered to beat the girl, but Joy said, "No I can handle it." Maxine was at least four or five inches taller than Joy. The cousins gathered around. Joy grabbed Maxine, threw her down, got on top of her and punched her in the face repeatedly. Maxine fought back. Like a girl. But Joy, fought, like a boy. The cousins could not believe that little person could fight like that!!

When Maxine returned to school, she told the principal that Joy had fought her. Mr. Butcher, called Joy into his office, along with Maxine. He was known to beat the children with a strap for fighting. But when he saw this little girl and how Maxine towered over her, he did not believe the story, and sent them back to class. At lunch time, Maxine and her brother, "Wild Boy", were hungry and asked Jim, who came to school that day, for half of his lunch. Jim asked, "Where's your food?" "Our mama and daddy said that we was too old to have lunch." "Well, you not too old to ask for mines." "I should beat you anyway, for sticking my sister with a pencil." "Matter-a-fact, I think I beat both of you!' But his cousin Will, Buddy's oldest Son, who spoke with a slow tongue, said, "Come on Jim, you don't want to do that." Jim gave them his lunch. Jim could not stand to see anybody hungry.

J. Buddy's second son, along with Will took their cousin Jim to eat with them in the cafeteria. This was Jim's first time eating in the cafeteria. He did not like the taste of the food. He said, "Man, I wish I kept my own lunch." So, he just drank three bottles of milk. Will and J told Jim, "The food is always good to us." "Our new mother is not the best cook." "But she tries real hard." "Daddy said she will learn." J said, "Man, she's better than she was." Jim said, "Nobody can cook like Madea." "But Aunt Pearl is a good aunt." "We all love her." This was true. Every niece and nephew loved Aunt Pearl. Joy was no longer afraid of her and could not stay away from her house. Nor could she stay away from her cousin Chrissy.

After school, everyone went their way. When Mary's children returned home after school, they went in alone, Mary was not home. Boonie and Jim went to draw water, but was unable to get water, because Lawrence had threw a cat in the well, and the cat drowned. Kitty spanked his behind. There was no other well, other than Deacon Ginn and Mother Ginn. Deacon Ginn, was an old man in his eighties, that lived next door to the church. He walked with two cruthches and it took him about ten minutes to walk a half a block. He had a little store, in which he sold sodas, cookies, bread and peanuts. The whole neighborhood brought sodas and peanuts there. Deacon Ginn had never let anyone draw water from his well. But after hearing what had happened to Joe's well, he allowed them to come up the hill and draw water from his well. He did not want anybody to draw water at night. Mary's children could care less. They slipped out at night, and drew water from the well, because they knew that it would take him a long time with those two crutches to see who it was.

Mary was never too tired to make dinner for her children, no matter what. They often ate late. Sometimes, Emerson made dinner when he came home on the weekends. All he knew how to make was biscuits and fried fatback. This would be their dinner for that night. Mary allowed this sometimes. She always wanted the children to have vegetables. Emerson did not know how to cook vegetables or beans. The children was happy with what their father cooked. But Mary wasn't. She taught Ruthshel how to cook greens. Ruthshel was not good at washing the greens. Being so young, sometimes the greens were gritty, but tasty.

Mary did not allow her to cook often, only when it was necessary. But Joe and Kitty's children, on the other hand, knew how to make the whole dinner and taught Joy to make cornbread, which Mary would never had allowed. Mary's children knew how to clean the house. Emerson Jr. and Jim kept the yard clean. Other children would come by and play in the yard. One day, a girl, by the name of "Blackgal", had a fight with Emerson Jr. Ruthshel burned her with a hot iron on her arm. "Blackgal" ran to Kitty's house with a third degree burn. Kitty took care of her wound. When "Blackgal's' mother came to Kitty's house, she was angry. Mary and Emerson took care of the doctor bill, until the arm healed. Ruthshel was not punished.

The doctor bill was not cheap. But they were the kind of people that were responsible. The families was friends. All was forgiven. "Blackgal" never fought Emerson Jr. again. Emerson Jr. gotten into more trouble. This day, Joe was home and took care of the matter with a belt. Emerson Jr. knew he was not allowed to cuss grown people, but not to cuss at all. For some reason, he cussed Miss Maggie out. The reason was, Miss Maggie's son Percy, had stolen his ball and Miss Maggie let Percy keep it. Junior got mad with his Uncle Joe, went down to his Grandmother Hodges' house, where his Uncle Willie was home from the Army, crying. Boonie told his Uncle Willie, that Uncle Joe beat him for nothing. Willie stormed out of the house, with Boonie to find Joe. Unknown to Boonie, his father, Emerson and Joe were talking about him Cursing Miss Maggie.

Willie saw Emerson talking to Joe. "Emerson, that bow-legged nigger hurt my nephew." Emerson said, "Shut up, Willie." "He is my son, and when you hear what he did, you will beat his behind too." Willie had not asked Boonie what had happened. When he heard the truth from Boonie's mouth, "Now, Boy, you want your uncles fighting over you?" "They ain't gonna be no fighting here today, or no other day," replied Emmerson. "We always got along." "And we gonna kept on getting along." "Somebody's betta tell me something", said Willie. "I done already told you." "Now, go home." Boonie was afraid his daddy was going to whip him. "Don't worry, Emerson Jr." "Your Uncle Joe done already took care of everything." "And when I ain't home, Joe always look after y'all and wife." "Now, you tell your Uncle Joe, you is sorry." "And when your mama come home, don't worry her with this." "I don't want nothing to be upsetting her, when it don't have to."

Mary was the kind of mother that got up every Sunday morning and send her children to Sunday school. She did not attend because of her lack of Education. On Monday evenings, she sent them to Sunshine Band. Sister Beaulah, who lived with her mother, in an old house with cat skins on the wall, was the president of the Sunshine Band. This lady would have the children tarring for the Holy Ghost. That Monday, Joy was lying on the floor of the church, pretending, as a girl named Betty was into it. Emerson Jr. came into the church, and told Joy to get up and stop playing. Sister Beaulah said, "Emerson Jr. leave her alone, she's under the spirit of God." "No, she's not, she's playing." He pulled up her. "Joy, you better stop playing, I'm going to tell Madea." Joy got up and stopped playing. Sister Beaulah said, "Emerson Jr.. you should have left her alone." He said, "Madea, don't want us playing with God." "She said, if we play with God, when we are children, we might still be playing when we grow up."

Sister Beaulah walked Betty home with the rest of the Sunshine Band children following. As they walked down the street to the small house, where Betty lived, next to Grandma Hodges house. Grandma Hodges came over and talked to Betty. She said, “God don’t let nobody be out of control.” “He always keeps up in order.” “And this is out of order.” Betty was forming out of the mouth. Betty was not the brightest person. Grandma Hodges knew how to talk to people and not make them angry. Mary didn’t know her children was there at Betty’s house.

That same night, there was a fight between Miss Edna Logan and her husband. He stabbed her in the heart and she died. Mother Hodges and the grandchildren went up to the Logan’s house. When Mr. Logan saw her coming, he ran into the woods. She went over to Miss Eunice’s store and called the police. People heard the noise from the house. Mrs. Logan’s brother, Mr. Edward saw that his sister was dead and asked what had happened. One of the children told him that her husband killed her and ran into the woods. Mr. Edward ran after him and found him hiding behind a tree. The police work was easy. Because Mr. Edward had beaten his brother-in-law to

death. He dragged him out of the woods and told the police, he was ready to go to jail. He only served a few months and was then set free.

Chapter Twenty-five

Mary Starts a Fire!

After he was released from jail, he came to see Mother Hodges and asked her to pray for him. Emerson was also there visiting his mother. While he was gone, Mary was trying to fix a light fixture in the backroom. Emerson Jr. said, "Madea, leave that light alone, before you start a fire." She did as he asked. Joy had just had a bath. Jim was in the washtub taking his bath, Suddenly, Emerson Jr. heard something sizzle. "Junior, what is that?" "Madea, the house is on fire!!" She gathered the children and they all ran out of the front door. Everybody had on clothes, except Joy and Jim. Joy was wearing underwear. Jim was naked. They ran over to Joe and Kitty's house. Silas gave Jim some pants to put on and Joy put on one of Barbara's dresses. Emerson heard the firetrucks' sirens from his mother's house. He ran up the street to see what was happening, and saw it was his OWN HOUSE!! The firemen were able to put the fire out, with very little damage to the house. After the fire was over, the children came home. David said to his father, "You should stay home sometime." "You are always going off." Emerson couldn't help but laugh. Repairs had to be done after the fire. Mary's brothers, James and Joe did the repairs They had everything looking as good as new. Except for the fact that, Emerson and Mary had to buy new furniture for the boy's room.

A lady named Miss Julia and Mr. Ernie, who lived across the street, had a bed they wanted to get rid of. They knew about the fire. So, they gave the bed to Mary and Emerson for the boy's room. Mr. Ernie, was the brother of Mr.

Hambone, that lived next door to each other. Mr. Hambone's wife, was Miss Celey. Hambone was very good to Celey. But Ernie beat Miss Julia every Saturday night. Miss Julia was very good to the children. When they heard him beating her, and how she cried. No child liked Mr. Ernie. The day, they heard Miss Julia crying, early. Mary thought, he was beating her again. Miss Celey came over to Mary's house and told her, that Mr. Ernie had been electrocuted on the job. No child was unhappy. Nobody was unhappy he was gone.

Mary had a black dog. Although, Ernie was gone, Hambone was still there, and didn't like dogs. Mary's dog went into his yard. He poured hot water on the dog. When Mary saw the dog, she and everyone else knew it was Hambone. Celey told Mary that Hambone didn't like dogs, and she saw him pour the boiling water. She knew that he was not cooking anything. A few minutes later, she heard the poor dog barked. She knew her husband, Hambone had hurt her dog. She told Mary she was very sorry and would take care of any bill. But Mary didn't need any help. She loved her dog and knew what to do. It took a while for the dog to heal.

Emerson wasn't as crazy about dogs as Mary was. He told Mary, that she needed to take the dog to a vet, and have him put to sleep, because he felt the dog was still suffering. "Daddy, come and take a look at him." To his surprise, patches of hair had began to grow into the burned skin. "Wife, you did a good job." "You know how to take care anything." "I got something I got to talk to you about." "Evan called me from Pascaguola, and said, there was a lot of work down there" "He is not working at the paper mill and there's a Ingalls Shipyard there too." "And, I might be able to get a job." Emerson and Mary talked it over. "Daddy, I don't want to leave my mama." "Who will help me with the children, when you and me go to work?" "Wife, when I want to move to Chicago with my brothers, Rob and Benny, you didn't want to leave your mama then." "Now who is you gonna choose?" "Your mama or me?" "I didn't like having to leave you and the children at 4 a.m., when its dark every morning and coming back home when its dark," "My daddy is dead and my mama needs me." "I tell you what I'm gonna do, I'm gonna leave you here, until I can save enough money." "You and the children can come later."

Emerson went to Pascagoula, got a job as a steel bender at the shipyard. It was hard work, but the pay was good. The pay was better than when he worked at the Railroad Shop. It was a good thing, that Mary did not go with Emerson. Ellen was having headaches every day. She was diagnosed with a brain tumor that was cancerous. She was taken to Jackson, Mississippi, to a hospital that was equipped to treat her condition. It seems there was no help for her thirty-one year old sister. Mary went to Jackson with Mose. While sitting in the waiting room praying, she said, "God I know you can do anything." "But it's my sister's head." She heard a voice. She believed it came from Heaven. The voice said, "I'm over the head as well as the body." Mary said, "Thank you, Lord," and wiped away her tears. Ellen came through the surgery. The Neurologist said, sorry, we cannot remove the tumor." " All we could do was clamp it with a steel clamp, in hopes that it will not return."

When Ellen recovered, Mary then moved to Pascagoula, Mississippi. The day of the move, was Joy's ninth birthday. The ride was horrible for the children. Jim, Joy and David sat in the back of the truck. While Ruthshel, Darnell and Hue sat in front with the driver. Their Uncle Buddy rode in the back with his niece and nephews. Joy was angry with her mother for making her ride on the floor of a truck, surrounded by furniture. Uncle Buddy sat in the middle of the children with blankets and pillows to rest on for the four hour drive. The ride was still awful. As they were driving across the bridge, called Singing River. It was called Singing River, because Indians have drowned themselves there. Uncle Buddy let them look under the cover of the wagon, to see the big river. It was the most water the children had ever seen. Finally, they made it to their new home.

Chapter Twenty-six

Living in Pascagoula

Mary and the children were met by Emerson along with Evan, Laura and their four small children. Excitement filed the air. The house had a bathroom inside. This was the best news ever. They would no longer have to go to the oddhouse. Joy wanted to be the first one to take a bath in the big, white tub. Her younger cousin, Bo (Deborah) showed her how to turn on the water. She was so excited. Bow then showed her how to clean the tub after her bath. Although, Bo was younger than Joy, there were good friends. Next, Jim took a bath. Then David and Hue were just as excited playing in the water, having enough water to cover themselves. This was much different from the little water in the big washtub.

The people in the neighborhood came out to meet their new neighbors. They couldn't help but notice, Mary's beautiful red softa and chair. Although, the house was smaller than what she was used to, she didn't mind, because she no longer had to draw water and gather wood for her heater and stove. An electric refrigerator, gas stove, and hardwood floors. Now, she thought, "Where am I gonna put all my children?" They put two beds in each bedroom. Jim and Hue slept in one bed. David and Darnell slept in the next bed. Joy and Ruthshel had their very own bedroom. Mary and Emerson pulled out a roll-away bed every night and slept in the livingroom.

This neighborhood was called, "DuPont Circle" There was a house on the corner, next to Mary and Emerson, where the Brown family lived. Miss

Shirley Brown and Mr. East Brown had twelve children. The four oldest ones were not living at home any longer. If Mary and Emerson, had seven young children and the Browns had had twelve children, in a two bedroom house. How on earth did they make it? But they were a loving family. On the other side, lived Reverend and Mrs. Samuel Johnson with four daughters. Mrs. Johnson was so in love with her husband. Everyone who saw them together, could see how much she loved the Reverend and her four daughters. In the center of the circle, lived Laura and Evan Mitchell and their four young children. Next door to Laura and Evan, lived Miss Johnnie with one son, Bradley. Next door to the Johnson, lived the Paige family, a mother with two daughters. The next house, lived the Post family, a husband and wife only. This completes the circle.

Emerson felt this was a good place for his family to grow up in. There were children the same ages as his children, and two boys of the Brown family, that was around Junior's age. Emerson regretted letting Mary persuaded him into leaving his son behind. Sunday morning, it was time to go to the new church. He said to Mary, "Wife, tomorrow I gonna send for Emerson Jr." "I don't care, if he want to come or not." "I'm the man of this house." "Daddy, I know you is right." "I got to stand up to mama." "Somehow, I'll find the courage." "Let me call mama today, Daddy." She went to Laura's house and made a telephone call to her mother. Before she could tell Idana that her husband wanted Junior to come to his new home, "Hello, May Lee, said Idana, I got some good news for you." "Ellen is fine and she is gonna have a baby." "Oh, mama, I'm so happy about that." "But Emerson, said, that Junior has got to come with us." "May Lee, I don't think he is gone like that." "His daddy said, if he don't come, when he send for him, he'll come and get him himself." That was not a problem. Junior was there the next week.

It was September, everyone was in school. Emerson Jr. was introduced to the three brothers next door. The older brother, Lawrence had already graduated that May and was getting ready to go into the Army. Danny and Patrick were in the same grade as Emerson Jr. They were all ninth graders. Danny played football. Patrick was in the band. Danny persuaded Junior to join the football team. Junior told him to call him, Boonie, because that's the name his sisters and brothers called him and other family members. When he told his mother, Mary Lee, he wanted to play football, she said, "No, you might get hurt." "Madea, stop being so scarry." "Daniel plays football." "I still say, NO."

"I'm gonna ask my Daddy." Emerson stood up, when Junior asked him if he could play football, gave him a big hug, "Boy, do you think you tough enough for that?" "Daddy, I'm your son." "Well, the answer is, yeah." "Daddy, I told him, NO." "Why didn't you talk to me first?" "Oh, wife jus let my son be a man." "He's fifteen years old, he can't be your baby forever." Emerson Jr. was allowed to play football.

Emerson Jr. was a good player. One of the best on the team. He played Defensive End. For a small person, he was a force to reckoned with!! He was 5'11 and 150 pounds. Ruthshel is a thirteen year old, ninth grader, was meeting new friends and excited about school. Jim had played hookie so much, now he is in the same grade as Joy, but in a different classroom. When it came to math, Jim was the top. There was no math problem he could not solve. He was a good math student and very protective of his sister Joy. David was two grades behind them. He was an excellent speller and reader, but very quiet. He was calm and loved by his classmates. He and his first cousin, Rob were in the same grade. Rob had been bullied by other boys. Now, when someone wanted to fight Rob, he would just say, "I have my cousins with me and they got BIG FISTS! "My cousins, Boonie, Jim, and David will help me beat you." David stood there quietly. Rob knew David had his back. This family still stands together.

Mary thought everyone was happy in school. Ruthshel wanted to go to Catholic school for that year. For some reason, or another. So she had to catch the bus everyday to Biloxi, along with Marcel her friend. There was not a Catholic High school in Pascagoula, so many children rode the Greyhound each morning. This school was best for Ruthshel. She loved it there. Mary found a job working for Mrs. Bradford, to help pay Ruthshel's tuition. Mrs. Bradford had six sons and no siblings of her own. She told Mary, "You're not my maid, you're my sister." So, they cleaned the house together. Washed the clothes together. Mrs. Bradford took clothes out of the washer and Mary would hang them on the line. The both of them, fold clothes together and put them away. At the end of each day, Mary was given ten dollars. She worked there three days a week.

Mrs. Bradford did not know Mary couldn't read. She left a note for Mary, saying, she had to go to the hairdresser, and she needed her to make dinner. Not being able to read, she could not read the note. After Mrs. Bradford left the hairdresser, she went shopping. Mary's ten dollars was lying on top of the note. When Mary was finished for her daily duties, she picked up her ten dollars and went home. The next time, she went back to work, Mrs. Bradford told her," She was fired." Mary cried all the way home. She told her children that she did not have a job anymore. "What happened, Madea,"? Joy asked. "She jus told me I was fired.'"Madea, there must be a reason?"

Two days passed. Mrs. Bradford came to apologize and asked Mary, why didn't she make dinner that night? She said, "Mary Lee I got home late. Mr. Bradford and my boys did not have any dinner ready." "Were you sick, was that the reason you didn't make dinner?' "Mrs. Bradford, you did not ask me to make dinner." "I left it on the note." "You mean that piece of paper, with my ten dollars laying on it?" "I'm so sorry, Mrs. Bradford." "I did not want you to know that I couldn't read." "So I didn't know the paper was for me to read." She kissed Mary on the cheek. "Oh Mary, I knew there had to be a reason, why you didn't cook dinner." "From now on, I just tell you what I want." "And I will never leave you a note again." "Will you please come back to work?" "We need you." "You know we care about you Mary, and I will never let you go again. "Now, are we sisters again?" "Yes we is." "I see you on Friday." "I'll be there."

Mary told her children that it was a misunderstanding and that she was not fired. "Mrs. Bradford left me a note and I didn't know it was for me, asking me to cook supper." "I left early and didn't cook supper, because I didn't know what the paper said." "Now, she knows that I can't read." "I'm just as dumb as I ever was." "Madea, that is not your fault," said Jim. "Your parents should have made you go to school, like you made me go." "Even though, I'm not in the right grade, I can read." "I thank you and Daddy for making me go to school."

Mary was so proud of Jim and the encouraging words he gave her, "Jim, the next time go to work, I'll take one of my children with me, if I go to another job to fill in the other two days." "Madea, said Jim, we can't go to work with you in the day time, we're all still at school." "And you know, you and Daddy is going take us to church every Tuesday, every Friday, and every Sunday." "Jim, what are you worried about" said Boonie? "You know you going to run off, when everybody's on their knees praying?' Well, Boonie was telling the truth. Jim did not come back to church, until the Benediction. He always made it in time.

Chapter Twenty-seven

Street Ministry

Emerson is now preaching on the street, downtown, in the village, or whoever will let him have church services in their home. There were many people, who allowed him and his family to come into their homes. Mary was not able to go, as much as she has been going. She was expecting her eighth baby. Her sister Ellen, at the same time was having her second son, Mose Jr. Mary now longer had to have babies by midwives. By Emerson working at the Shipyard, she had good insurance and will be able to have her baby in the hospital. This was not an easy pregnancy. Mary was sick most of the time. But not as sick, as she was having Jim. She could still go to church.

Emerson had not been assigned to any church at this time. So, he decided to start his own church. He rented a run-down building in Moss Point, Mississippi. Between services that day, Emerson went to talk to a perspective member. Mary and the children were sitting outside the building. The children were playing a game called, "Long Step." When it was Jim's turn, he felt to the ground. Mary ran and sat on the ground, pulling Jim across her lap. She began to pray, "Lord, God, don't let my child die!" She didn't know he was having a seizure. Joy was screaming at the top of her lungs People began to gather. Joy would not stop screaming. Mary kept praying and calling on the Name of the Lord. "Lord, please." "Lord, please God, don't let my child die." Emerson must have been close by, when Joy saw her father coming toward them. She stopped screaming, "Daddy, daddy, I don't know about

Jim." Emerson said, "Don't worry, Joy." "We got to talk to God." He took Jim from Mary, as Mary held on. He prayed as he took Jim to the car.

He kept praying all the way to the hospital. "Daddy, what's wrong with our child?" "I don't know, wife." "We'll just keep praying and we see what the doctor says." "But I know, in my heart, God is gonna work it out." Jim was in the Emergency Room. They ran all kinds of tests and decided that Jim had an enlarged heart. This was not something that was going to take his life, but with the right medication, he will be alright. He might have another seizure or two, they just kept giving him the medicine. The next morning, as the other children was getting ready for school, Jim had another seizure in the livingroom. Boonie picked Jim up and laid him on the sofa, as tears rolled down his eyes. "Y'all don't think I love my brother, but I do." "I love all of my brothers and sisters." Mary began to pray again and did not stop praying, until Jim came around. Nobody went to school that day. They all were concerned about their brother.

That was Jim's last seizure. Mary said, "Prayer has brought us through once again." "Now, let us all thank God for all the things that he has done for us!" "Now, Madea, said Ruthshel, you need to rest." Mary was able to rest and not worry about Jim. Jim went back to school, the third day after the seizure, as if nothing had happened. "It is so wonderful how God works, Daddy," said Mary. "You, know wife, that boy won't even stay in church until prayer is over." "I believe it is because of our prayer, and our mama and daddy's prayers." "I believe, that is true, Daddy." "Daddy, do you think your daddy made it into Heaven?" "Wife, I don't know what was between him and God." "I don't know why I ask you that." "It ain't my business in the first place." "I know God is good and we can't stop prayin and praisin Him."

When Jim came home from school, he said, "Madea, I feel fine." "I played basketball during recess." "Everybody told me to take it easy." "Jim, it don't seem like playing basketball is takin it easy," "Okay, Madea." "I see what you mean." "Tomorrow I just shoot marbles." "I just lay on the ground and get dirty." "Don't you be playing with me, Jim." He put his arms around her and kissed her on the cheek. Her children were very affectionate towards each other.

Mary was not as affectionate as her husband. Emerson came from a family often, where there was love and closeness. It was important to love your brothers and sisters. His parents taught their children, that if you had a dime, five cents of it, was your brother's or sister's and how to share whatever they had with each other, which was not much. They were always hugging and kissing each other.

Mary had much love for her husband, as well as her children. But she did not know how to show her affection, that they showed toward her. Her patience was short. Maybe it was, because she had gone through so much as a young child. There were times, when she needed a hug and encouragement. She did not receive it, because she was in white people's home working trying to please them and her parents. She didn't have much time to think of herself. HER SUN WAS SOMETIMES GRAY.

Emerson would try to kiss her in front of the children. She would just push him away and say, "Leave me alone." Emerson had his way of making his children see love and punishment at the same time. One day, Joy and David had a fight. David told Joy, "if you don't leave me alone, I'm going to throw you behind the bed, like Daddy did Aunt Cele." David did not know it, but he almost got the best of his sister, and she decided not to fight him again, because next time, he would be the winner. Now, Hue was so sweet. There was no reason to fight him. As far as his brothers and sisters were concerned, no one should lay a hand on Hue. One morning, Mary was whipping Hue, before they went to school. For what reason? No one understood. Hue did not want the family next door, to know he was getting a whipping in the hallway of their home. For every lick she gave him with the belt, he did not cry. All he would say, "Yes, madea, yes madea." Why would a mother beat her child the first thing in the morning? What could he have done? There were little girls living next door. Hue did not want them to hear him cry. He just went into the bathroom, washed his face, and brushed his teeth, as if nothing had happened.

When Emerson was home, Mary would sometimes fuss so much about nothing. All he would do was take a chair in the backyard, put a towell over his shoulders and read the Bible, with a glass of ice water on the side. If she was fussing at his children, and it lasted too long, he would just look her in the face and say in a calm voice, "Wife, I think you had said enough', without hesitation. She did not say another word. Other times, she was as sweet as pie.

Chapter Twenty-eight

Difficult Pregnancy

It was the month of May, and the eighth baby was coming in July. Sometimes, Mary would just lie on the floor, kick her legs up and cry, and say, "I feel so bad." The children did't know what to do. They did all they could to help their mother. Her blood pressure was extra high. She was afraid to take medication, because she was afraid it would harm the baby. On July 27th, she had a baby boy. He was born at the Singing River Hospital. He weighted seven and a half pounds. Mary was still very sick. This is the second time she had been this sick, since Jim was born. With Jim, she could not walk and her blood pressure was not high. But with this baby, her blood pressure was high.

Now what is Mary and Emerson going to name their new baby boy? There was an old deacon, by the name of Herbert Lee Cross, who wanted the baby named after him. So, they named the baby, Herbert Lee. Deacon Cross never told anyone his age. Maybe, he didn't know how old he was. Emerson held his new baby boy in his arms, as he held his wife's hand. "Wife, the doctor say, your blood pressure is down some." "And if it keep goin down, you can come home in a few days." "Daddy, how is my children?" "Wife, Ruthshel is doin a real good job, with the help of the other ones." "What about Emerson Jr.?" "He is there." "Is he giving you any trouble?" "No, he ain't." "He is behavin hisself." "Thank God for that.'

"Daddy, he ain't been the same, since he had to kill his own pet rabbit." "When you first got down here, on the Gulf Coast, I can't help but think about, how he cried, when he skinned the rabbit." "He didn't even eat that night." "Wife, we got to make it up to him, somehow." "We should've all gone hungry that night." "It hurts me what I had to do to feed my babies." "Don't you concern yourself, about that now, wife." "I been prayin for you to get better and come home." "Because, we all need you well." "Miss Shirley Brown, next door, say she is got a present for the baby." "And when you get home, you know she be right there for you." "She's a good friend to me, Daddy." "You is a good friend to her, too." "We understand each other." "And our children get along well together."

Boonie was angry. He felt that since, he was in high school, and his mother was too old to still be having babies. When Miss Shirley came in, she saw the look on Emerson Jr.'s face. "What's wrong, honey?' "Miss Shirley, I'm embarrassed." "My mama is still having babies." "Why is you embarrassed?" "I have a daughter, who has a daughter three years older than my youngest child." "Is you afraid that the children is going to tease you in school?" "Yes, ma'am." "Danny is teasing me already." "Junior, you know Daniel is always teasin' somebody." "I'll get on him when I get home."

In her hand she held a brown piggybank with two silver dollars in it for the new baby. "Miss Hodges, I'm so glad that you're feelin better and able to come home." "Let me see that baby." "He is a fine baby!" "Do you got everythin you need for him?" "What can do for you?" "Miss Brown, you done enough." "I know you was looking out for my children, while I was in the hospital." "I am so glad, that we move down here." "I didn't have to worry about nothing." "The nurses took care of me." "Miss Hodges, is this your first time havin your baby in the hospital?" "Yes, Miss Brown." "I always had a midwife." "It shore feel better this time." "I hope this is your last time?" "I don't know." "if its God's will, it will be my last time.'

Chapter Twenty-nine

A Good Friend

Miss Brown left Mary to go to the store. Whenever she brought fresh vegetables for herself, she also brought them for Mary. Today, she brought cabbage. One large one for herself and one large for Mary. Mary got out of bed, went into the kitchen and started supper. She then, felt very dizzy and had to return to her bed. Ruthshel was able to finished the supper. Every time Mary had babies, her oldest daughter, did all she could to help, without complaining. Now it seems, as if Ruthshel was almost living the life, that Mary lived. Taking care of the family. This was too much for a young girl to do. But say again, this is the way it was.

It is now time for the children to return to school. Junior had worked all summer, cleaning yards and helping to paint other people's houses. He had given a large portion of his money to Mary to save for him. When he asked for money to buy his school clothing, there was not any. Jim had worked also and saved his own money. Jim never told the truth about the money he earned, because he knew his parents would take half of it. If he earned twenty dollars, he would tell them he earned ten. This was a smart move. Jim was able to buy new clothes. Emerson felt bad, that all of Junior's money was spent. He went downtown to the Clark's Department Store, where they brought clothes on credit and brought a few things for Junior,

Junior did not like the clothes at all. They were not of the best fabric. Jim was at least four inches taller and very well built and so was Junior. Jim loved nice clothes. Junior became jealous and nasty. He didn't show love for his brother anymore. But the boys next door loved Jim. Jim was a good person. Emerson Jr. and Daniel had a fight. They were rolling in the grass and talking about each other's mother. "Boonie, your mama's hair is so short, she can't even curl it", said Danny. Boonie said, "Your mama walk like she got a stick stuck in her ass." Danny punched him again. No one stopped them from fighting. They fought until they were tired. Danny's younger brother, Patrick said, "Man, you guys oughtta be ashamed of yourself" "You call yourselves best friends." "And best friends don't fight like that!" "Soon we be graduating from high school and we will be grown men." "You guys should shake hands and forget about it." Danny held his hand out to Junior. "Man no handshakes for me", Boonie said. He turned away and went into the house.

Jim is now playing football. He has developed his body with lifting weights. He has become a big guy and strong. His teammates, calls him, "The Mule." He is the strongest person on the team. It is time for the Football Banquet, and Jim needs a cumberbund. "Boonie, can wear your cumberbund, to the banquet." "No, you can't." "You big, ugly orky-mouth." Jim wasn't bothered by what he said, because he knew he was good-looking. He just went next door and asked Patrick, if he had one he could borrow. It was a little large for Jim. Patrick used needle and thread to adjust it. Mary thanked Patrick for his kindness toward Jim.

Soon it was graduation time. Mary and Emerson are excited that their son is graduating from high school and is going off to college, and so is the other children. The night of the graduation, the whole family is getting ready to go. Mary is dressed in a pretty green dress. Emerson is at Laura's house. When Junior saw Mary dressed in her green dress, he asked, "Where are you going?" "I don't want you there." "Your belly is still FAT!" Mary slapped his face. He held her hand and said to her, "Who do dash in my face!" "I dash in your face." She slapped him again. Just then, Emerson walked in. He picked up a chair, "Boy, you don't talk to your mama like that!" "Wife, is this the way he talks to you, when I'm not here?" Mary did not answer. She just stood there with her hands up, to keep her husband from hitting her child with the chair. Joy took the chair from her daddy's hand. "Daddy, you can't hurt my brother!"

Everyone calmed themselves and went to the Football Stadium to the graduation. After graduation, Junior apologized to his mother, saying that, he would never do that again. "I promised, I will never do that again! Emerson blamed himself for being away from home, working different jobs and not knowing what was going on in his household. "Never again, will I leave my family." "My son is overbearing and ain't got no respect for his mama."

No one was unhappy. There was going to be peace in the house. Although, Mary loved her son very much, felt that it was a good thing that he was going off to college. She was also concerned about is well-being. Whether he would get along with others well, or that someone might hurt him. She told her husband, "I hope he can keep his mouth closed at that college." "Get his education and be a newsreporter." Emerson Jr. always wanted to be a journalist. Believe me, he has the mouth to do so!

Now that Junior is away from home, there is a little more room in the bed, The boys have been sleeping three in one bed. Now, there was two in one bed and three in the other. Mary decided, that it was not fair for three boys to be in one bed, and two in the other. So, she and Emerson slept with Baby boy Lee between them. Emerson had gained a lot of weight. So, there wasn't much room in that double-size roll-away bed. Mary had also gained weight, over the years. But know where close to Emerson's.

Joy loved babies. One night while Emerson and Mary were sleeping, Joy took her younger brother and put him in the bed with she and Ruthshel, and this is the way they slept for the next two years. Mary is still going to work for Miss Bradford. She and Mary remained "sister-friends". It was very uncommon for a White woman to call a Negroe a sister and mean it.

While ironing clothes, at Mrs. Bradford's house, she felt faint. Mrs. Bradford told her to sit down and that she would finish ironing, "Mary Lee, I think you're pregnant again." "I know I am." "You got to tell me things." "I don't want you here, if you don't feel well." "What is you going to do without me?" "Maybe, your girls can help me." Joy and Ruthshel knew how to clean. But there were really too young to cook a whole dinner. Ruthshel was working for the Ellis'. "Can Joy work?" Joy was only twelve and did not know how to cook. When Mary asked Joy, did she wanted to work for Mrs. Bradford, her answer was, "Yes, ma'am." She went to work, while Mrs. Bradford went on vacation to visit her mother in Laurel, Mississippi.

Joy came to work. She cleaned the house. Mr. Bradford asked Joy to fry porkchops for him and his three youngest sons. Joy burned the porkchops. She was afraid to fry anything, because of fear of burning herself. When Mr. Bradford saw the porkchops, all he said, "Don't worry, Joy, I just scraped the burnt part off." He did exactly that. He and the boys ate the porkchops. Joy did not want to sit down with them and eat the burnt porkchops. Mr. Bradford asked Joy, if she mind staying with the boys until he came home from work at 4 p.m. and that he would give her an extra five dollars. Joy was happy to stay.

When Mrs. Bradford returned from her mother's. Joy continued to come to work five days a week. She made the beds, swept the floors and washed dishes. Mrs. Bradford asked Joy, if she wanted to be a maid someday? "I'm just helping my mother." "I will never be nobody's dumb maid." "And I don't want to come back here anymore." "Did you hear what she said, "Mrs. Bradford said to her husband. "Yes, I heard her." "I guess you won't ask her that again." Her face turned RED. She was furious with Joy. Mr. Bradford, on the other hand, thought it was funny. She drove Joy home. Joy told her mother what Mrs. Bradford had said to her and that she told her that she was not going to be a dumb maid. Mary said to Joy, "Maybe, I should not send you there anymore." "Madea, I'll go back." "I'm not afraid of her.'

Ruthshel and Joy worked the whole summer, and so did Jim and Junior. Jim was often late coming home from work, because he went to visit other people. When he was asked by his parents, why he was late? He would lie. Jim said, "Daddy, I got so sick, I had to go lay down on Mr. Kidboy's porch." "Boy, stop lyin." "Why ain't you sick now?" The truth is Jim did not like to be home or confined any place. He was a free spirit. Jim worked at a place called, "The Big Pig." Sometimes he worked the nightshift and brought home left overs. His little brothers and Emerson, his father, would eat anything. Emerson was like his mother, he loved to eat. Mary didn't eat anything, nor did the girls. Mary said to Emerson, "You had your supper, and you is eating again?" "You know the both of us have got to watch our blood pressure." "Well, wife you stop eatin greens late at night." Mary could eat a plate of greens and drink a quart of water anytime of the night. Jim often said to his mother, "Madea, you should not eat like that." "Emerson Hodges brought this food, and I'll eat it if I want to." Jim just left her alone.

Chapter Thirty
The New Church

They were a praying family that believed in God. Although, they were not perfect. As Mary often stood between them, when Junior was home to try to keep peace, Junior never tried to fight his father. He just could not stop talking back. It was hard for Emerson to deal with him before leaving for church. There was not enough room in the car for all the children. He did not have a car of his own. Deacon Hall would drive him and his family, along with one or two of his daughters, Bebe and Judy. I don't know how so many people could fit in one car? Mary Lee and Emerson sat in the front seat with the baby in her arms, beside the driver, Deacon Hall.

Jim and Junior were left behind. Jim did not mind at all. He was told to go to church. He only went to Sunday school. Jim was a Bible Scholar, as well as a student. He could explain everything he read with a good understanding.

When they arrived at Bay-St. Louis, Mississippi, the members of the church were in Sunday school. After Sunday school was the eleven o'clock service. Sometimes, the deacon of the church and his wife would have the pastor and his family over for dinner. Mary took food she had prepared with her to Deacon Williams' house. He said, "Sister Hodges, please don't bring food here again." "We folks is able to feed our pastor." The next time, Mary did not take food with her. There was not enough food for everyone. Deacon Williams' said to his wife, "Why didn't you cook more food?" "You make me feel shamed." "Honey, you know I ain't use to cookin for nobody but you and me." "I know that we have plenty of food in our freezer." "Very well, honey, I'll cook more the next time."

The next time, they came back to Bay-St. Louis. Sister and Brother Grace invited them to dinner, as well as Deacon Hall, who drove them. Sister and Brother Grace went into the kitchen to prepare dinner, Mary said, "Let me help you, Sister Grace." "No, Sister Hodges, you just sit and talk with your husband, and let the children play outside." "Me and my husband will call y'all when the food is on the table." "Sister Grace, I can't let you do all of this cooking, while sit down." "I'm going to help you." "Sister Hodges, I can't do nothing with you." "Come on in here." "I'll tell you what you can do." "What is that," said Mary? "Finish frying this chicken in this pot." "Is that all?" "No, you can take the cornbread out of the oven and put it on a platter." "I was glad to help you." "When we get finished, my girls can wash dishes." "Not in my kitchen." "Let the children be free," said Sister Grace. This woman was not a good cook. She was a great cook.

Mary felt at home. There were other families of the church, who loved their pastor and wanted him and his family to have dinner with them. She would rather, to have gone back to Sister Grace's house. Mary wanted to be the best pastor's wife she could be, More people were becoming members, God was working miracles through Emerson, by the "laying on of hands". The lame were beginning to walk. Demons were being casted out. As the Bible speak of when Jesus walked among men, there was a certain man in the Bible, who sat in the graveyard among the stones. When Jesus asked him his name, he said, "Legions." Which meant many. Jesus casted all the devils out of him and he became an ordinary man.

"Daddy, why is all of these things happening to other people, that comes to church?" "Why can't we have peace in our own house?" "Wife, sometimes, we have to go through it." "We will pray and God will work it out." "Daddy, pray so hard for my children, for others, and their children." "Wife, I pray for everybody." "God don't want nobody's soul to be lost." "Why don't people listen, Daddy?" "Wife, since God created Adam and made Eve, they didn't listen to what God told them." "And if they hadda been listen, they would've obey him." "Daddy, you is talkin like my daddy." "I guess, so." "He taught me real good and I listen to every word he had to say."

Within a few days, the Superintendant of the District, came by Emerson and Mary's house. They wer sitting in the livingroom, watching television.

When Superintendant Addison, came be, "I see you got yourself a television," as he rubbed the top of his head. "Ain't many saved folks got no television." "I guess they don't." "But my son brought this television." "My wife likes it and we is gonna keep it." "Elder Hodges, want to appoint you to the church in Biloxi, also." Emerson said, "Two churches might seem to be too much." "I know you can handle it," said Superintendant Addison. Emerson took the appointment. It was too much having people to drive him here and there. So, he brought himself a black Buick and named it "Lizzie". He now had room for his two sons, Jim and Junior, whom his brothers and sisters called, "Boonie'. Boonie was out on summer break.

Junior (Boonie) had gotten a job at a hardware store, where he had brought the television. He had gotten tired of his brothers and sisters peeping through other people's screen doors watching T.V. Sometimes, Emerson Jr. would let the children watch T.V. with him, while his parents were away, and there were times when he turned the T.V. around, so that nobody will watch it but him. When he was asked to turn it around, he would just say, "This is my T.V." "I'm paying for it, not you." They decided, this day, they had enough! Jim turned the TV around so that everybody could see it. Junior punched Jim in the face. Ruthshel said, "Let's take his clothes off, put him on the porch and lock the door." And they did just that. He went to every window and door trying to get in. They would not let him in. Finally, Daniel saw him and gave him pants and a shirt to put on. "Boonie, have you been beating on your brothers and sisters, again?" "No, man they beat me up this time." Daniel walked with him next door to his house. Jim opened the door, and Daniel stayed there until Mary came home.

When she saw Daniel, she knew immediately that it must have been trouble with Junior. "Hello, Daniel, it good to see you." "It's good to see you too, Miss Mary." "What have you boys been up to." "I've been trying to help Boonie put the screens in the windows." But Mary saw no screens. The house was run-down. Emerson had been laid off from work and the church offerings were less than fifty dollars a month. They were dirt poor. There was a hole in the bathroom floor, that was so large that you could see under the house. Mary covered it with a board that was not nailed to the floor. The sink in the kitchen was leaning to the side. The backdoor had no lock, except for a small piece of wood with a nail in it to lock the door at night. The roof of the house was leaking and when it rained, Mary had to move the beds and used pots to catch the water from the roof. Her sheets on the bed began to rot. She would sew them by hand. They were uncomfortable to sleep on.

The children did not understand why the sheets were sewn. Joy would take her hand and pull the threads out from the torn sheets. The next day, poor Mary sewed the sheets again. Uncle Evans told Emerson, if he brought the shingles he would repair the rooftop. Uncle Evan was not the kind of man who made inside repairs. No one knew, how poor they were, because everyone always looked nice. Just about everything the children wore, were hand-me-downs. There wore black-and-white oxfords, that Jim got were new, was given to David, then to Hue. By the time Hue got the shoes, they were so worned that the children in school, called him, "Hue with the raggedy shoes."

On the other hand, Ruthshel and Joy had better clothing, because Mary sometimes, worked for Miss Nunion, who had daughters their size. When they cleaned their closets, their clothes were given to Joy and Ruthshel. When Ruthshel outgrew the clothes, Mary took them in and gave them to Joy, They were given many pairs of shoes that Joy could wear. Her classmates and friends thought she was wearing new shoes, but they were all hand-me-downs, that she was glad to get.

Chapter Thirty-one
Baby Val

That July, Mary had a new baby girl. Joy was jealous, because Emerson would say, "I got a little girl." "Daddy, you told me that I was your little girl." "Joy, you is twelve ." "You will always be my little girl, but you have a little sister." "I didn't want a sister." "That's what God gave us." At first, Joy wanted no part of her little sister. Ruthshel and the brothers adored her. After watching Ruthshel with the baby, Joy began to join in and fell in love with her little sister. Every time the baby cried, she wanted to give her a bottle. Mary told her, "Every time a baby cry, she don't need a bottle." "Sometimes, she might be wet." Joy did not want Mary to do anything for the baby. She and Ruthshel took full charge of their little baby sister.

Before you knew it, the baby girl was walking. Mary got a telephone call from Idana, saying that Ellen was sick again. Mary immediately went to Comb City, to see about her sister. They had taken her to Jackson, Mississippi to the same Neurologist. He told them this time, that they were more tumors in her head, and if they operated, it will kill her. Ellen had had her second child, which was a boy. She was no longer able to take care of her children, Mose allowed Mary to bring the two boys home with her. The oldest child, was four and the baby was six months old. It was Joy's responsibility to take care of the baby boy. He was the most muscular baby she had ever seen. He was not a problem. Mary had four little children to take care of each day while the older children were at school. Ellen's older son, Brad threw an object in the toilet and stopped it up. He was afraid Mary was going to spank him. Which she wasn't. He told his cousin, Lee, "just say the gal did it." "If you say, I did it, she will beat my ass." Mary didn't care who did it. She just called for Mr. Kidboy, who was the neighborhood plumber that came and fixed it. He also came to fix her kitchen sink. He was placing a board underneath the sink, when Mary asked him, not to put it there. She said, "Wait until my husband come home, and come back." After Mr. Kid boy, had left, Mary was thinking to herself, "I don't want Kidboy back in here.' "He can't do nothing right."

Emerson had gone back to work. When he got home, Mary told him about the toilet and that Kidboy had fixed it. She had decided that she did not want Kidboy to fix anything else. "Daddy, all you do is let Kidboy come in here and mess up my house." "Why don't we let Sister OraLee's son come and fix everythin." So, young Herbert came and fixed the kitchen floor and well as the sink. But not the hole in the bathroom floor. The board which Mary had placed over the hole was still there. Mary trusted Herbert. With her girls, Herbert was trustworthy.

Junior had left college and moved to Chicago. Herbert had taken his place as an older brother.

Emerson allowed the older children to join Elder Mack's church. It was very hard on those children going out of town and sometimes not returning home until two or three in the morning. Herbert patiently stayed with them on Sunday nights, until their parents returned home with the younger children. Jim and Herbert became best of friends. He teased Joy, and told her she was his girlfriend. He was being playful, because he did not like little girls. He loved older women.

One night, Joy had a dream. She saw Herbert's car in a wreck with Herbert in it. Jim was known to ride with Herbert very often. The next morning, she said to Jim, "Please don't ride in Herbert's car today." He pushed her away. Joy ran after him. As she looked up at him, she said, "Jim, you got to promised me that you will not get in that car today." "Joy, do this really mean that much to you?" "Yes, Jim." "Something bad is going to happen today." "Why, is you always seeing things?" "If it means that much to you, I promise I would not ride in that car today." The same day, around noon, everyone heard a loud noise. They went outside to see what was happening. Joy was getting her hair done. Half of it was done, half was not. They ran to their Aunt Laura's yard, and saw Herbert inside the car. He had been shot in the head, lying there dying. This was the most saddest day of their lives.

Someone had went to get Herbert's mother, Sister OraLee, who Mother Moore was trying to console her, as she sat there weeping on Mother Moore's front porch, knowing that she could not help her child. Herbert was taken to the hospital, where he died that same day. He was shot in the head, by Mr. Chuck Robinson. An old man in his late sixties, that had a young daughter and a wife. He was also going with Herbert's girlfriend. His girlfriend was renting a house from Mr. Chuck Robisnon. He told Herbert, that she was his woman, the people said. Herbert told him that, he was an old stupid man and started to drive away. As Herbert was pulling away, Mr. Robinson shot through the passenger's side, where Jim usually sat. Someone had told Jim what had happened, he left his job and came home. He did not plan to go to work that day, because he and Herbert was going to Biloxi and to Mobile, Alabama. But after Joy had told him her dream, he went to work. He saw Joy crying. He said to her, "if I hadn't kept my promise to you, it would be dead." They loved each other so much. They both stood there crying. They knew that they would never see Herbert again.

Mary, Emerson and Laura went over to Mother Moore's porch just to be there with their friend. Who had now lost her son a few months, after her husband, Deacon Dale had been electrocuted on his job tragically. She had two other sons and a daughter. But Herbert was the closest. The others had moved out on their own. Herbert was always by his mother's side. He was obedient to his parents. Loved by the neighbors and friends. No one had anything bad to say about Herbert.

After Herbert's death, Sister OraLee left Mississippi. And never returned. Mr. Robinson was found guilty and sent off to prison for five years. Mary was broken by this incident. She could not imagine losing a child. She prayed to God, that she would die before her children. No mother or father wants to lose their child. Only God knows why these things happen. Mary became so afraid and nervous, that if one of her children were out, and she heard a siren, she would walkthrough the house, praying saying, "Lord, is that my child." "Please don't let it be my child." This she did continuously.

Idana called Mary and told her Ellen was better and Mose was coming to get the children. It was hard to let the children go, after keeping them over six months. Mose told her, "The doctor made no promises." "But Ellen was up and about and was able to take care of the children again." "But one thing I don't understand, Mary, the medicine they gave her has made my wife fat."

"Mose, you mean my sister is fat." "I wouldn't exactly say fat." "But she's much thicker than she was." "Mose, you need someone to ride with you." "You cannot take these babies in that car by yourself." "Daddy, do you mind if I go with him for a couple of days?" "I want to see Ellen for myself." "I'll be back, as soon as find out that she is alright."

Idana was glad Mary was there. She told Mary, "I don't want you to stay long." "I going to keep the children and make sure Ellen is alright." Ellen seemed to be fine. "You're right mama, I think she will be okay." "I guess, I can go home." Now, her youngest brother, Sam Jr. loved to tease his mother. He came down, one afternoon, after work, to tease his mother. He said to Mary, "I'm going to go in here and make mama say her words." After a few minutes of teasing, Idana said to him, "Shit, shiit" "Boy, leave me alone." He thought it was funny. This caused Ellen to laugh. Ellen had a laugh, that when she laughed so hard, she would lie on the floor and roll. She would say to Sam, "Why in the hell, you make mama cuss?" "You are a preacher!" "You need to stop it!" He would only laugh and return home.

Mary asked Sam, "Would you and Nora like to drive me home?" "Mary Lee that's four hours there and four hours back." "Just let me put you on the bus." "You know Nora's having another baby." This was baby number ten for Nora. Mary returned home sick. The doctor said she had a tumor in her uterus and they had to remove it. Mary was admitted to the hospital. The doctor told Emerson, it was not a tumor at all. She was about to have a baby. When Mary was released from the hospital, she told her children that she was having a baby within a month. She asked Joy, to go downtown with her to buy clothes for the new baby. Joy said, "Madea, why do you always have to have babies?" "We don't have any room in the house already." "I wish I could five somewhere else." Mary began to cry. "Joy, I can't help it." "Why do Daddy have to sleep with you?" Mary didn't answer

After she brought the baby's clothing, they came home. The baby was born within two weeks on a Sunday morning. The baby had to be delivered by a midwife, Emerson was laid off again and had no insurance or money. Joy had a job babysitting at the White church. It was called "white" because all white people attended. When Joy returned home with her six dollars, Emerson asked for it to buy the baby milk. Joy gladly gave him the money and went to see the baby. She looked her father in the eyes, and said, "Daddy, are we going to have anymore babies." He said, "No, this is the last button on Joe's coat."

This was the "last button om Joe's Coat. It was baby number ten. He was born on February 21th.

Ruthshel stayed home out of school again. The principal came from her school to talk to her parents. He said,' Mr. and Mrs. Hodges, Ruthshel said she would have to stay home and help with the baby, until you was out of bed." "This is not right." "This child needs to be in school." Mary did not like what was being said. But she remembered being spoken to before, concerning her daughter being absent from school. Mary decided she would do the best she could and send all her children to school. They would be no more missing days for Ruthshel. They named the baby, Lamar. He weighed eleven pounds.

Chapter Thirty-two

Idana's Visit

Idana came to stay with Mary and take care of the baby. One thing Emerson did not like Idana being there, was when he brought home is paycheck. She would say, "Emerson, let me see how much you make." He would just say, "Sister Idana, I don't let nobody see my check, but your daughter, Mary." "Now, wife tell your mama not to ask me again." "I mean, no disrespect, but it's not her business." Of course, Idana was not in the room.

Idana stayed for three weeks. She went to church with her grandchildren. When one of the deacons of the church saw her, he grabbed her and looked at her and pulled her hair and said, "Stick, is that you?" "Sam, where did you come from ?" "Stick, I have been living down here for forty years." She told her grandchildren that Sam was her first cousin. This was surprising to the grandchildren and to Mary, because he had a young son that stayed at Mary's house more than he did at his house. Boy, this was strange, to find out, that the best deacon in the church, was your grandmother's first cousin. Idana was shocked to see her first cousin, that she had not seen since she was a child, living in the same town that her daughter Mary Lee lived. They lived a few blocks away from each other. Sam took Idana home with him after Bible study to meet his younger wife and his son. They had a very large house. They invited Idana to spend the night. "Sam, we ain't seen each other in a lifetime." "Yet, it seem like we be runnin and playin in the woods, while our mamas and papas be workin in the fields." "This all seems like yesterday." They reminisced for awhile.

Idana had brought Hue and David with her. They were watching television with his wife, Rosa and their son. Idana, says to Sam, "Your wife is a sweet girl." "She don't really know me." "Next year when I come to visit Mary, um gonna spend a few nights wit you, if its alright with your wife?" When Idana returned to Mary and Emerson's, she stayed there until she returned back home. She told Mary before she left, that Sam was her first cousin. Nothing changed between Sam, Rosa, Mary, and Emerson.

Sam and his wife, Rosa was close to Mary's children already. Joy asked Rosa, if she had some work she could do, because she wanted to buy herself a Can-Can slip. Rosa gave her fifty-cents every week. One night after Bible study, Mary, Rosa and the children were standing outside of the church. Rosa said to Joy, "Do you have enough money to buy your Can-Can yet?" Mary interrupted, "What slip?" Joy was afraid to answer. "You know, I don't want you beg nobody for money." "I didn't beg her, she just gave it to me." "Sister Rosa, I'm so sorry." "Please don't give her no more money." "I'll buy her the slip." Joy said, "Madea, you know we don't have any money." "Who told you we ain't got no money?" "I thought, you said that we didn't have enough money, Madea?" You must have thought it. I didn't tell you."

Mary had a smart mouth. When one of the children did something she didn't like, when she got disdgusted, she would say, "You can't do me this." Or she would say, "Dog bites kitty licks." When Hue would hear her say that, he said, "Madea, what do you mean?" "I simply mean, what I say." "A dog will bite and a cat will lick you." Hue could be as funny, as Mary was mouthy. He would do anything for a laugh. Sometimes, watching him could make you laugh, without even trying. Mary said, "Boy go out and play." "Madea, is a kitty gonna lick me?"

"Maybe, one will if you can find one outside." "I ain't gone say another word to you." "Alright, Miss Madea."

Mary could remain calm once in a while. It was very hot inside the house in the summer. She did not have fans. So, she took part of a newspaper in her hand and went from room to room, fanning her children while they slept. She prayed as she walked. Joy said, "I don't know why Madea always praying?" "We don't have nothing." Joy understood that if you were sick, God will heal you, because once a year, mostly in the fall, Joy was unable to walk. Her brothers had to carry her from the bedroom to the bathroom. Jim didn't mind carrying her. He just was not going to stay around that long. David Complained.

Hue never complained. He carried her with a smile on his face. That is who Hue was. Darnell and Lee would bring food to her bed. This only lasted about three weeks. After which, she was up and running.

This was Ruthshel's senior year in high school. The children are growing up. Soon, Ruthshel would be away in college and Mary would have to depend on Joy and the boys. After work each day, Mary came home, washed clothes by hand in the large bathtub. She no longer had to draw water, Emerson saw this washing was too much for her. He brought her a washer from the place where Junior had worked. This made all the difference in the world to Mary. Mrs. Brown kept the babies, Lamar and Val. Darnell and Mrs. Brown's two little daughters went to kindergarten. Once in a while, Mrs. Brown went to work on Saturdays. Mary did not have to babysit her children, because she had older daughters who took care of the younger ones.

One night, Mrs. Brown came by the house, while Emerson Jr. was packing to move back to Chicago. "Junior, what are you doing with that suitcase?" "Is you going back to college?" "No, ma'am." "I'm going back to Chicago live with my Uncle Dieyall and Aunt Ree," "I was hoping you would go back to college." "Tell your mother, I need to talk to her." Mary came into the livingroom and asked Junior to leave them alone. "Miss Hodges, I was jus walkin down Bilbow Street, and when I walk through the darkest part, I heard chain rattlin." "Miss Brown, maybe it was your imagination." "No, Miss Hodges, I think it was a token." "Well, let me pray and ask God let everyone be a right." Mrs. Brown went next door to her house. Later that night, Mary heard a noise and looked out her front window. She saw someone helping Mrs. Brown into a car. It was Mr. East, her husband and another man. They drove away in a hurry.

The next day, Mary went to the house and asked one of the children, was something wrong with their mother? Edna, said, "She got sick and my father had to take her to the hospital." "Did anybody hear anything today?" "No, ma'am" "Do you think Elder Hodges can take one of us to see our mother?" "Well, he's at work right now." "But when he gets home, I can go with somebody to see how she's doing." Emerson and Mary drove three of their daughters to the hospital with them. They had prayer. After an hour or so, they left.

Mrs. Brown seemed to be doing better. Although, she died the next week. Mary never asked what was wrong with her. All she know was that she lost a friend and that she would do anything she could for the children. The body was brought back home for the wake. Mary did not go to bed. She sat in the chair in the bedroom, looking out of the window at the people, as they came in and out of the Brown's house. Emerson said to her, "Wife, you need to lie down." "You gonna make yourself sick," "If you don't take care of youself, you ain't gonna be here to help the children."

Chapter Thirty-three

Suffering Losses

After Mrs. Brown's death, Mary begin to come around. It was a very cold winter that year. Snow was all over Mississippi. It was the year of 1962. Idana called Mary on the phone, crying. "Maylee, I have bad news for you." "Mama, I know its's my sister." "Yeah, May Lee, my child is dead." Mary dropped the phone. It was late night, when Idana called. Emerson caught her as she was falling. "Wife, is Ellen dead?" "Yes, Daddy." "My only sister is dead." "I got to go, Daddy." "I got to go now "Wife, we can't leave tonight." "We have to wait til mornin." The next morning, Laura saw Mary Lee and Emerson put their suitcases in the car. She ran out in her bathrobe. "Emerson, what's wrong?" "Laura, Ellen is dead." "Lord, have mercy, Mary!" "I'm so sorry." "You know I'm coming too." "As soon as Evan come home, we will catch the bus." "What about your children, Laura?" "Don't worry, Mary." "I got somebody that I know can keep them." Mary laid her head on Laura's shoulders. The both of them cried. "Mary, do you want me to watch your children?' "No, Ruthshel will be home." "She can watch them." Mary took her three youngest children, Lee, Val and Lamar with her.

Lamar did not talk. He would just point to whatever he wanted and suck his thumb. As they were getting ready to leave, the other children came out to say, goodbye and to give Mary her hatbox. She could not take the hatbox, because she was holding Lamar in her arms. Emerson said, "Wife, put that baby down for a minute." Lamar took his thumb out of his mouth, and said, "Why, you always talking about people." Emerson could not move Mary was so surprised. One of the older children said, "Madea, when did that baby start talking?" "I don't know, he never said a word to me." Lee said, "Madea, Lamar always talk to me and Val." "Val, why didn't you tell me your little brother could talk?" "I don't know." "What do he say to y'all?" "He says, get me some milk, I wanna cookie." Lee Said, "Madea, he say everything we say." Now the jig was up. Everybody knows Lamar could talk!

On the way to Comb City, Lamar talked until he fell asleep, "Wife, you know that boy is smart." "He had all of us fooled." "Even the older children." "I guess, the young ones, thought we knew that he could talk." "Daddy, I thought, that he was slow, because I was so old when I had him." "We both was old.' 'Wife, I know he's the last button on Joe's coat." Mary knew that there would be no more children for her. "Daddy, he is a change-of-life baby." "The doctor told me that lots of women have babies during "the change". " "Daddy, I guess, he is the last button on Joe's coat."

It took them six hours to drive, because of the snow and ice, Mary went straight to her sister's house, so that she could be with her sister's children. When Mary's older children arrived, Mary wanted them to stay with her at Ellen's house. "Please, Madea, don't make us stay here," Jim replied. "We can stay at Grandma Ginn and Grandma Hodges's house. After the funeral, Mary asked Mose, if she could keep her sister's children. Mose told her that he and his mother would raise his children.

Mary was exhausted when she returned home. She laid on the floor, crying. Emerson sat beside her rubbing her legs. Joy said, "Madea, get up off the floor." "You not going to die tonight." "Your sister died, not you." "You might as well go to bed, Madea." "So that Daddy can rest." "Ruthshel and I can take care of the children tonight." Mary went to bed. Finally, she fell asleep. Lee came into the room and laid beside his father. "Daddy, want to sleep with you." "Because you a cool Daddy." "if I sleep with you, I can get strong." He held his arms up to show his muscles. Emerson placed him in the bed beside him and Mary. This is where Lee slept for weeks.

After the death of Ellen, Idana came to visit Mary. Idana stayed longer this time. She said to Mary. "May Lee, don't know how I gone live wit out my child?" "Mama, you'll make it." "We all will make it." "May Lee, Dieyall said, (Dieyall is Mary's brother James) that he and Ree might be comin back home to live wit me." "I don't like bein in that big house by myself." Sometimes,

Sam Jr.'s children spent the night with Idana. "I am so lonely, without Ellen." I so use to seein her everyday." "Mama, I miss her as much as you." "I love my sister so much." "May Lee, you know she loved you too." "Mama, Can you remember when my children were little, how she and Mose would pretend to be Santa Claus and bring the children toys to my house on Christmas Eve?" "I never told them that it was Ellen and Mose." "Until one night, she laughed, and they all knew it was her."

"May Lee, did I ever tell you bout the time, when she brought me fresh greens out of her garden and Miss Taylor was sitting on my front porch?" "She ask Miss Taylor, I bet you would like some of these greens, wouldn't you?" "And Miss Taylor, said, "Yes, I would." "I ain't gone give you none," and she broke out in that laugh she always did. "You know May Lee, that gal didn't giv her no greens." "Mama, you know all that liquor she kept in the house, she let my children drink it sometimes." "How do you know that, May Lee?" "She told me." "And she will let them say bad words, she thought it was funny." "Mama, I miss her so much."

"Mama, how long is you going to stay?" "I guess, I stay til my son-in-law tell me to leave." "We better build you a room." "You know my husband, would never tell you to leave." Jim was glad she was there. When it was Jim's turn to wash dishes, she washed them. Matter-of-fact, she cleaned the kitchen everyday. She even made dinner, at least three to four days a week. She was a big help to Mary, just as Mary has been to her when she was young. Now, that Idana is older, she has learned how to be a mother,

One day Mary received a letter. Mary opened the letter and looked at the writing. Idana laughed and said, "You know you can't read", as she pointed to Mary. Jim became furious at her. "Grandma, don't you laugh at my mama." "It's not her fault, it's your fault." "You should have sent her to school." "Madea, don't you dare cry," "I don't care if she is your mother." "She should have sent you to school." "Jim, I didn't want to go." "I didn't want to go either, Madea." "You and Daddy made me go." "I'm glad you did." "Jim, that's your grandmother, say you sorry." "Why should I say that, I don't mean it." Jim did not say he was sorry.

Idana was having those headaches she had in the past when Mary was a young girl. Unable to get out of bed, Mary gave her aspirins. Nothing seem to help. Emerson took her to the hospital. After Xrays and bloodwork was done, they discovered that she was having migraine headaches. They had not just started. Mary suddenly realized that, all the years she thought her mother might have been lazy. But the pain was real. Now, they knew what was wrong with Idana. Another doctor came in, and told them that she also had diabetes that have never been treated. So, all these years, Mary thought, nobody would find out what was really wrong with her mother. She was not lazy. She was just sick. Now, Mary wanted to do more.

Idana felt she had stayed long enough after a month. Although, she had promised her cousin, Sam that she was going to spend more time with him. He understood, why his little cousin, Stick was not able to stay in his house. He did not have any bad feeling concerning the matter. He knew that the next time, she came down to the Coastal area, that they would have time together and everyone could get together and just be one big family.

Chapter Thirty-four

Sealed Friendship

Mary was still working for Mrs. Bradford. All six of her sons was out of the house. The two oldest are married. Mrs. Bradford, oldest son, married a poor girl and her second son married a rich girl. The third son was dating a girl, who was crippled from polio. He wanted to marry her. But Mr. and Mrs. Bradford, told him, "this was not the right thing to do, because she was going to need care that he could not afford." So they thought. But this young woman with braces on her legs, was able to get around, go to college and open her own business. In which, she became rich. She had two large clothing stores in different cities. So, the third son ended up marrying the first son's wife's sister. The fourth son, was unlike his brothers. He loved Black people. They were his best friends. The youngest two, became priests. So we guess. Mary and Mrs. Bradford had a friendship that would never end as long as Mary lived. She and Mrs. Bradford would be together two days a week for the rest of their lives.

Although, Mary had no biological sister anymore, no one could ever take Ellen's place. But there was true love between she and Mrs. Bradford. Most Black and White women did not have that kind of a relationship. Mary also worked at a trailor court for people that was also as poor as she, except they can afford to have their trailors cleaned. Behind the trailor court, lived Mr. and Mrs. Cummings. People called them as well as the people, who lived in the trailors "poor white trash." Mr. Cummings would come over to the trailor court to make sure that Mary was safe, because the men and women were heavy drinkers. He liked Mary because she and her daughters cleaned he and Mrs. Cummings nasty house. It was the nastiest house they had ever seen. The floors were filthy, the stove was impossible to clean. Mr. Cummings were overalls that was dirty from the tobacco juice that he let run down out of his mouth as well as snuff.

Mrs. Cummings was as watchful as her husband. Nothing ever happened to Mary or the girls. They also had a daughter who lived across the street with her Cuban husband and eight children. Mary, sometimes, sent Joy to clean in the Summer. When Joy came home, she said, "Madea, I am not going back to that dirty house." "How can you go down there and clean for those people?" "Joy, don't judge them by their dirty house." "Why?" "Because they is good folks and they pay good." "You know some people don't know how to keep nothin clean." "Madea, that house is very large and all their children have their own beds." "I wish I had my own bed." The boys were still sleeping two or three in one bed. Joy slept with her little brother Lee and sister Val.

Val was a pretty little girl. Mary kept her hair in long braids. Mary was outside hanging clothes on the line. Lamar was sleeping. Lee told Val, "I'm gonna make you look pretty, hold your head still." He cut one of the braids with scissors that he had gotten from the kitchen drawer. As Mary walked through the back door, she saw a long braid of hair on the floor. Lee still had the scissors in his hand trying to cut another braid. "What is you doing to your sister?" "I'm making her look pretty." Val said, "Madea, he said I look pretty." "Baby, Madea don't want your hair to be as short as hers." "When I was a little girl, I had long hair." "Madea, you are pretty." "Did my daddy cut your hair to make you look pretty?" "No, baby, I got sick and lost my hair." "I had malaria fever and it didn't grow long no more." "Give me them scissors, Lee." Mary put the scissors on top of the kitchen cabinet. "Lee don't you ever cut your sister's hair again or I spank your behind!

Lee was always into something. If Mary fell alsleep on the floor after work, Lee cooked hotdogs, put them on a fork and served them to his smaller sister and brother. One day he decided to serve them on a slice of bread. There was a large jar of mayonnaise in the refrigerator. It was too large for his small hands. Mary heard something break. The jar had fallen from his hands. "What is you doing in there, Lee" Mary said? "I'm sorry Madea, I made a 'stake." "Please don't beat me!" "How long have you been using my stove?" Lamar took his thumb out of his mouth. "He feed us all the time." Val said, "He's a big boy, he know how to cook." "When you're taking a nap, Lee use the stove." "He said me and Lamar is too little to use the stove, because we might burn ourselves." "I guess, I better not be going to sleep, when we be by ourselves." "Madea, be tired after work." "Next time you want food, you better wake me up, or I beat your behind with a switch." "Y'all come in here and watch television."

Mary was getting tired of Working and coming home washing and cooking. She was in no wise going to let her children go hungry or be dirty. She made sure Emerson's white shirts were starched and ironed when they went to church. The men and preachers wore white shirts in the Pentecostal religion, Mary knew how to be a good mother and wife at the same time. Each day she made dinner and there was always some kind of desserts. She would make teacakes. They were made with flour, butter and molasses. She also made Jell-O with fruit cocktail. There was always good food. On Sundays, it would be roast beef or fried chicken, one or the other. There was always potatoe salad, greens, or green beans.

Chapter Thirty-five

Lives are Changing

The children were getting older. Jim and Joy are in high school. David, Hue and their first cousin Robert are also in high school. They all went to Carver High. That was the only high school in Pascagoula. David was also a football player. He has grown to be as tall as Jim. Jim had his own friends that was older than he. He stayed out late at night. Emerson would whip his boys if they did not obey his rules. Jim was always getting a whipping. Joy said to Jim, "Jim why don't you come home on time?" "And stop putting those dirty dishes in the oven." "If you don't want to wash them, I'll wash them for you." "I hate it when Daddy whip you." "Don't worry yourself, a whipping don't last no longer than when you get it." Mary and Emerson was sleeping in the roll-away bed in the livingroom. Jim often tipped through the room without waking his parents and baby brother Lamar.

When he was very late, one of his siblings would let him in through their window. So that when Emerson got up to check to see who was in the house, he was in bed, and if he wasn't there, Mary would get upset and nervous thinking something might have happened to him. In order to get some rest, Emerson would just get up and go find him. Most of the time, he was sitting around, talking and drinking soda with other young men from high school. There would be only men and boys. Jim never gave his parents any trouble, except for staying out too late.

Emerson Jr. had came back in town for a little while from Chicago. He married a girl by the name of Lisa. The day he and Lisa were married, he wore a black suit, white shirt, and black boots. He looked very handsome. Lisa wore a black tight dress. She had the body for it. "Getting married in a black dress," Joy said. "This marriage would not last." Sometime later, Mary asked her son, "Why did you marry that girl?" "I felt sorry for her, because her parents was not good to her." "Well, maybe they were alright, she was always working." Emerson Jr. and Lisa gave Mary and Emerson their first grandchild. It was a boy.

Emerson Jr. and Mary walked to the hospital. It was a very hot day in June. She wanted to see her grandchild. "Emerson Jr., this baby looks just like you when you were born." "Madea, you mean look that good." "You sure did." "Lisa, how is you?" "Do you feel alright?" "Yes ma'am." "I didn't have a hard time havin the baby." "What is you gonna name him?" "We don't know." "Do you have a name for him?" "After ten children and fifteen pregnancies I ain't got no more names," "I don't think we're gonna have ten babies!" said Lisa. "I sure hope you don't." "When is you gonna come home?" "I'm already discharged." "Madea, Daddy said he be here soon," said Junior. "He want to see his grandchild." "We will name him as soon as Daddy gets here." They named the baby Michael. A few months later, Junior went back to Chicago and sent for his wife and baby. She did not want to leave Mississippi. So he stayed in Chicago. Lisa brought the baby over very often. Mary kept him for days. She and Junior went their separate ways. Junior came back to Mississippi on vacation, to see his son that was now walking and talking. Mary and Emerson loved the baby, it was though they had had another baby. Jim felt like he was the baby's father. He was a good uncle. He told his mother and father they were the grandparents and he would take the role as the father.

While Junior was still in Mississippi, he got involved with an older woman, who had a daughter as old as he was. She was almost as old as Mary and Emerson. Emerson did not like this. Mary said that he was a grown man and had to live his own life. Junior was jealous of Jim taking the role of a father to his son. He told any lie he could think of on Jim. The kind of lies he told could have gotten Jim killed. Jim would say, "I don't pay my brother any attention." "He is crazy." Jim was a grown man working at the same shipyard with his father.

That summer, Jim met a girl from Tylertown. He brought her by to meet his parents. She was gorgeous. Mary said, "Jim that girl is gonna be your wife someday." "Madea, you think you know everything", as he got up from the kitchen table and washed his hands in the sink. Some of Mary's children are grown-up and moving out. Ruthshel had met a nice fellow named Floyd. He was one of the nicest fellows Mary had ever known. The night before their wedding, Floyd came over and fixed all the broken chairs and whatever that needed to be fixed. Mary made redbeans, rice and fried chicken, iced tea to drink, with teacakes for desserts. Floyd ate well.

Floyd called Mary, "Madea' and Emerson, "Preacher." They were married in the livingroom. The pastor was so nervous that he had Floyd put the ring on the wrong finger. Floyd became a brother to all of her brothers and sisters. He and Emerson Jr. had played football years ago as rivals in high school. The night after the wedding, Junior shook Floyd's hand and said, "Man, I love you like a brother." "But if you ever put your hands on my sister, I will kill you." Ruthshel, Floyd, Jim and Junior went out with their friends.

Joy and her friend, Martha was allowed to go to their high school cafeteria along with their other girlfriends to a "Sockhop", which means everyone danced in their socks. Girls really do like having fun. No one went out to be with a boy. Boys were there, but not with them. All the girls danced and went home. Some of them came into Mary's house, ate leftovers from the wedding and cleaned the whole place. Jim came home drunk for the first and last time. David, Hue and Darnell let him in through the window and did not tell their parents anything.

Mary knew something was different about Jim. His eyes were red the next day. "Jim is you been drinking?" "No, Madea, you know I'm not going to drink in this house." "I didn't say in this house." "You come home mighty late!" "Madea, I want to talk to you about somethin." "Jim, is you gonna marry that girl?" "Madea, I told you, you think you know everything." "Yes, ma'am." "I'm gonna ask her to be my wife." "She is staying with her older brother, I would ask him first." "He and I get along well." "I told him that I was in love with his sister already." "Jim, Jim, when is y'all gonna git merried." "It will be soon."

The wedding is going to be in Tylertown. Judy, Jim's fiancee' and Joy became best friends. She asked Joy to be her Maid of Honor, Joy, Jim, Emerson, Ruthshel, and Floyd were going to Tylertown. Floyd drove Emerson's black Buick. They had drove at least fifty miles. When Emerson asked Jim, "Do you got everythin you suppose to have?" "Yes, Daddy, I do." "How bout your license?" He searched himself. Everyone looked about in the car. They weren't there. "Oh, boy, I left them at home!" They had to turn around, go back to Emerson and Mary's house and get the license. Mary wished she was able to go to her son's wedding, but that was the only car that would make the trip and there was not enough room. So they started out to Tylertown again. The people in Tylertown were waiting. Idana and Luella, Jim's grandmothers were there dressed in their Sunday best. Judy was in her wedding gown. They were four hours late. The car had given out of gas. Jim and Floyd had to walk to the gas station and back. It was midnight when they arrived in Tylertown. They were married. The reception was held at Judy's parents' house.

Judy came back to Pascagoula with Jim to the room he had rented for the two of them. Now, there were three people out of the house. Everyone lived close by. Mary could see her children almost everyday, for a little while. Now, Joy was the oldest at home. Darnell was Joy's shadow. Everytime there was a ballgame, Darnell had to go with his sister. After the game was over, some big tall boy wanted to walk Joy home. When they got home, Darnell would say to Joy, "Why do you like those big boys?" "Darnell, they only want to walk me home." Darnell was protective of his sister. He wasn't going to let no boy get to close to his older sister. Darnell was also the big brother for his younger sister and two brothers. He had to clean the house as well as iron. He could clean and iron, as well as David and Joy. Hue didn't care, whether his clothes was ironed or not, as long as they were clean.

Mary had taught her children well. If Joy did not want to wash dishes, she would say to David, Hue or Darnell, "Madea, said for you to wash dishes today." If she told David or Hue, there was no problem. They would just wash the dishes. When she told Darnell, he said, "Madea, didn't say that." She pushed him toward the kitchen, he pushed her back. Hue pulled off his belt, "Boy, don't you hit your sister." Darnell was not about to talk back to Hue, his brother, who was four years older than he, and at least six inches taller. Mary didn't worry when she and Emerson had to leave the seven alone. She knew they would take care of each other.

On Fridays, Emerson, Mary, Evan and Laura went their separate ways to the market to buy food for the week. At Evan and Laura's house, you could eat anything you felt like. It one child wanted a cold-cut, he could have it; if another wanted fried chicken, they could; it one wanted hamburger or steak, it was alright. Meanwhile, at Emerson and Mary's house it was hamburgers and hotdogs, Kool-Aid and milk. When they had eaten as much as they wanted, Emerson would say, "Wife, look at them long mouths." As Mary made hamburgers for them, "Daddy, I love to see them happy." He would then say to his children, "Eat it all up!" "You ain't gonna git no more til next Friday."

It was up to them to try to make the food last. Often they drank up all the milk. They only brought two gallons at a time for seven children, and four which were teenagers. Mary and Emerson just looked as the children carried on.

One of the Brown sisters, asked Mary, if Joy could go to work in her place. The job consists of ironing clothes for Miss Gena, who's a white lady that worked at JC Penney. "How much does the job pay?" Mary asked. "Six dollars every Saturday" said Edith. Mary wanted to know if the lady was going to be home. "Yes, ma'am, she will be there." When Joy got to the house, a man answered the door. Joy was wearing a red dress with soft gathers with a wide belt around her small waist. "Hello, sir, my name is Joy." "I came to iron for your wife in Edith's place." "She's in the back bedroom," he said. She went into the back bedroom, she saw no one. "Where is your wife?" "I meant she's on the phone, lying on the bed." She picked up the phone, the person on the other end was his wife, who gave her instructions. She was to iron the clothes and hang them in the closet. When she was almost finished, she saw the tall, big man looking down at the small 5'3 tall black girl. "Did you know you're a pretty nigger girl?" He pulled her to him, picked her up, kissed her and took her to his bed. She knew she was in trouble.

She thought this man was going to rape and kill her and hide the body. He looked so sick. She kicked him in his groin. As she flipped over the bed and made two somersaults, unlocked the door. She ran into the next room. Joy picked up the iron and came toward him, "You won't burn me, would you?" "Try me." He moved back as she ran out of the front door, holding the iron in her hand. When she was out of the door, she threw the iron inside the house and ran as fast as she could. Not knowing where she was, she did not know where to go. She cried loudly. "Lord, please help me to get back home." Before she could turn around, Mr. Lewis, the cab driver that drove her younger sister and brother, as well as her two young cousins to kindergarten every day. He was also a friend of the family was driving by. He stopped and told her to get into the cab. She told him what had happened to her. He took her home and told the story to Emerson and Mary. "Madea, he was trying to make love to me." "Make love, nothing." "That honky was trying to rape you," Emerson said. "Daddy, he was just here and gave me Joy's money." "He gave me much more than what he suppose to pay," said Mary. "I ask him where was Joy, he didn't answer me." "He just drove away." "Daddy, before I could tell you, Joy was here."

The news spreaded so fast. The whole neighborhood was there, as well as Reverend Johnson. The story was told to Reverend Johnson. The Reverend was known to cuss. "That honky needs to be killed." "Preacher, don't let your young girls work for no white folks." "Keep them home where they belong," said the Reverend. Mary asked Edith, "Did he ever try anything on you or your sister?" "No, Miss Hodges." Mary said, "Why Joy?" She did not believe her. The police wasn't called, because they did not want their child to go through the same thing another black girl had gone through earlier. The young girl had been called a liar by blacks and whites. They did tell his wife what happened. She said Joy was a liar. "He did not try to rape her, nor did he tear her clothing." "She tore her own clothing." In less than two weeks, he raped his step-daughter. Now, she believes Joy's story. This saved Emerson Jr.'s life, because he was going to find him and kill him. In Mississippi, for a blackman to kill a white man in cold blood, he would have been electrocuted or hanged.

Joy had not given up on God. Mary and Emerson had not give up either. "Daddy, this child goes through so much." "Every year she can't walk for a month or so, and all of her other sickness." "Wife, I'm sorry about his wife's daughter, but God don't like ugly." "And I don't know what reason Joy goes through." After this incident, Joy was so upset, she was unable to go back to school. When she did go back to school, the principal called her to his office, and said, "I'm sorry Miss Hodges." "For such an awful thing you had to go through." "I know you are a nice beautiful young lady, think all of us black men should just get a gun and just shoot them all up." "All the white men." "Mr. Jackson, my Daddy said we should forgive them and pray for them." "Miss Hodges, I got so angry, your father is right." "You may go back to class."

Chapter Thirty-six

Changing Character

As time passed, Emerson Junior and his older girlfriend went to New York. Junior became a different person. Now, he can get along with his whole family. He and his wife were divorced. She continue to bring Michael to visit his grandparents. Michael was well taken care of in that house. The older boys took Michael wherever they went, Although, Mary did not let them take him out of the circle. Laura's boys loved Michael also and helped to take care of him. They treated him like a little king. Lamar did not like the attention that was taken away from him. He would not share anything he had with his nephew, because Michael had taken his place. Mary thought of a way to make him happy by making him a chocolate cake and have everyone sing "Happy Birthday" to him, even though, it wasn't his birthday. From then on until he was four years old, whenever someone made a chocolate cake, he thought it was his birthday.

A friend from church come over to see Mary on a Sunday afternoon. It just so happened, that Mary did not go with Emerson to church. She happened to be in town while the lady and Mary were visiting. Lamar said to Miss Dorothy, "Come have some of my birthday cake with me." "Lamar, I didn't know it was your birthday." Mary whispered to her, "It ain't." "Everytime someone makes a chocolate cake, he thinks it his birthday." She had a slice of cake and sang "Happy Birthday" to him. Later that day, after Miss Dorothy had left, Lee became ill. His body was hot. His eyes were rolled back in his head. All you could see was the white of his eyes. All Mary knew to do was pray. David, Hue, Darnell, even Lamar were praying. Joy said, "God please don't take my little brother, take me instead." She did not know what she was asking God. Not realizing that God does not trade. God was able to work as many miracles in one second, then she could imagine in one day. Because HE IS GOD.

Emerson was called and drove home as fast as he could. He prayed with Mary. The child's body was still hot. "Wife, we done prayed, now git in the car and let us take him to the hospital." "It may be Daddy, that God will work through the doctor's hands." "Wife, I don't know how's he's gonna do it." "But, I do know my son will make it." Mary wiped her tears. She believed what her husband had said. They were told that Lee's tonsils were very large and that it was not enough time to operate. Something had to be done then and there. The doctor was an American Indian. His name was Doctor White Cloud. He told them that he will have to burn his tonsils out. No one knew if he used a laser or what. With prayer, the treatment worked. He did not have to stay in the hospital. He was sent home. God again, had given Mary the wisdom. The same wisdom. He had given her years ago to take care of her small nephew. She nursed him back to health.

Living in Pascagoula, was much different than living in Comb City. Hospitals and doctors were closer. They could treat whatever illness they had in the same hospital. Unlike, having to go out of town, when Joy had polio. She did not have to leave her children. If she could, she would have kept all of her children as close as possible. But she knew she had to let them go. She was not worried about Junior, Ruthshel nor Jim. Ruthshel and Jim had married people that loved them. Judy loved Jim and Floyd loved Ruthshel. Judy and Ruthshel were sister-in-laws that cared about each other, as well as they did their husbands. They both had been taught by their mothers how to keep their houses cleaned and to keep the boys in check (their husbands).

Mary was still praying wherever she was at home or at work, She had a prayer in her heart. She was not praying out loud, she often prayed, "God please let me live to raise my children." "Please keep my mind and my soul." Mary did not tell anyone that she was still grieving her sister's death. She had to keep on being strong for her mother's sake. There was also small children of her own to take care of. She had asked her brother-in-law in the past to raise his two boys, because Ellen had told her, if anything were to happened to her to take care of her children. Ellen knew that the love Mary had shown her, she would love her children in the same manner that she would keep them in church, as she would her own. This she had expressed to Mary the second time she became ill, Mary had taken the boys home with her.

Although, in Comb City, Mose took the children to Idana and Sam Jr., who would keep them overnight. It seemed to Mary as if it were yesterday when she losted her sister. She said to Emerson, "Daddy, you know my sister was only forty-one years old." "She died so young." "Wife, I know she died so young," "it must be hard." "I never loss no brother or sister, thank God." "I love Ellen, like she was my own sister." "Daddy, she love you the same way." "It look like to me, the doctor could have done somethin to keep her alive." "Wife, when God gets ready, you got to go." "It was her time." "Daddy, I know I am getting better, because I can stand to talk more about her," "But I wish, he would let me have the children." "Wife, you know them is his children." "Don't bother him again."

There was an explosion in Comb City, at the place where Mose worked. He was badly burned. When Mary heard the news, she went straight to Comb City to be by her brother-in-law's side, whom she loved very much. Mose didn't make it. His mother kepted the children. Mary said to Idana, "Mama, why don't you fight for your daughter's children?" "You is much younger than his mother." "Miss Ida is eighty years old, and you is in your early sixties." "Why thank you ma'am, I know how old I is." "His sister stays there too." "She's younger than Ellen was." "She ain't got no children." "They was real close." "I don't want to fight them over his children." "He always been nice to me." "He drove me anywhere I want to go and brought me anything I want to eat." "He's never been disrespectful." "Yes, mama, he was the best brother-in-law."

Mary was refolding her clothes in her suitcase. She found an old ragged girdle. "Where did this old thing come from , it's not mines." She had brought with her a new girdle that she had never worn with the tags still on it. "My goodness, this rag, my money is also gone!" "Mama, who's been here?" "Ain't nobody been here, but Sister Francis,"(Sister Francis was one of the church members.) "Auntie, (a friend of Idana's) and your cousin Bessie." "Mama, I know Bessie is too little to were a girdle." "Count her out." "I won't accuse anybody." "I'll borrow the money for my bus ticket from Cleve." "And send it back to him when get home." "May Lee, I think that is the best thing to do." "Because your little brother Sam ain't got no money wit all dem children."

"Mama, is you still keeping the children everday." "Yes, I am." "Everyday God sends the sun or the rain." "Whatever God sends, I got the children." "You know Nora, ain't got time for them children." "She follow Sam everywhere he go 'cept work." "Mama, both of them where so young when they got married." "So they is still being teenagers." "Fifteen was too young for them to get married." "Nora, still got more sense than Bessie." "May Lee, that is the truth." "Yesterday, all them children were fighin, Sam's children and Bessie's children." "I told Nora and Bessie about it." "Nora told her children to stay in my house." "All Bessie said was the was fightin them." "I said Bessie tell them children to stay in the house, she still say the was fightin them." "Mama you know there is more crazy folks walking around than there is locked away." "Bessie is my Daddy's dead sister's child." "And her thoughts ain't never been right." "But when push come to shove, she is always there for me." "One thing about Bessie she only goes to work and church and like me, she takes care of her husband and children." "She ain't never ask nobody for nothing.

Cleve brought the money to Mary and told her that she did not have to pay him back. "Mary, I'm your oldest brother, you can always depend on me." Mary caught the bus the next afternoon. Emerson met her at the Greyhound Bus Station. When she got home, everything was in order and everybody was alright. The house was clean. Clothes were washed and ironed. "Daddy, who helped you do all this." "Wife, you know, where there is a will, there's gonna be a way." "I guess, you ain't gonna tell me nothing, Daddy." Lamar, the thumb-sucker wanted to tell. Val put her hand over his mouth. Mary knew then were going to Stick by their father's side. "Well, I guess, it ain't nothin for me to do here." "Maybe y'all wanted me to stay gone." "No, Madea, we want you home." Darnell said, "We have dinner ready." "Just wait a minute." He came back into the kitchen with his shirt off and a necktie around his neck and said, "Let's have dinner." The children called Darnell, "Crazy Cousin Ginn." He did the same thing almost everyday. Hue, on the other hand, just wore his pants inside out. "Mr. David', had to be neat and clean.

After the boys had eaten dinner, they would just wiped their hands on the kitchen curtains, which made Joy so angry, she called them, nasty and stupid. They just picked her up and said catch, as they threw her from one to the other, this was Hue and David. Joy just played along with them, until they were tired they let her go. She washed the curtains at least four times a week. They would do the same thing over and over each day. Maybe if they had napkins, they would not have wiped their hands on the curtains in the first place. Papertowels were not heard of in that house. Emerson's sister, Laura had napkins in her house and plenty of toilet paper. The Hodges did not always had what Laura had. Why would anyone use newspaper to clean themselves and flush it down the toilet? It was common for them to use newspaper, because it was not enough money to buy all the necessary things they needed. Most of the money was spent on food and bills. Mary's boys wore hand-me-down clothes from one to the other. Mary took care of their clothes. She brought the best fabric she could, because she knew that at least three children would have to wear the same shoes and clothing down the line.

As for Joy, she was able to make her own clothing, as well as Mary's and her baby sister, Val. She also learned how to do hair. If Joy was too busy sewing, and was notable to do Mary's hair, one of the Brown girls, who was a third grade teacher came over and did Mary's hair. Neighbors were neighbors. On the other side where the Johnson family lived with their four daughters, one could always depend on Reverend Johnson. He was the kind of man that would do you a favor and never take a penny. Mary had very coarse veins in her legs. One day, one of the veins bursted, blood was everywhere. Reverend Johnson came over, wrapped Mary's leg with a towel and took her to the hospital. Twice, Reverend Johnson took her to the hospital. Emerson tried to pay him for his trouble, he just said, "That was not any trouble at all." "That's what neighbors do, we help each other."

The other neighbors in the circle had small children around the same age as Mary's youngest ones. The children came to Mary's house to play with her children. Mary's children were only allowed to go into the Browns and Johnson's house, and of course Laura and Evan's. Laura's oldest daughter, Bo visited Mary almost every day. Laura said, "Mary, this child is more like you than she is me." Bo was more like Mary, than Mary's own children. She never gave anyone any trouble and she never talked about anybody. She would keep a secret forever. Bo was a few grades behind Joy. They were in the girl's bathroom, when Bo showed Joy her homework, Joy said, "Bo, you need to write that over, your paper is wrinkled."

Bo misunderstood and went home and told Laura and Evan that Joy was talking about her in school. They became upset with Joy. Laura called her niece while Evan was at home. Joy came over. Laura said, "Why did you talk about your cousin at school?" "All I said, Aunt Laura, was Bo you should write your paper over because your paper is wrinkled." "Bo, said Madea, you know I can't hear good." "is that all you said Joy?" "Yes, ma'am." "Right, Bo." "Yeah, that's what you said." Evan said, "Laura you ought to beat Bo's behind for having us upset with Joy." Joy said, "Bo why should I talk about you and who would I talk about you to?" "I wouldn't be crazy enough to have said anything about you ever." "I'm very proud of you." "Your grades are all A's." "I don't have all A's." "I got two B's." "I hate when get a B, but it's okay." "Just keep the good work up little cousin." "Give me a big hug." "Please don't ever think I would say anything bad about you."

They were fine and was never another misunderstanding. Uncle Evan was still the same caring man towards his nieces and nephews, When Laura was away, Jim would go over and get money from Evan. He never said no, and if Laura was home, and if any of Mary's children needed money from Uncle Evan he gave it to them. He treated them the same way as he did his own. When she was there, she would say, "Evan we need that money." He would say, "Oh, Laura." Evan would just keep giving. On Saturday nights, Laura made cakes. Laura and Emerson would spread butter on a cake, that was made with butter and eat it. Mary said, "Daddy, all that butter is gonna make you have high blood." Both Mary, Emerson and Laura had high blood pressure. They ate and fed the children too much fried food, although, there were vegetables as well. Sometimes they could not eat as well, when Emerson was laid off from the shipyard. They were given something called "commodity" they had to get food from a certain place that were given to poor people that could not feed their families. They had to stand in long lines. Some of the items were: chicken in a can, about eight pounds of butter, dry milk, bologna, corn meal, and flour. The children hated the dry milk and would not drink it. It was a good thing that Ruthshel's husband, Floyd worked part-time for a company that sold bread and other sweet items. He brought them home and gave them to his mother-in-law. The children loved the sweets.

Mary's part-time jobs enabled her to buy fresh chickens and vegetables. On Sundays, Mary fried at least three chickens and what was left, Floyd came over and ate it. Sometimes, Mary wanted to have leftovers. Floyd would eat anyway. One Sunday, they were five pieces of leftover chicken. When Mary saw Floyd Coming, she told Joy to hide the chicken. "Joy put the chicken in the oven." Joy would stand by the stove. "Floyd said," Madea, I know you have leftover chicken, where is it?' He looked into the refrigerator, found no chicken. As he looked around the kitchen, he asked Joy," why was she standing by the stove?" "No reason, I'm just standing here." He said, " Madea, are you tryin to hide chicken from me?" Mary didn't say a word. "Move Joy." "Let me look in that oven." He pushed Joy aside. Took two pieces of fried chicken out of the oven and ate it.

"Stop it Floyd, "she said and closed the oven door. Holding the chicken leg in his hand, "Joy, you know you're my nigger, if you don't git no bigger." "Floyd, you are just so crazy." "Madea, why did you hide that chicken." "I didn't hide it, Joy did." "Madea, you told me to." Floyd was not upset nor angry. Neither was Mary. She knew he would take anything he wanted. He was just another son.

Chapter Thirty-seven

Mary's Upset

This was Joy's last year in high school. She and her friend Betty was chosen to ride in the parade. Joy and Betty rode on each side and Carrie rode in the center. This was her second time being chosen to ride in the parade. They rode in a Ford Convertible, sitting on top of the back seat, waving at the crowds. When they were returning home from the parade, the car caught on fire and the car was pulled out of the parade. Their teacher, Miss Gibbs was driving. She had to call her boyfriend to come and get them. Miss Gibbs was in her late twenties. After the boyfriend came in his new car, she took them into town to get stockings to wear. They were happy to have new stockings. Joy came home all happy and told her mother what had happened to them, and that was why she was late getting home.

Mary said, "Where did you get those stockings?" "You ain't got no money." "Madea, I told you Miss Gibbs brought them for me." "You is a lie." Joy got undressed out of the gown she was wearing and redressed herself in regular clothing. Mary had one of Emerson's belt in her hand. "Tell me the truth, some man brought you them stockings." "You little whore." "Madea, why would you say something like that about me?" Mary hit her on the hand, as hard as she could, on her arms, back, chest, and neck, until she bled. The pain after the beating, was worse than the beating. When Emerson came home and saw Joy's arms and neck, and the blood on her back; he turned blue. "Wife, why?" "She told me a lie." "Daddy, I told her the truth." "The car we were riding in caught fire and we were pulled from the parade." "My teacher, you know, Miss Gibbs, Daddy." "Her boyfriend came and got us, she took us downtown and brought all three of us stockings for our Homecoming tonight."

"Wife, what is wrong with you?" "Anytime a sixteen year old girl would tell her own daddy, she asked the boy to come home with her and lay on the sofa and kiss, and when he try to rub her behind, she beat him out of the house wit a broom." "I told you she ain't up to nothin'. "I tell you this, she is going to the football game tonight." Mary tried to speak. She said, "Daddy." Emerson said, "Wife, it ain't no reason for you to beat the blood out of her." "You know how low her blood is and all the problems she's got." "I'm just gonna pray for you wife." Emerson gently washed Joy's back and sprinkled baby powder over her wounds. Joy had a long-sleeved green dress that she wore to the game. She was so happy to be there. She almost forgot about the beating. Mary did not apologize. But Joy forgave her anyway. Joy did not tell her brothers or anyone. Only Val and Lamar knew she had gotten the beating. They did their best to console their older sister. They were too small to help her.

Chapter Thirty-eight

Mary Learns to Write

Now, it was Prom time. Mary took Joy to the best fabric store in town. She brought the most expensive fabric in the store for her to make for the Prom. The dress was made from pink organza and pink satin roses at the bottom of the dress. The Prom was held in the Recreational Center, two streets over. This was the fourth prom Joy had gone to. She had gone to the first two proms with a boy from Mosse Pointe, by the name of Thomas. Her junior prom was with Anthony. The senior prom with Zell. One night, Mary overheard Joy saying to Zell, "I'm going to ask my mother, if we could walk to the store and buy sodas for everyone." "But you and I will go to the Recreational Center and dance." He said, "I'm not going to take you anywhere." "Unless we ask your mama if you can go." When Zell left, Mary said, "I like that boy, he's got more sense than you." "He said, he was not going to take you nowhere, unless you ask me first." "Mother, why were you listening?" "I was not at first, but when heard you, and he said, no." "I really like that boy." Zell was the boy whom she would marry. Mary let her go but she had to be home by midnight. There was no problem. No one wanted Mary to worry about anything.

The older two boys left, David and Hue. David was the star football player. Hue was in the stands cheering for his brother. David got knocked out in the game, he was not hurt. He just got the wind knocked out of him. Emerson was at the game. He did not come inside, he watched the game outside the fence. The reason he did not go inside, was because preachers from the

Church of God in Christ, was not supposed to attend football games. He never thought that rule was fair. He stayed outside to keep people from talking. Emerson told his superiors, that he stayed outside and that he wanted to see his boys play football. Emerson wanted to be a part of everything his children did. Mary was embarrassed to go to Sunday school and PTA meetings. She was afraid that someone would ask her to read something. Emerson was never embarrassed or ashamed of his wife. This was all in Mary's mind.

Jim decided that he was going to teach his mother how to write her own name in cursive and to become a better reader. Each day after he and his wife, Judy had dinner, he would come to his mother's house and have her write. Finally, she learned how to write her name and became a better reader. He also taught her math, which she was very good at. "Now, Madea, you don't have to be ashamed of yourself anymore." "Your children have never been ashamed of you." David agreed with Jim.

Hue and David asked Mary, if she wanted to go with them to look at cars, because they wanted to buy a new car before David's prom. "Where are you going to get the money?" "Madea, we both working." "Floyd said he will help us." Floyd helped Hue and David buy their first car together. David went to the Prom in his new car with his girlfriend Joyce. He was late coming home. Mary walked the floors, looking out of the window every five minutes. The whole house was awake. No one slept until David came home about 2:30a.m. Mary did not ask him why he was late. All she cared about was that he was home and well. Now everybody could go to sleep. And sleep a little later. It was Saturday morning, Hue would have to get up and find a new job. He had just finished working his last week at the old job, cleaning yards on the beachfront for the wealthy. No one lived along the beachfront, except white people. There was only a small part of the beach for black folks. As long as black people stayed on the part they were given, and not try to mix with them, everything was fine.

White people didn't care whether you live close by them, as long as you stayed in your place. Your place was to clean their houses, not to talk back, and if you work in their houses, you ate your food after they had finished, and clean the kitchen. Mary asked Hue, "Did you work today?" "Yes, ma'am." "I helped Mr. Jack put a roof on a house." Hue didn't really want to work. He always hoped someone would say no, when he asked for a job. When he went out to find a job, he would walk into a grocery store and ask to speak to the manager. He would say, "Mister, you don't need nobody to work do you?' The manager or whoever he asked would always say, "Yes," it was just his luck. No one ever turned him down. Hue always had a few dollars in his pocket. He had a walk that was so cool, but natural. Women loved his walk, as well as his looks. Mary and Emerson had good looking children, because they was good looking.

Hue was as comical as Darnell. They both can make you laugh. What they wanted most was to see their mother happy. All of Mary's sons loved their mother. They would do anything they could for her. But no one was going to keep her from going to work for Mrs. Bradford. Even on Thanksgiving and Christmas, she would go there at six a.m. and return home by noon to be with her family. Mary asked Emerson, if he wanted her to stop working. "Wife, I ain't telling you what to do." "If I say stop, you say you can't." "And if I say, keep working, you won't stop." "So, um gonna keep my mouth shut, "Daddy, you know we had a hard time for years." "You had a good job at the Railroad Shop." "You let people talk made you stop." "You know we ain't got much money."

"Now we're living in Pascagoula, you're making more money." "I got gas and water in the house." "And I don't have to worry about my children goin to no outhouse no more." "But we need a bigger house." "I been making do too long." "I was so glad to have all the things we got." "I didn't think too much about how little this house is." "Wife, um gonna see if we can add a few rooms on to this house." "I can't afford a new house." "I know you can't afford it." "If you could, we wouldn't be living in this old mess." "You say, you is glad we got water, hot and cold, nobody has to go to no well to draw water." "Or outside to do their business." "How do you call this house mess?' "You don't fix nothin, all you do is have Kidboy come and you and him mess up everything." "Floyd can fix things." "Wife, that boy works hard." "Well ask somebody who know what they're doing."

The Reverend Emerson Hodges was always helping others. The members of the church came often to borrow money. Some needed to pay their electric bill, their rent, or needed to buy food. His offering at the church was still a small amount. This preacher-man had to find a way to please his wife. He knew a high school shop teacher, who lived on the next street. So he asked Mr. Baylor, if he could add two rooms on to his house. Mr. Baylor told him, he could assign a few boys out of the shop and he would assist them, as they added bricks for the new rooms. Mary did not like the idea of having high school boys working on her house. The boys came and laid bricks on to the front of the house. They made a doorway and four window frames. The rooms were never finished. It was left open with no rooftop. It was so embarrassing for the older children. They all had jobs and still didn't finished the rooms. They just didn't! People much poorer than they were, added new rooms on to their houses. Evan and Laura had two large rooms added on to their house. Everyone in the circle had enlarged their houses, except for the Hodges. Although, the children never went hungry or dirty, she did not have many sheets or towels, but she kept the ones she had clean.

Chapter Thirty-nine

They Grow Stronger

Mary worked many different jobs as a maid. Sometimes she worked two jobs in one day. She often worked too hard, no one could stop her. Every now and then she took a break. But never a break from church, never a break from prayer. Now that they were no more babies coming, everyone was growing up and moving out. Joy and Zell eloped and was married by the Justice of the Peace. David was away in college. Hue was in his last year of high school. Darnell is a quarterback on the football team in high school. He keeps the children on Saturdays when Mary goes to work and have girls over, which he knows that Mary did not agree to that. He didn't have to worry, because the younger ones was not going to tell. Lamar told Lee and Val, what to do as if, he was the oldest. Lee allows his little brother to boss him around, but Val didn't.

Joy came to see her mother everyday with her new baby boy Zell Jr. Zell Jr. was born early. He was so small that you could only hold him on a pillow. Jim and Judy came often with their six month old son Jim Jr. Jim Jr. was a happy baby that loved crawling under the kitchen table. When Mary pulled the tablecloth up, she would say, what is my big boy doing under the table?" He laugh and crawl away back into the livingroom. "Wife, I think that boy wants to eat," Emerson said. "He's not hungry," said Judy, "he just likes to play." Then he would crawl to his father Jim. When Jim reach for him, he would crawl away again. Zell and Jim got along like brothers. They both had played on the same football team in high school. Jim said to Zell, "Man, I never knew you would be my brother-in-law." Zell, said, "The first time I saw her I knew she would be my wife someday." "I told her she was going to be my wife, and she said I would not marry you even if you were the last man on earth."

Joy, Judy and Ruthshel were like sisters. Ruthshel had a job teaching American History in the next town. Floyd, Ruthshel's husband, was just as close to Jim and Zell as their wives were to each other, The three men worked at the shipyard and played semi-pro football on weekends with the Pastpoint Steelers. Their wives thought this was crazy. This was what they wanted to do. Mary could talk to Floyd and Zell, as well as she could talk to Jim her son. She said to them, "you is men with families, now Jim and Zell you have babies, what if you get hurt." Jim and Zell did not get hurt. But Floyd got his leg broke. That was the end for Floyd, Zell and Jim after a year of playing semi-pro football.

That summer David came home from college. After he had put his things away, Val went into his room and went through all of his mail. At six she could not read much of the letters, only a few words, but she knew they were from his girlfriends. She said to David, "David you are too old to be living here." "You are supposed to have a wife." "Do you want your big brother to move out?" "I don't know." But what Val did know that if someone was going some place, she wanted to go too. Mary didn't always comb her hair the way Val wanted her to do. Mary was never good with hair. Val's hair was too thick and too long. If Ruthshel or Joy didn't help their little sister, it was too bad. Because if Mary had to do Val's hair, and if she didn't hold still, Mary would peck her on the head with a hot straightening comb. Val would put on anybody's shoes, a small one or a large one. She would say, "Wait for me." "Val you can't go, you're not ready," Ruthshel would say as she and Joy was leaving Mary's house. Val would say, "I'm a sister too, please let me go." Mary would say, "Val, come help me with the baby." Then the two of them would leave. Val loved holding the baby on the pillow, She would rather play with the baby, then travel with her older sisters. When they returned home from wherever, Joy would say, "Val, you can go the next time." And that was good enough for Val.

Mary and Emerson now have three grandsons, which Mary loved to keep. Joy had gotten a job working at HeadStart as a teacher. Once in a while, she would be late picking up her son. After an hour, Joy had not made it to Mary's house. Mary became angry. "Where is she, Daddy?" "What on earth could she be doin?" The door opened. Joy walked in with three large bags and gave them to Mary. She had brought her a pair of shoes, a new dress, and a new hat. "Everytime I get mad with you, you go and buy presents for me." "Mother, you won't let me pay you for keeping the baby, so this is my way of paying you."

Joy and Mary was sitting in the living room alone. "Mother, may I tell you something?" "Tell me what!" "I'm a grown woman and I don't have to lie to you," "Do you remember the day you beat me when I came home late from the parade, you said a man had brought me the stockings I had." "The story I told you then, that was the truth." "I didn't lie to you, mother." Joy has been calling Mary mother since she was eighteen. "I didn't know or did I ever understand that when I was a little girl, and sat on my own daddy's lap you would say to me, Get off my husband, he is my husband not yours?" "How could a child have a husband and what did you mean?" Mary did not have anything to say for herself. "Mother, I was thinking you were playing with me." "You don't even know how to say I'm sorry." "I'm sorry beat you that day, I don't know what I was thinking," Mary said. "Sometimes my nerves gets the best of me." "Mother, I know you are a saved woman." "But you need a person to talk to ."

Chapter Forty
Mother and Daughter Relationship

They became friends that day. Mary told Joy more about herself within the next few months, than she had ever told since the day Joy was born. Joy began to understand her mother better. Mary realized she could talk to her daughters, both Joy and Ruthshel, as well as Mrs. Bradford. She even told her things she had kept to herself concerning her mother and father, what a powerful man her father had been in Christ and how the women been after him, and that she believed he made a few mistakes, and how he asked God every morning for forgiveness. Before he went to bed each night, he would call his children and asked them, "Did I do anything wrong to you today, and if I did I want you to forgive me and God to forgive me?" He would also asked Idana the same question. Then he would say, "goodnight." She also said, "There are some things that happened to me that I just have to pray about." "The next time me and your daddy goes to church, I want you, Zell and the baby to come with us."

Emerson did not have to drive far anymore. He had a church ten miles from home. He had to carried some of his members to and from the church. One lady in particular, was Sister Simmons. Sister Simmons always said she was sick. Sometimes, she would get down on her knees in the back of the car and say, "Elder Hodges, please pray for me." I am so sick, I don't know what to do." Emerson would pull over, Stop the car, he and Mary would pray for her. The lady had the worse body odor. Lee, Val and Lamar rode in the back seat with her. The children say, "Daddy, that lady stinks," when they got home.

Lamar Said, "Daddy her butt stinks so bad, she needs to throw it away and get a new one." They knew she had a bad odor. Joy said to Mary, "Mother, I don't believe she is sick as she say she is."

It was a Tuesday night, one of her daughter's called for Emerson and Mary to come and pray for her mother. When they got there, she was dead. "Elder Hodges," said her daughter, Mamie, "If you had made it here in time, I don't think mama would have died." "Everytime you prayed for her she got better." "There is nothing I could say that is going to make you feel better." "I do believe your mother is with God." "Daughter, your mother was a woman that lived by faith. Mary put her arms around th three girls and cried with them. All the words Mary spoke was comforting. "This was God's will." "She ain't suffering no more." "Let me know what we can do to help you." Maybe, Mary should not have asked that question.

Early the next morning, there was a knock at the backdoor. It was Sister Simmon's three daughters. They came in. "Elder Hodges, we ain't got enough money to bury our mother." "What about your daddy?" "He spends all his money on alcohol." "We have been doin the best we could do." "Mama had a job, she spends it on us so we can stay in school." "But when she got really sick, she had to stop working." "We are so sorry to ask this of you." They looked toward Mary. "Sister Hodges, you think the church will help us bury our mother?" "Honey, my husband don't get a good thirty dollars on Sundays. And we have to pay the church the electric bill out of our pockets." Emerson could not help with the expense of the funeral, but he would talk to the man who owned the funeral home and see if he would take care of the funeral arrangements and bury their mother, and would let them pay in small payments.

Mr. Alexander agreed to help the family. Mary said, "Daddy, you know we is going to help them people make the payments." "We help everybody, except ourselves." "Wife, when you help other folks, God will help you," "Daddy, I know you is telling me the truth." They were glad they was able to help them. There was a time when they didn't have money to help someone that needed food. They would give food out of their own refrigerator and cabinets until it was almost gone. Mary wanted her children to have enough to eat, no matter what. She remembered in the past, when she had to fry bread on top of the stove in a large black skillet and they ate it with butter and syrup. The bread was called hole cake that was for snacks before going to bed. There were not any potatoe chips or cookies for snacks.

Chapter Forty-one

Sudden Changes

The children were sometimes asked to go to the store by the older people in the community. Sometimes, they would give them five cents or a dime and even a quarter. They could buy cookies two for a penny. They could share with each other the whole day. Coconut cookies were the best, they thought. Lee, Val and Lamar ate cookies all day. If they were given a quarter, they walked to Miss Delphine's store. Miss Delphine was said to be mean to most of the children. They didn't know if she was white or black. Miss Delphine was not mean to Mary's children. Hue loved cookies and milk, and this he would share with his little brothers and sister in the summer. Hue would buy milk during the week, because he knew there would be no more milk until Friday. Lee asked people if they wanted him to go to the store, so he could buy cookies and soda. Val and her cousin, Catherine, Laura's youngest daughter, didn't go to the store as much as the boys. They mostly played inside the fence at Laura and Evan's house or they would be inside Mary and Emerson's house. Most of the children were drawn to Laura and Evan's yard because there was a swing set. The yard was always full of children, No one was asked to leave, unless a fight broke out. Only then, would Laura say, "Go home to your mama and daddy, we don't fight in this yard."

There was never any fighting among the Hodges and Mitchell cousins. They could always make things right between them. It has been the same way between the older Hodges and Mitchell cousins. They were going to stand together as they did with their cousins in Comb City, Laura and Evan had eight children. Mary and Emerson had ten. Somehow, they had kept the children in church. Even the older ones, except for Emerson Jr. He said to Mary when he had called her on Mother's Day, "Madea, I love you, but I'm sorry haven't been going to church, as you asked me to." "Emerson Jr. everyone at least goes to church and know they ain't saved." "But I know they might get saved." "Madea, I can't go to church because everytime I go the spirit of The Lord comes over me."

"Baby, mama just want you to get your life right with God." "And stop living with women you ain't married to." "Why don't you marry that woman?" "Madea, I still believe that you not supposed to have only one wife." "Boy, you is living in sin." "Why don't you marry the woman you livin with now?" "The truth is, Madea, she is too old." "And I can't marry anyone as long as Lisa is living." "Madea, you know what Daddy always say." "You know what Daddy taught us, he said the Bible said a man is supposed to have only one wife and read it too." "And a divorce is not right." "I still love Lisa." "My life is all messed up, Madea." "You said you marry Lisa, because you felt sorry for her." "I lied, I do love her." "I know we will never get back together." "Madea, that's not why I called you. "I called you to let you know I got a new job that pays me twice the money I was making in Mississippi."

He told her that with the extra money, he would send her a few dollars once in a while. That was a lie. He did not send his mother any money. Mary was not disappointed. Instead, he used his money buying alcohol. What he loved most was women and alcohol. Mary was glad to hear from her child and to know he was doing well. She still wished that she had moved to Chicago, when her husband had first asked her, She imagined how different her life would have been. She might have had a chance to live in a larger house and that Emerson would have been living in the same place with his brothers, that he might have been as prosperous as she thought they were. Because when they came to Mississippi to visit, in their pretty cars and nice clothes, Rob and Emerson looked so much alike, they could have been twins. Rob's wife was also named, Mary Lee. Mary remembered the first time she met the other Mary Lee that Rob said to her, Mary, this is my wife Mary Lee and she's lighter than you." Mary said to Rob, "I never thought much about my complexion, she looks alright." It seems as though everyone who left Mississippi was doing better than the ones they left behind. This was just a thought in her mind.

She was happy in Mississippi. Most of her blood relatives were still in Mississippi and if she had moved to Chicago she would not have been there for Ellen, or for Joe, Cleve, and baby brother Sam, nor her mother. Her children would not have known her family. Family meant everything to Mary. "Daddy, what do you think we might be doing if we were still in Comb City?" "Wife, we will still be be goin to the outhouse." "Ha, ha, ha." "I ain't gonna ask you what you are thinking about no more." "Oh, wife, I don't think about the "what if', I just think about what we got to do next." "Darnell want to go to college someday." "And I got to git the money somehow." "Daddy, we ain't got no money to send nobody to college." "He is a good quarterback and his coach says, he might be able to go to college for free." "That's good news," Mary said. Just then, the phone rang. It was Laura crying. "Emerson, mama's sick." "They said she had a stroke." "I got to leave Emerson, I got to leave now."

Emerson and Mary went over to try to calm her down. "Wait, Laura we don't know everything." She called Evan at the Paper Mill. When Evan got home, the three of them were praying. The children had not gotten home from school. When the prayer was over, Laura laid her head on Evan's shoulders. He ran his hand through her hair gently. "What ii the john-brown is wrong?" "Evan, mama is sick, I got to go see about her today!" Evan said, "Preacher what is you going to do?" "Me and wife is gonna call somebody." "I can't get no sense out of Laura." "All she's telling me is mama had a stroke, and we was in here praying." "I know a stroke is serious, don't forget she's my mama too." "Preacher, you know I love your mama, but I have to think about my children." Before they could finish talking, Mrs. Wynn, a friend of the family called.

There have been an accident. She told Laura, her daughter's husband, his mother, and three of their children were killed in a car accident. One of the boys were Darnell's classmate. The other two were Jerome and Lee's classmates. Their problems had doubled. Laura and her children left the next day on the Greyhound Bus. Mary, Emerson, Val, Lamar and Lee drove that same night. Emerson was upset over his best friend and his family being killed. Mary wanted him to wait, but he insist on driving. On the way there, the car drifted off the road into the woods and hit a big tree. Emerson and the children were not hurt, but the doctor's told Mary after an x-ray that a small blood vessel had burst in her head. But she would be alright. They drove on to Comb City.

Chapter Forty-two

Difficult Times

They found Laura and her two sisters at their mother's bedside. She was unable to speak or walk. She was released from the hospital within three days and was taken to the oldest daughter's home. Laura stayed behind. The doctor in Pascagoula told Mary, that there have been very little bleeding in her head and that it had stopped. Mary had no after effects. She did have a slight headache for a little while. The headaches might as well have been from her high blood pressure. She said to Emerson, "Daddy my head been hurtin me for a while." "it ain't no bad headache, it jus a slight headache." "Wife, don't you know that the doctors said you should have another x-ray?" "Daddy, the doctors don't know God." "Pray for me." He laid his hand on her forehead and the headache stopped. Mary had the faith to believe that the prayers of the righteous availeth much. She had already experienced the healing from the malaria fever, how her father took her to the church and the pastor laid hands on her, and she began to walk. She also remembered how her father laid hands on her mother's side and miraculously enough her mother was healed. She knew that what man thought was not possible, it was possible with God. For this reason, she and Emerson always prayed together.

When there was prayer going on, the children Stopped talking or playing. Whatever they were doing, they stopped when prayer was going on. Lamar said, "Daddy pray for me." "You know I was killed one time, I don't want to be killed no more." "Baby, when were you killed?" "When you drove your car into the woods and hit that big tree." "Lamar, you didn't die." "And you are not dead," said Val. "We did die." "That boy is crazy, Daddy." Val went into the room to play with her dolls. Emerson told Lamar, "Let Daddy put his hand on you, so you won't die no more." He just rubbed his baby's head. Lamar went away smiling. Older brother Lee was a strange kid. He thought if he could make a potion out of baking powder and water and sit it in a window, and drink it the next day, it would make him as strong as his father. Mary saw the cup in the window. "What is you doing, boy?" He dranked it as fast as he could. "I asked you Lee, what is you doing with that cup and what is that stuff you drank?" "Madea, it was baking powder and water." "Why did you drink that?" "It's gonna make me strong like the cool daddy." "Who is that?" "Your husband, my daddy." "Don't do that, it can make you sick." Lee was always making some kind of potion. Whatever potion it was, he kept it in the windowsill in the bathroom.

Lee also told his cousin, Jerome about his potion and that Judy, Jim's wife had a large nose. Jerome asked Lee, why you talk about her? "Lee, I look at her nose too." "It looks like white people nose." "Jerome, you shut up!" "You can't talk about her." "You were talking about her first." "Yes, I know that, she is my sister-in-law." "I can talk about her, but you can't!" "At least, she's almost like my sister-in-law." "Because Jim is like my big brother." "And my brother Earl is your big brother, too." "So why can't I talk about her nose?" "That don't mean she's not pretty." "You still can't talk about her." Mary and Emerson now have four children in the house. Hue has graduated from high school that May. He is attending the same college as David. Darnell is in the eleventh grade. With two boys in college and Darnell almost ready for college, Mary still wanted a new house.

Chapter Forty-three

A Patient Man

Emerson is pastoring at a church in Biloxi. The people loved him as well as his family. Sister Ruby and Sister Bell were sisters in Biloxi. He also had members in Pascagoula, that drove their cars to Biloxi along with Emerson and his family to the church. Things had gotten better. He was not laid off from work anymore. He had a church full of people that actually paid money in church. The church needed to be enlarged. He put some of his money into the construction and the members paid the rest. He and his family was living much better. Although, he had a Deacon that stole money from the offering pan. Emerson, Mary and other members saw him steal the money. Mary said, "Daddy, you should put him out of the church." "Now, wife, God called me to preach, not you." "What is you going to do about him stealing that money?" "Nothin." "You got to do something." "Wife, when he gets saved, he will stop." "He ain't takin no more than two dollars." "Daddy, you teach our children, if you don't put it down, don't pick it up." "Did you mean money?" "Money or anything else that ain't yours."

"I guess you is going to let that man run all over you." "Wife, every time the money is prayed over in the church it becomes God's money." "He allows the preacher to use some of it." Sometimes it is for the church." "Bills got to be paid to keep the church going." "Man, why do you always give the right answers." "I told you wife, I learned everything from your daddy." "Well, I mean everything I know about the church and the people in the church."

"That man loved God and God worked through your daddy." "I just don't know nobody like him." "If his mind was on something, it was just on that one thing, there was no way in the world that no one could persuade him not to teach the Bible as it was written." "Daddy, I guess we should get some sleep for church tomorrow."

It was a Sunday night in Biloxi, when a large woman came in the church and sat in the back row. After Mary had sung, the woman got out of her seat, walked to the front of the church, while Emerson was preaching, she started saying all kinds of crazy stuff. She said she was the pastor and not Emerson. She went to the pulpit and tried to pull him out. Mary saw that she did not have a weapon. She grabbed that woman as if she was a man and sat her down. She came back again, this time she laid on the floor. Her dress flew up. She was wearing men's boxers. Everyone could see them. This time, the three deacons put her out of the church and locked the door. The next Sunday, the same thing happened again. The police was called and locked her up. They never saw her again. But another lady across the street from the church, came running into the church saying, "Somebody call me, somebody call me from this church." She was crying. Emerson said to her, "No one called you." She said, "I want to become a member." Sister Dorsey joined The Church of God in Christ, she was a faithful member until the end.

Sister Bell's husband didn't come to church as often as his wife. When he came he sat quiet and still and said he loved hearing Elder Hodges preach. Elder Hodges can preach and sing. His favorite song, after preached was "Two Wings Fly Away, Heaven Is Going To Be My Home." When Emerson sang that song, everyone in the church had to move. The power of God was upon him as he sang. His body would be wet with sweat. After church, everyone would shake his hand and say, "Pastor, I hope you sing that song again the next Sunday you come." Preachers did not wear robes in those days and did not bring a change in clothing. At least most of them didn't have robes. Whether it was cold or hot, they went home with the same suit they had worn that day and night, because they have morning service and evening service. He was not concerned about himself, as he was about the church. He just wanted to be a good pastor and the best that God would allow him to be. Mother Hodges had always told her children, as well as Mary, "whatever you do in life, be the best."

Mary's mother-in-law was an example of what she had taught them. She was the best church-mother, mother, wife, and grandmother as she could be to her family. She did not allow them to say that she was the best, she would say, "I'm the best to you, because there is other people who think they have the best as well." "That person is the best to them, but not to you." She told her sons and daughters that your wives and husbands should be the best to you and that you should be the best to them. Mary didn't believe in saying that anyone was the best. When she heard someone say that their preacher was the best, she would say to herself, "they are the best to you."

Monday evening, Emerson's older sister called and said that she needed help with her mother. Laura and Emerson talked to their other brothers and sisters and they all decided that Laura's house was the best place for their mother to five. Laura went to Comb City to get her mother. In the meantime, Ruthshel and Floyd, Judy and Jim, Joy and Zell got together, went over to Laura's house and said to their Uncle Evan they had came over to get everything ready for their grandmother, They cleaned the house, washed the clothes, changed the sheets and towels in the room where their grandmother was going to be sleeping. Evan was surprised when he saw that things had been changed in his house to make everything nice for Laura and her mother. "How much do love y'all?" "Uncle Evan are you kidding us, "they said. "You are the best uncle in the world to us." "We would not take one penny from you." "Goodnight." They all left and went to their own houses.

Mr. Whitehead drove Laura and her mother home. She had a wheelchair with a built-in potty. She wasn't sick at all, she was a stroke victim that could not walk or talk. She spoke a few words. She could say, Yes or No, Lord have mercy, and Jesus. Although, she was the way she was, when Mary brought her dinner to her, she would eat, Smile at Mary and say, "Jesus", then she pointed towards the church. The church was in the back of Mother Moore's house. Mother Moore was a church-mother in Pascagoula, who also brought breakfast for Mother Hodges. Mary called her mother-in-law, Mother Hodges and so did Mother Moore, who was only a few years older than Mary and Emerson. The two of them have been friends for years, even before her husband, Big Hand was killed. They sat with Mother Hodges, while Laura went out and took care of whatever she had to do.

Ruthshel and Joy came often to give their grandmother a bath. Rob, Laura's oldest son, would put his grandmother in the bathtub, because she was afraid that Ruthshel and Joy might drop her, and they might have. Everyone pitched in. They gave Laura breakfast food to cook for their grandmother, as well as fresh fruit and vegetables. There was plenty of help in Pascagoula. Emerson kept her fingernails and toenails cut and cleaned as well as possible. The grandchildren pushed her to church in her wheelchair. During the church services, you could hear her saying, "Jesus." This woman had been faithful to the church and God. In times past, she walked miles and miles on hot sunny days, selling Sweet potatoes pies that she had made from scratch. She walked at least three miles with those pies in a box. She sold them for twenty cents a slice for her church. She washed and ironed white folk's clothing and cleaned their houses. She grew her own vegetables, raised chickens which she sold for her income.

Although she was in a wheelchair, unable to speak, she never forgot the days that the people of her faith was suppose to fast. Somehow, she knew when it was Tuesday and Friday. On those days she would not even drink. No matter how someone try to convince her that she was sick and needed to eat, she would just say, "Jesus" and point her finger toward heaven. She stuck to her faith and what she believed in.

Chapter Forty-four
Family Visits

Mother Hodge's brothers, Moese and Bias came from other parts of Mississippi, along with her two younger sisters, Aunt Beulah and the youngest of the two was Aunt Feo. Aunt Beulah smoked a pipe. She knew Emerson did not allow smoking in his home. When she came over to eat dinner, that Mary had made for the whole family, Aunt Beulah sat down, crossed her legs and it her pipe. Emerson said, "Aunt Beulah, you know better!" "Shut up, Emerson, I'm gonna smoke my pipe." She stood about five feet even and could not have weighted more than one-hundred and ten pounds. The youngest of the two, Aunt Feo, who had been living in Chicago over fifty years had a hearing problem. Feo spoke very LOUD and wore her dresses too short, with lots of makeup and jewelry. Aunt Feo asked Emerson to go to the store to buy sherbet for her. It took him over thirty minutes to walk there and back. He and Mary had to buy a few things for themselves.

Aunt Feo said to the others, "Do y'all reckon the preacher steals?" "No, Aunt Feo he had a long walk." "Where do you think he's at?" "It's taken him a mighty long time." "Aunt Feo, my brother doesn't want your money," said Rose, Emerson's youngest sister. Emerson came in laughing, because he had heard his aunt talking about him, "I don't steal, Aunt Feo." "And my wife don't steal either," "I didn't say your wife, said YOU." "That Mary is too pretty to steal," Aunt Feo said. "I used to be pretty, Aunt Feo, but after ten children I look alright." "You still pretty Mary Lee, with them big ol' pretty legs." Aunt

Beulah was still smoking her pipe. "Aunt Beulah, what did I tell you about smoking in my house?" "Emerson, I done known you since you was a baby, you can't tell me where um gonna Smoke my pipe." "Daddy, leave her alone." Mary pulled her husband aside, "Daddy, she's old and set in her ways." "She's only gonna be here for a few days."

Mary was clearing the table, while everyone sat in the living room. She heard a voice, saying, "Hodges Hotel." It was Emerson's two brothers, Willie and Buddy. "Mary, you got any more of them big steaks that we can eat?" "Yes, I do." Aunt Feo said, "Y'all sit your behinds down, y'all jus got here." "I knew it was you when heard your big mouth." Mary just took two T-bones out of the refrigerator and cooked them for her brother-in-laws. She and Emerson had no problem entertaining the family when they came to town. The brothers left around midnight after visiting with their mother. Aunt Beulah, Aunt Feo and Rose stayed with Mother Hodges. Mother Hodges loved having her youngest daughter who also lived in Chicago, her sisters, as well as her brothers Moese and Bias visit. Her youngest brother, AP had been hit by a train. Her other brother Willie died of a heart attack and her oldest brother Samuel was also dead.

It was only a four hour drive from Comb City to Pascagoula. Emerson was not worried about his brothers driving from Pascagoula to Comb City, he knew the two of them would make it home before morning. Days later, Beulah, Rose, and Feo left. Rose and Aunt Feo went back to Chicago. Beulah went back to her home in the upper part of Mississippi. Laura's house stayed full of people, as well as Mary and Emerson's with family visits. On occasion, Nora and Sam came with their younger children. The two of them were so much in love, they had to go everywhere together. They loved each other as much as anyone on earth could love. They came on overnight visits. Sam would not let Nora sleep anywhere, other than where he slept. Mary and Nora were both pastor's wives and could share information about things that were happening inside the churches.

She said to Nora, "Your brother has a deacon that steals from the offering pan, and he won't do nothing about it." "All he would say to me, is I'm the pastor." "And that God has called him to preach not me." Nora said to Mary, "You remember when your daddy was pastoring and that woman, Sister Morris, who had twenty-one children and no husband, how she had to stand in front of the congregation twenty-one times asking forgiveness from the people, as well as

God's forgiveness?" think that woman," said Mary, "must have had those children by the same man." "They all dressed nice and she lived in a big, nice house." "But this, Nora said, "was between her and God." "The Bible says every child is a blessing."

"Nora, I always say don't ever talk about anybody's children, because you don't know what yours might do." This they agreed on. They knew their children didn't always do as they was told. When Mary took her youngest children to church, they had to sit on the front seat with Mary, the same as the oldest ones had done. This way, Mary could keep an eye on them. Now that most of their children were grown, she didn't have to worry about a thing, because the older one watched out for the young ones. She and Emerson were free to move about and be together. Although, Mary was never going to leave them for a long period of time, even though she prayed for them and with them. Emerson said, "Wife, you need to stop worrying so much." "I can't help myself." "You need to rest more than you do." "Daddy, I'll be alright." He knew within his heart she would not be alright. Maybe, she would be alright with God and that his wife needed to let go and just rest. He knew, he should have put his foot down, and insist that she stop working, but he was not going there! Mary didn't know anything other than work, which she had done all of her life.

Chapter Forty-five

No More Whippings

Emerson was a man with strong will. But when it came to his wife, he was soft. He didn't want to hurt her feelings in any way. There were times when he had to be the man. When it came to disciplining the children, he had a way of making them think without using the belt. He only used the belt when it was absolutely necessary. Once when Jim was a teenager, Mary asked him to go and find him, because Jim had stayed out too late, Mary said, "Daddy, I think that boy is got to be doing something wrong." When he found Jim he was sitting on the grass with other teenagers eating candy and telling jokes,

Jim saw his father standing in the front of him. He said, "Fellas, got to be goin." He took off running. Emerson ran behind him saying, "Wait, boy, I'm gonna beat you back." He rushed past his father, as Emerson tried to Swing his belt. Jim ran home as fast as the speed of lightning. "Jim, where's Daddy?" Darnell asked. "He's up there in the street, lying on his big, fat belly." "He fell trying to hit me!" "Did he hurt himself?" "No, but I think he bruised that big, fat belly." After walking home all Sweaty and tired, he just went to bed and said to Mary, "I ain't gonna look for that boy no more." His stomach was bruised, as Jim said. His brother Willie had told him to stop trying to beat grown boys. "You is hurting yourself." "Them boys ain't hurt." He was right.

Nora and Sam had Come again and stayed overnight. As Nora and Sam was leaving with their small children, Mother Hodges sat in the window waving goodbye. The grandchildren were very helpful. Laura rewarded her children by giving them whatever they wanted to eat. She gave them money if she had it. Someone was always there for Mother Hodges. Bo, Laura's oldest daughter, made meals for the family when Laura was not there. Marie, the next daughter, loved to sew, as well as buy expensive clothing. The next sister, Lou, cleaned the house and was the director of the church choir. Catherine and Val washed dishes. Jerome was very bright in school. He and Lee played together and fought each other's battles. Escoe and Mike played with Lamar. They all came to see Mary everyday. There was as much love between these cousins as there were sisters and brothers.

Evan and Laura were praying with their children. When Emerson came in, Evan was praying quietly. Laura and the children prayed out loud. Emerson came in when they had finished praying, Emerson said, "Evan, that is the sorriest prayer I have ever heard." He and Emerson always had words, but never in anger, "Preacher, I ain't praying to you, I'm praying to God." It was not Emerson's place to say such a thing to Evan. Mary was told what Emerson had said to Evan. "Daddy, I know you's a preacher, but you don't know what's in Evan's heart." "Why do you do that?" "Wife, you know how me and Evan is." "We like talking to each other in that kind of way." "We've been arguing with each other since the day we met." "He is a good brother-in-law."

Mary felt the same way as Emerson felt toward Evan, about all her brother-in-laws and sister-in-laws, even Marge. She loved Cleve, Marge and all of their children. Cleve Jr. would come to see his aunt and cousins every time he had a chance. When he was a teenager, back in Comb City, she, Marge and Kitty were always close. Even when Joe and Kitty moved to Pascagoula, and rented an apartment, Mary was happy to have her brother Joe near her.

Mary asked Joy to walk with her to Kitty and Joe's apartment, while Ruthshel was keeping little Zell. Joy was expecting her second child. Mary said to Kitty, "I hope this is her last baby." Kitty replied, "Let her haw'em." "I had six it didn't hurt me." Joy said, "Mother, don't talk about me as if I'm not here." "Don't think of me as being sick, I have an affliction." "Now, the two of you have fun, I'm leaving." "Mary Lee, do you think I hurt her feelings?" "No, you didn't." "She is the same sassy woman, she was when she was a little girl." "She would have told you." "That little thing should have learned how to close her mouth." "Kitty, our children, at least half of them is grown." "Mary Lee, you forgot, all my children is grown, you just didn't stop having them." "Kitty, you say anything to me."

Joe came home Smoking his cigar. "Mary Lee, see you and Kitty is together again." "Somethings never changed." "The two of you is as thick as thieves." Mary kissed Joe on the cheek. "Joe, I am so glad I am living down here on the Gulf Coast with you." " I miss my big sister." "This is the first time I lived outside of Comb City since got out of the Marines." "I like my new job and the money is okay." "Joe, I wish you would do one thing for me, little brother." "Mary Lee, you know I'll do anything for you." "Okay, come to church with me on Sunday." "That, I ain't ready to do." "Maybe, one day, I'll come." "All I can do is pray for you boy." "You is one of the best brothers anybody can have." "I will be the happiest sister in the world, if all of my brothers was in church." "I miss Dieyall." "He said he was leaving Chicago when Emerson Jr. was up there," "Junior said Dieyall drink too much." "But I think they both drink too much."

"Joe I never thought, a child of mine would be a drinker." "I know it's in the family on both sides. I know my husband got at least one brother that drinks." "I don't know about the ones in Chicago." "I never saw Buddy take a drink or heard anyone say that he drink." "Well heck, Mary Lee, what the hell." "The only difference in them and me is that I drink the best liquor." "They drink that cheap stuff." "Mary Lee, you know he's right." "The money he spends on that stuff, he could be giving it to me."

Joy came back and spoke to her uncle. He pinched her on the cheek as he always did. "Uncle Joe baby, you still treat me like a baby." "You know you always be my baby girl." "Well, you know you better not let my cousin Barb hear you say that." "Awww, heck, Joy, she loves you as much as think you love her." "You're right, Uncle Joe baby, I do love my cousin," "Mother, are you ready to go?" They walked back to Mary's house. "Joy, where did you go, when you left?" "I went to Zell's mother's house to check on Fat Sam." "Why did you bring him home?" "He don't like to leave her at night." "Mother, you know what, she still don't have any dishes, glasses, or plates, or nice pots." "I thought, we were poor growing up, but I never seen anyone with nothing." "She works harder than you." "Joy, you don't talk about your mother-in-law." "If she don't have dishes, you buy her some and anything else she needs." "You is married to her son." "Mother, I love her, I'm only telling you." "Don't tell me." Mary was serious. She believed in loyalty. She knew that Joy's mother-in-law loved her daughter and she was not going to stand in the way of Joy loving her. This woman has always been good to Joy and Mary knew this for a fact, Joy's younger brother and sister were close in age with Zell's baby sister. Val was a year older than his sister, Terry. Terry was a year older than Lamar. The two of them were together a lot. Terry and Lamar had physical fights. Terry would say to Lamar, as they visit Joy and Zell, "This is my brother's house." Lamar would say, "This is my sister's house." "You go home." They did this every single time they came for a visit. The two of them didn't like their nephew Zell. They felt he was taking their place.

There was a nephew before Zell. Now that Zell was born, Lamar had two nephews to be jealous of. He was not jealous of Jim Jr. guess, because Judy wasn't there as much as Joy with the baby. Jim Jr. was tall like his father, beautiful eyes and brown skin. Zell Jr. was light-skin with red hair. His hair was as red as a carrot top. He was not as tall as his cousin. He was the image of his father. Mary and Emerson had three grandsons and no granddaughters, yet, Judy was also pregnant with her second child. She would have her baby two months before Joy.

Laura told Mary, "Joy was going to have the baby in the street, if she didn't stop walking so much." "Laura, I guess she is glad she can walk for a little while." "Mary, what do you think the reason is why, she can't walk every year for a while?" "Laura, I don't understand it." "The doctors can't tell us why." "Mary, it might be that old polio that's acting up." "Laura, we have to pray that one day it will stop." "We have to pray for that old asthma to stop making Mark sick." "We can't stop praying for our children, as long as we live." "Laura, hope that they will keep the prayer going." Mother Hodges could not join in the conversation, all she could say was "um, Jesus, Lord have mercy." Because prayer is what she had taught her children all of their lives. Papa Hodges stood by his wife's beliefs. No one ever said papa was a holy man of God, All they said that he was a good man that loved his family.

Emerson was very much like his father in that way. He was patient, he took the time to listen to what the child had to say, even if it made no sense to him. Mary, on the other hand, patience was short. She had to get her housework done before night. If someone had left their homework on the kitchen table overnight, she sometimes ripped the sheet of paper in half to light the oven from the eye on the stove. Once she ripped a report one of her children had worked on for days. When the child saw the torn paper, he said, "Madea, didn't you know that was my homework." She cried and said, "I'm sorry, I'm just so dumb." "I should know not to do that." "I saw a book and a pencil lying their too." "I'm just dumb." He said, "Madea, can do it over." "And don't say you're dumb, it's not your fault." "I have other classmates that have parents that can't read." "You can read and spell some." "You just don't take the time to look." She did everything in a hurry. She did not get angry with the child, because she knew the child was right. Mary learned not to tear notebook paper with writing, before asking anyone if the paper is any good.

Chapter Forty-six

Mary Realizes that God is in Control

There was lots of things Mary had to learn. She learned that she could not keep Joy well. She had no control over the situation, Concerning her walking and having babies. Joy had said to her mother," hope when I have my baby it will be easy this time." Judy and Jim had a baby girl. When the family saw their first granddaughter in the hospital, Joy said to Judy, "I hope my baby is half as pretty as she is." "asked God to give me a little girl." "Don't worry Joy, that baby is going to be beautiful and it will be a girl," Judy said. The baby was a girl. She was pretty with big eyes and beautiful brown skin. Joy had a hard time giving birth. Her Uncle Sam was in town, running a revival for the pastor in Pascagoula. He was also Joy's pastor. She no longer went to church with her mother and father out of town. Because Zell didn't like his son being up so late. He wanted the baby in bed by eleven o'clock. When she out of town to her parent's church, it would be as late as 2 a.m. coming home. Mary said, "Joy, if your husband wants his baby home early, then you have to have that man's child home when he want him there." "Mother, you are the best mother ever." "What do Daddy think?" "He agrees wit me."

The night before Joy had her baby girl, she had been in labor over twelve hours. Unable to give birth, the doctors thought they was going to lose her. Mary and Irene, her mother-in-law, was standing by her side. Mary said, "Push." Irene said, "Don't push." Nothing was working. The baby was breeched. Elder Ginn, Joy's uncle, along with Elder Grove, Joy's pastor came to the hospital. Mary was carryon so the staff had to push her out into the hallway for her family to see her. Zell did not know what was going on or what to do. Joy said to Zell, "if I diel want Ruthshel to raise my children, because I know she would keep them in church and would treat them as her own." "I don't care about myself." "I want you to please let Ruthshel and Floyd raise the children." "Joy, don't say that." "First of all, you ain't gonna die." "And second of all, I'm keeping my children." Her uncle reached over, put his hand under her gown, over her stomach, and her pastor placed his hands on her head and prayed. Emerson was watching the clock. The nurses took her back into the delivery room. The doctors was getting ready to prep her for a C-Section. But somehow the baby positioned itself, and she was born the normal way. The doctor said the baby was born at 11:58p.m. But Emerson said it was 12:02a.m. The baby's birthday went down as July 24" not July 25", as Emerson had said.

Mary and Irene was standing side by side, Irene said to Mary, "That baby looks like Zell, she got his eyes already." Mary said, 'They is Zell's children, nobody looks like Joy." Irene was just as proud, as Mary and Emerson. Mary and Emerson have five grandchildren. Irene has two. A few hours later, Joy woke up and asked her family, "what was the baby." "Irene said, We got a little girl." Joy looked at them and her husband and said, "I can't believe I have a little girl." "Thank you God."

Mary and Emerson were just getting started with the grandchildren. There would be plenty more to come. Although, she loved her grandchildren, it was too much to have them all there at once, along with their mothers. She was not at all like Idana. Idana has as many as twelve grandchildren inside her house and in her yard. When they misbehave, Idana Spanked them. Mary was not about to spank any of her grandchildren. They got away with everything, and so did Lamar. Having small children and grandchildren at the same time was not easy. She was sleeping more and more. When she was supposed to be babysitting for Joy, she left her granddaughter at the table with a pan of cornbread and a jar of jelly was left sitting on the table. Mary Elizabeth was in her little pink highchair, as her grandmother slept on the floor. Val saw her little niece with jelly all over her face, ran to her mother, "Madea, that baby ate all the jelly." Mary was so afraid, she did not allow Joy to take the baby home. She said the baby might get sick from eating too much sugar. She was not doing her job. Emerson prayed for his little granddaughter. They both watched her through the night hoping that nothing would happen.

The baby girl could talk at eighteen months. Mary felt that this was strange. She would crawl and say to her uncles and aunts, "Y'all better come and get me." "Pick me up." Ruthshel said "There's something wrong with that baby, the way she crawl is, she's dragging one leg. She and Floyd was the second parents to Joy and Zell's children. The baby, Mary-Elizabeth was taken to the doctor by her parents to see why the baby was not walking. Doctor Moore checked the baby out and measured her legs. One leg was three inches longer than the other. No one had taken noticed, until Ruthshel mentioned it. Doctor Moore told them it was nothing to worry about, she would just have to wear a built-up shoe. They told their parents what the doctor had said how their daughter would have to wear a built-up shoe on her right foot. Emerson told them, "God is able to let both legs be the same length." Well, guess it was no surprise to anyone, that Mary Elizabeth began to walk and never needed that built-up shoe. "God is in control, not no doctor", said Mary. "Daddy, God had done brought us from a mighty long way." "That is why we have got to keep the prayer wheel turning." "Wife, you is right about that."

"Prayer is all I know." "I'm glad our folks taught us about God when we were young." "Mama and papa didn't have no money, like your folks." "All we have was love and each other." "Why, you think we didn't have the same thing." "I didn't say that, wife." "I only meant, that was all we had and we ain't never had no house with nice stuff, like y'all." "Daddy, ain't nothing wrong with y'alls house." "Your mama just don't like to clean no house." "I told her I would clean the house for her and she said, no." "Wife, I know you is right." "When I was a little boy, they said company was comin." Everybody was just sittin around the house and it was dirty." "I got some water and I poured it on the floor." "Did your mama get mad at you?" "No, but that was the only clean spot on the floor, after she swept the water away." "Did the company come?" "Yeah, there was a preacher and his wife." "Mama sometimes cook dinner for the preacher." "Her and papa ate with the preacher and his wife." "After the preacher has finished eatin as much chicken as he could, we got what was left."

"Daddy, I know that was in your past, but was there enough food for everybody?" "Sometimes." "You mean, y'all didn't get enough to eat?" "That's about right." "I can say, one thing, when mama and papa went off to take care of business, I cook food for everybody." "What did you cook?" "I would cook two chickens." "Mama didn't know how many chickens she had, and papa didn't know either." "I would put the chicken's head through the hole in the hog pen and the hog would bite their heads off." "Everybody was happy when cooked and got enough food to eat." "One day, Laura wanted to tell, but she didn't know how." "Mama asked us once, what have we been doin?" "Laura said, "Mama, you know the Bible said, when you get some food, you supposed to eat is all up." "I guess she said that, because told them we had to git rid of everything." "By then, we had learned to clean up."

I didn't understand why we have to move so much then?" "But I understand everything now about sharecropping." "And how them white folks cheated the colored folks out of their money." "Most colored folks couldn't count and they was too scared to say anything to those white folks." "Like my money ain't right." "You know wife, you have to be careful, because they might hang you," "I wonder if we colored folks, would ever BE FREE," "Daddy, you know what they say, ain't nobody free in them days, but a black woman and a white man." "The white man was always the boss." "Daddy, I know you work and preach hard." "Wife, I don't always like what they say to me on my job, but I take it because I have a family to take care of." "Daddy, the leaders of the church don't treat you right." "They laugh and make fun of each other." "They be holding stuff against each other." "God ain't pleased with none of this!" "I hope that someday, our children and their children wont have to put up what we put up," "Wife, you know that fella that is havin all them marches tryin to git people to change their mind about black folks?" "We betta pray for him." "Daddy, we got to pray for everybody, even the white folks and God would change their hearts." "Daddy, say, we ain't no better than nobody, and ain't nobody better than us black folks." "Wife, you sound like your daddy." "You is jus like your daddy and so is your baby brother." "That young Sam stands for the truth and he loves my baby sister." "They both is still so young." "He had to grow up quick to take over where your daddy left off.'

"Daddy, I don't know why we is having this conversation." "I know, because it's time." "There's a time and a season for everything under the sun." "This is our time." "Well, alright now." These are the words that Emerson would use he has finished the conversation. The children were all in bed. Emerson felt hungry. He and Mary went into the kitchen and began to prepare their usual hole cakes of bread. The smell of the food would wake the children and Mary fed them as well. Now when Joy brought the children for Mary to babysit, Mary Elizabeth was walking with those little skinny legs. Judy's little Sharon was much healthier looking. Sharon loved her granddaddy, not that she didn't love Mary, but she was granddaddy's little girl. Mary was so proud of her little granddaughters, their being pretty didn't hurt. Emerson was still not a babysitter. All he would do is sit and watch them play.

As they grew older, he would tell them Bible stories and about his childhood. He would say things like, "Do you know you lookin at a dead man's son?' To the girls he would say, "Your dolls is dead." He made them cry and they would punch him on the arm and on his back. "Girls, you can't beat your granddaddy." "Well, stop saying my doll is dead." Mary would say to him, "Stop teasing my grandchildren." He could be very playful with them. Someone gave Little Zell a small baseball bat. Emerson had to take the bat from him and hide it, because he was hitting the walls of the house and breaking up Mary's knickknacks, trying to learn how to swing a bat. Mary didn't like him taking things from her grandchildren. She told him to give the child the bat, take him outside, and show him how to use it. "That ain't my job." "His daddy is younger than me, let him teach em." Zell did not teach him, Floyd did.

Chapter Forty-seven

Determination

Floyd enjoyed the children, as well as he did his younger brothers in law and his younger sister in law. Ruthshel kept a very clean house and did not want anyone to make a mess in it. She had always been clean since she was a child. Mary said she had to change her dress if she got one spot on it. Joy was different, she was a tom-boy. As a child, being dirty was not a problem for her. Mary would have to make her come in and change. They were all visiting one day, when Mary had one of her nervous spells. She said, "All of you go home." "I'm tired, I need some rest." They all left and did not return, except Joy and her child. After Zell had come home from work, he said to his wife, "I want you to stop going to your mother and father's house everyday." She looked at her husband and said, "You don't stay home." "You go wherever you want to." "Can't nobody tell me when I can see my mother and father." "You don't tell me when I can see them and I won't tell you when you can see your mother." She turned and walk out the door with her son and left him with the baby. She and her son were in her mother's livingroom watching T.V. with her younger brothers and sister. Mary heard little Zell call, "Mamaw." She said to Joy, you can't hurt some people feelin." "No, Mother, you can't hurt my feelings, I came back to make sure you was alright." "Maybe I would stay home, and maybe I wont." "Mother, go wash your hair, and let me press and curl it."

"I want you you look nice tomorrow when you and Daddy go to the store." "I got to go to work, girl." "I don't want my hair done today." "Stop, carrying on and wash your hair lady." "Why can't you go home and be with your husband?' "I will, later." "I wanted to show him that he can't tell me when can see you and Daddy." "Now, for the last time, let me wash your hair." Mary had her hair done. "By the way, Mother, Ruthshell and I have something pretty for you to wear Sunday." "I'll go home and be with my husband now."

"Madea, you look pretty." "I like the way Joy do your hair,' said Val. "Is you going to let her do your hair, Val?" "No, she hurts my head." "You know your sister ain't going to hurt your head." "Do you want me to do it?" "No, ma'am." "You make me look funny." Mary did not know how to do the poor child's hair. Val like for Carol, the teenage girl next door, to wash her hair and Joy to press it. Mary loved going to fabric stores, where she could buy fabric by the pound. She brought as many colors as she could for Joy to make clothing for Val to wear to school and church. What was left of the fabric, Joy made little dresses for Mary Elizabeth and Sharon, who they were now referred as May-May and Shay Shay.

Judy's mother came to town to visit. She and Mary met at Judy and Jim's house. Judy's mother was some kind of a lady. She was very spiritual and the words she spoke out of her mouth was always encouraging. She and Mary found out how much they had in common. They both loved their families and God. Judy's mother could sew as well. She made clothing for Judy and Sharon. Mary brought fabric for herself as well. Mary knew how to make patterns out of newspaper. She could sew by hand. She could also look at clothing in stores and catalogs, and could visualize them in her head. Joy had learned from her mother. The gift was passed down to her.

During that summer, Joy must have made over thirty outfits for Val, as well as sewing for others. She charged six dollars a dress. Sometimes she made a dress a day, sometimes two a day. She gave Mary half of the money, and she kept the rest. When it was time for Holy Convocation, Mary would have dresses made for herself and Emerson got new suits. Emerson didn't have new shoes to wear to Memphis, Tennessee. He borrowed a pair of shoes from his son Hue and never returned them. Hue said to his father, "I see you enjoying those shoes." "Boy, them shoes feel so good on my feet, I feel could jump out of a tree." "Daddy, I don't think you should jump out of a tree." "You don't have to buy me any new shoes." "I just brought myself two pair of new ones." David did not have to be concerned about his father borrowing his shoes, because he wears a size fourteen. David has the largest feet in the family, although he, Hue and Jim was the same height.

Jim's mother-in-law came to town again, because of an illness. This woman was very sick and had to be admitted to the Singing River Hospital in Pascagoula. She had cancer. Joy told her mother, that Judy's mother has cancer. Mary said "I'll tell your Daddy to go and pray for her. Emerson along with Elder Grove went to the hospital and prayed for Miss Margaret. There were many others praying for Mrs. Margaret. Mrs. Margaret did not have a bathrobe to wear. Mary only had one good one and she gladly gave it to her. Mrs. Margaret was healed from Cancer. After her healing, she went to church and in her testimony she said to the people, "God took the cancer away from me, but He did not throw it away." " He gave it to someone else." Mary knew this woman was saved and if Mrs. Margaret said, "You have the victory." Which meant whatever problem you have it would be solved. In other words, God was going to bless you in some kind of way. She and Emerson had known, Mrs. Margaret and her brother, Elder Lee Rue Howard, who was truly a powerful man of God, who had been killed in a car accident. After she was given a clean bill of health, she went back to her husband in Tylertown.

Jim and Judy brought a house in Moss Pointe, Mississippi. This was good news to Mary. She and Emerson had also been looking for a house in Moss Pointe. They found one they loved on Eastwood Drive. This house had enough bedrooms for all of the children and a large bedroom for the two of them. They had not had a bedroom on their own since they left Comb City. If they were able to buy the new house, they would give the old ragged house to Joy and her two children and Zell would come over, if Joy would allow him to.

He could finish the rooms they were never finished. When this was told to Joy, she said, "I don't want to five alone in that old raggedy house." "Daddy, I want to move to the new house, if you don't mind?" "Girl, you is a grown woman." "All you got to do is pay your electric bill." "No, Daddy, pay the electric bill in your new house where you are going to move to." She had her father wrapped around her little finger, so did Val and Ruthshel. If it had been one of the boys, he would have said, "Boy, be a MAN." He had never spanked her or punished her, because of her illness in the past. Once and only once, he smacked her with a dry towel, and apologized.

The possibility of moving out of the old house put a spring in Mary's step. She not only had a smile every day, she sang loud enough for others to hear that beautiful voice. She went downtown with her daughters to buy new sheets and towels, so she could throw the old ones away, Ruthshel and Joy said,

"Mother, why are we looking at all these sheets?" "We have more than we need." "You can have them." "Mother, you know I have them," said Joy. "I can bring all of mine." "You should know that already." "You made me give Tammy a new set, after she had told all those lies on me." "Now, Joy, you can outlive a lie," "Mother, I don't have no idea what that means." "Honey, just take your mother's word."

Chapter Forty-eight

The New House

Mary told Mrs. Bradford she was moving. "Mary Lee, I'm so glad for you." "Are you going to be able to come to my house?" "The house is in Moss Pointe, and I ain't got nobody to bring me over." "How about your husband?" "He leaves for work at six every morning." "And you ain't up that early." "Why, I'll just have to come pick you up and bring you back home." "I didn't think about that, Mrs. Bradford." "Well, I did, Mary Lee." When she got home, Emerson was sitting on the back porch with a letter in his hand. "What is you reading?" "My sister, Cele, said her and Buddy had made arrangements to take mama back home." They asked Mother Hodges if she wanted to go back to Comb City to live with their sister Cele. She nodded, "Yes." His youngest brother Will, and older brother Buddy came and took her home. She was happy to go back home. Shortly, after returning home, she had another stroke and died. Buddy's second wife died of cancer shortly after his mother's passing. When his first wife died, his children were small. Now they were all grown. Dot, Buddy's oldest daughter, was the oldest granddaughter on the Hodges side. This is the same young girl who had named Mary's seventh child, Darnell. She had a bouncy personality who wore the most beautiful Smile. Chrissy, his youngest daughter, was beautiful and when she spoke she used the word, "really." Sometimes, she used that word when she did not agree with you or if she was surprised. His sons, Jay and Will were very tall and handsome. Will loved women to death. Jay called all of his cousins, "cuz." These children were no different than the other grandchildren. They loved their mother and grandmother.

Mary had met Buddy's wife Pearl at her father's church. She never called her children, "stepchildren", and they never referred to her as stepmother. Aunt Pearl was loved by all. Buddy, who Emerson loved so much, was alone again without a wife. His four children took care of their father. He seemed to be doing alright, but there was no Pearl. Cele, his older sister kept in touch with her brother. They often visit each other. His children had moved out on their own.

Emerson and Mary wanted Buddy to move to Pascagoula so they could look after him. But those children of his, was going to keep him close. His nieces and nephews were also there for him. He stayed in Comb City. His younger sister, Nora fived only a mile away. Dot and her family lived in the next town and so did Jay. Chrissy and Will visited him often from out of state.

Mary said to her husband, "Now, look who is worrying." "You tell me not to worry so much." "Wife, ain't so much worried like you, um jus concerned." "I remember when we were young, when things got tough, how he would go away. "God only knows where and make money." "The money he made he gave to mama and papa." "Then he would give us all a dollar." "Wife, tell you, them would be happy days." "But, Daddy, he was only a boy." "Yeah, I know that." "He was a boy that knowed how to bring money home." "He was at least fifteen when he started going away." "You mean, running away, don't you Daddy?" "I guess so..." "Before mama and papa knowed, he will be gone again." know one thing, mama stayed on her knees prayin for him." "Finally, one day he came home and stayed." "He later marred that good-lookin Val." "Daddy, he's a lucky man, who had two precious wives."

"Daddy, think you is going to out live me." "Don't say that, wife." Emerson did not want to tell her that God had already shown him in a dream that she was going to die before him, "Daddy, I want to live until all my children is grown, if it be God's will." "Wife, we can't do nothin that ain't in his will." "I wish I had my children when I was younger." "Wife, we ain't old, what you talkin about." "Most people our age is got all grown children." "When Jim was born, remember how sick you was." "I didn't want you to have no more children." "I shore is glad that God done gave us all ten." "Me, too, Daddy." "They been a great help to us." "Thank God they was all able to go to school." "Darnell is almost ready to finish." "Lee is ten."

"Lee's teacher told me, she said, Mrs. Hodges, Lee is always out of his seat, taking care of other children's business." "He says, Miss Brown, those children are not getting their lesson." "I said to him, do you have yours?" "His answer was, "I'm about to do my work right now." "Miss Brown, sent Joy to talk to Val's teacher." "She told me, that the teacher was prejudice towards black children." "Wife, you know Joy is going to tell it like it is, and you won't have any more trouble out that teacher." "As for Lamar's, we would never have worry about him with that big mouth of his."

"Daddy, think something is wrong between Joy and Zell." "Little Zell told me, his daddy ain't there at night." "Joy ain't told me nothin, I know if anything was wrong she tell me." "Miss Bradford asked me to bring him to her house." "I take him to work with me tomorrow." The next day, Mary took her grandson to her job, as Miss Bradford has asked. She and Mrs. Bradford was talking to each other. Mary answered, "Yes, ma'am." Little Zell, said, "Uncle Tom, Uncle Tom." Mrs. Bradford said, "Mary Lee, can't believe that little boy called you an "Uncle Tom." "Oh, he means Uncle Tom's Cabin." "No, I don't." "I mean, you said, yes ma'am to Bradford." "He is too smart, Mary Lee." "Can you say your ABC's for Bradford?" "Yes, Bradford." Then Little Zell said his alphabets.

"You know Mrs. Bradford, I had a friend over one day, he was doing something he had no business." "She said, you ought to beat that little boy." "He said to her, lam so glad I don't mess with other people's business." "The woman, said, "I'll see you later, Sister Hodges." "Mary Lee bring him back tomorrow." "I like him." "He's as cute as a button." He was no longer paying them any attention. He was too busy watching cartoons on television.

When she got home, she told Emerson what he had said. "Wife, you should beat his back." "You beat it." Of course, no one was going to spank this child. Her olderson said, "Madea, we wish you had stayed home with us and not spanked us." "You should stay home now." "Joy needs you." "I know somethin was wrong between her and Zell." "I go down to her house and ask her." Mary asked Joy what was wrong with her and Zell. She said, "Mother, he is going with that old lady next door." "Joy, she is old enough to be his mother."

Mary went to her house to talk with her, without Joy's permission. Mary said, "What is wrong with you? She told her that she wasn't doing anything wrong, because someone had taken her husband. "Mary, said, it is not my child who took your husband." This big, old, nasty looking woman begin to spread lies on Joy, accusing her of his younger brother, Joy came home from work one day, and found blood on her bed, curtains, and on her kitchen floor. She ran to her mother's house with her children. The police was called. The police told Mary that someone is trying to hurt your daughter. "I've seen this kind of thing happen many times." Mary and Zell's mother found out she was using voodoo on him. Irene, Zell's mother went down to the bar with her butcher knife in her purse. She told this woman, "You ain't gonna have my sons trying to hurt each other over a lie."

"My son don't want your old ass." She pulled the knife from her purse. The woman said, "I respect you." Irene said, "Respect yourself." This woman ran from the bar, got into her car and drove away. Mary and Irene worked together and got him away from her. Joy no longer wanted anything to do with him. She and her children lived alone. The woman moved away. Roger, Irene's second son, visit Mary and Emerson, as well as Ruthshel and Floyd. Her whole family loved Roger. He was sweet and kind to everyone. Jim loved to see him play football. Mary said to Emerson, "That is a sweet boy." "And he would do anything for his sister-in-law." He called Elizabeth, his gal and drove Little Zell around with him in his car. Mary felt no difference towards him, it was as if he was one of her nephews.

When Roger was killed in college, Irene and her family were stricken with grief and so was the Hodges family. Jim cried like a baby. Zell went to Texas to get the body and brought back the bloody clothing that he was killed in and placed it on the back porch. Joy could not stand to look at them. Mary asked Joy, did you see this in one of your visions, before it happened?' She said, "Yes." "Mother, why are we talking about this?" "Ruthshel told me, how God had shown someone was going to die, before Aunt Ellen died." "Mother, pray for me." "I don't want to see things before they happened." "God shows you and my other children things, like He do me and your daddy." "If we pray, sometimes God will change things." "Joy your husband comes and talks to me." "I want you to take him back." "It was not his fault." "Mother, please don't talk about him to me." "He been staying with us sometime." "I'm going to make him suffer."

"Joy, that boy loves you." "And I don't want no other man over my granddaughter." "Mother, I still love him." "I promise they would not be no other man over your Mae Mae, because I don't want another man." "Mother, when are you going to stop working?" "I don't know." Working for the Bradfords was her only job now, except for selling church dinners and candy. She and her daughters prepared and sold church dinners out of her kitchen. They sold dinners until they sold out. People would come to her backdoor asking for her potatoe salad. She was not going to let her customers down. She made more until it sold out.

The young people ages 18-30, also sold dinners from that old raggedy house for the church in Pascagoula. Ruthshel was over the choir. That girl could sing! Most of their children could sing, except, Junior and David. They could not carry a tune. Their cousins were also singers. Rob, Beau, Mark, Cille, Evan Jr. and Marie could sing. Catherine and Essco were backup singers. The reason the young people were selling dinners was to buy chairs for the choir stand. They sold enough dinners to buy the new chairs.

Mary said, "As long as they were keeping themselves busy in the church, they would not have time for trouble, but sometimes no matter what trouble will find you." Hue and David were standing on the drugstore corner where all the young black men gathered to whistle at the girls as they pass by, tell jokes, and go inside the drugstore to have ice cream. That evening, a car drove by full of white boys screaming at them. "Hey black niggers." You samboes, go home!" One of the black young men said, "Shut up, honkies." "You red-necks, go home." Someone picked up a bottle from out of the crowd, and threw it, breaking the back window of Mrs. Bradford's car, which her son was driving. Mary's Sons did not know where the bottle came from. But they knew how their parents felt about this kind of situation. So, they got into their car and drove home.

David said, "Mother, we were standing on the corner of the drugstore." "When a car full of white boys came by calling us names that I don't want to repeat." "One of our boys threw a bottle and broke the window of the car." "We did not have anything to do with it." Which was the truth. Emerson said, "I'm glad you had sense enough to walk away." "Trouble is the last thing we need." The next day, while at work, Mrs. Bradford and Mary were cleaning the house. She asked Mary, "Mary Lee Can you ask your boys, if they can find out who broke my car window?" "How would my boys know that?" "My son drove by some of your people." "What do you mean my people?" Mary thought to herself. "Why on earth does white people always refer to black people as "you people"? " mean some black boys threw a bottle and broke the back window of my car." "Was anybody hurt?" "No, but they could have been."

Mary told her boys what her boss had asked of her. "Madea, why didn't you tell her, no." "You know we don't know and even if we did know, we would not tell her." "Just tell her we don't know anything." "And that we could not have known who it was." Mary told her that her boys did not know anything about it. She said, "Mary Lee, I don't know why my son and his friends can't keep out of trouble." "They just young, Mrs. Bradford." "Mary Lee, why could you just say young and stupid." David and Hue decided to stay off the corner after dark.

Chapter Forty-nine
Problems on the Corner

There were not many places for Black Pentecostal young men to go. It was either school, work, church, or a friend or a family member's house and back home. Being young men, they were going to be out if they were not in church. They knew they had to obey the rules that were given. They did not say they were saved or they were going to pretend to be saved. Emerson told his children, never to play with God. These were the words that were spoken to him by his mother, when they were young. "Wife, that woman don't know your sons." "I don't know why she ask you such a thing?" "Daddy, you don't understand how we get along." "We is like sisters." "Wife, if you think that, poor you!"

"Wife, it don't matter how much they say they, love you." "Not all of them, but some of them." "They think, we not as good as they is." "She ain't like that." "I know some is like that, but not her." "She is my friend, and I'm her friend." "Well, forgive me, if I'm wrong." "You jus keep on working, if that makes you happy." "Daddy, I know you and me been used by some of them white folks." "But not her and her husband." "Remember, Mr. Bradford brought Joy her first sewing machine, 'cause we didn't have the money." "Ruthshel went to work a few times in my place and they treated her real good." "And even send her to work for my best friend's mother-in-law." "Wife, you proved your point." He got up from his chair and kicked his leg as high as he could. "I bet you can't kick that high?" "No, I can't." "Remember your age, Daddy, and the last time you tried to put your leg over head and fell on the floor." "I don't need you hurting yourself." "We would never move out of this mess, if you can't work." "You know been tryin to get you that pretty house in that white neighborhood." "And if we get it, you know they is going to move out when we black folks move in."

Emerson was right. They got the house. Mary never had a kitchen, as beautiful as this one in her whole life. Two nice bathrooms, large livingroom, setting off to itself; large closets upstairs and downstair. She said, "This house looks better than the house work in." She thanked God for the house. He had given her, again and again. It would have been better for Val, if Joy and her two children had stayed and fixed the old house, and not take the bedroom that would have been hers. Val didn't seem to mind sharing the room with her brother Lamar. She never said to her older sister, "I wish had my own bedroom." Instead, she showed love towards her sister, that had taken her out of her parent's bed when she was a baby and placed her in her bed. She also taught her to exercise. When Joy would exercise, Val would lay beside her on the floor. Joy said, "Val you can't just exercise, you have to watch what you eat and watch your figure." "You can't eat all of that candy, that you're eating." Val said, "I do what my figure, everyday in the mirror." Joy would do anything for Val, except move out of her bedroom.

There was not enough furniture for the whole house. Joy gave her mother and father her bedroom set. The bunkbeds she gave to her brothers. The rest of her furniture, she sold to her Uncle Joe, who never paid her a cent. When she asked him for the money, he said, "Girl, all the things I've done did for you, and you asking me to pay you money!" "Uncle Joe baby, was a child, I can't remember anything you did for me, except paying me my five dollars, twice when had polio. Since, you not going to pay me anyway, come over to mother's house Saturday and make donuts for everybody."

Joe, Sam, Cleve and James (Die-yall) were all bakers, who worked in the bakery in Comb City, Cleve served in the Navy, Joe the Marines, Die-yal the Army. Mary said to Joy, "Don't talk to your uncle like that." "May Lee, tend to your own business." "I promised to pay her." "That was our deal." "I come to your new house and make donuts for you next week." Those were the best donuts ever. He made enough to last for days. He stood by his sister, with his bow-legged self, with an unlit cigar in his mouth. He was not going to smoke in Emerson's house. "Joe, I want my children to know how you looked out for them when their daddy was out of town working." "You saw that we had wood for the stove to cook and the heater to keep us warm when we were cold." "You brought bread from work and helped me take care of my boys and looked out for my daughters."

"May Lee, you ain't got to tell them nothing." "I didn't do it for nobody to brag on me." "I did it 'cause I love my sister." "I thought, Emerson should have stayed his behind in town." "He oughtta not left that Railroad Shop." "Joe, it was too much pressure on him." "You know, how he was before he got saved." "Yeah, that big fella ain't scared of nobody or nothin'." "No, Joe, he still ain't scared." "It is God, that makes him hold his peace." "May Lee, when you start talkin like that, you gonna want me to go to church wit you." "Joe, you know I'm gonna tell you what's right." "You always do, what's going to stop you now." "May Lee, I got to go." He gave her a kiss and said, "I see you next time."

Chapter Fifty

Southern States Destruction

Mary became an Avon Lady throughout Moss Pointe and Pascagoula. For a woman who could not read, she got every order right. She would make a circle of every product and give the order to one of her children to write it out for her. When the packages arrived, she could bag them and remember what every person had ordered. After Emerson came home from work, he took her to every place she wanted to go to deliver her orders. She earned large amounts of money selling Avon. But, it did not keep her from the Bradford's house.

The weather was changing. It was hurricane season. Hurricane Camille was about to hit Mississippi, Louisiana, Alabama and other Southern states. Mary, Emerson, Laura, Evan, their children and their spouses, and their grand-children and other members of the congregation when to the church to take cover. (Sha-Sha) Sharon said to Mary, "Madea, you know my daddy had a drink in the car and didn't give his children nothing to drink." "He drank it all up." "I get him about not sharing his drink wit his children." "Jim, the next time you better share you drink with your children." In the south, most people call sodas "drink".

The wind was blowing very hard. You could hear the sound of the rain as it fell on the roof of the church. As fast as the wind blew, you could also hear trees falling. Everyone kept their children close. They prayed to God, "Please, don't destroy the church." While they were inside praying, the towns were being destroyed. People were being killed by the storm. No one knew how bad it was until the storm was over. The damage it had caused. There were families that were swept away. In New Orleans, Bay-St. Louis, Biloxi, they had lost many friends. But the old ragged house was still standing, There was a few leakes in the roof. Evan knew no one was going to fix the roof. Evan said, "There was no reason to let the house fall down." So, he fixed the leakes in the roof. It was still their house, except no one lived in it and they had no thoughts of selling it.

The new house wasn't danaged at all. Many people had given money to repair their damaged houses. Someone said to Emerson and Mary, "Why don't y'all go down and get some of that money?" "Say, that the hurricane damaged your house." "You can tell them you lost your food." "They would give you money for food and money to fix your house." They were not going to lie. They knew many people that were lying. She was happy that God had blessed her with this new house. Some of the same people that were lying, were members of the church. Mary loved the store down from her house. She could walk there and back. It reminder her of Miss Nunion's Store in Comb City, where she could buy food on credit and pay for it at the end of the month.

The children loved the area also. They made new friends. The grammar school was much larger. The teachers didn't seem to be prejudice. Things were changing for the better between the races. Little black girls and little white girls were friends and visited each other in their homes. But the little black girls was told to come in the little white girls' back door. Mae -Mae had a little white friend, named Shanna. Shanna and Mae-Mae came running to Mary's house. Shanna said to Joy, "My mother said Mae-Mae cannot come in our front door, she has to come in the back door." Joy said, "Don't worry Shanna, just tell your mother that you can't come in our front door, you would have to come through the back door, and so will she." Mary became nervous. "Joy, please don't tell that little white girl that." "You know she's gonna tell her mama." "Mother, I don't care."

The next thing they knew, Shanna and her family had moved away. Other white families began to move out, and more black families began to move in . The Hodges had saturated the neighborhood. It was a blessing to them to have a home. They even brought a large colored television. No one else in the family had a colored television at that time. On Sunday afternoon after church, everyone gathered in the garage, that had been turned into a large family room. The men monopolized the television watching football games and other sports. The women sometimes watched it with them. Other times, the men played basketball in the back yard. Jim was a dirty player. He was so large, that he would knock his brothers and cousins flat. No one got angry or wanted to fight. They would only say, "Man, you are dirty." "I'm not dirty, I'm just good." "You suckas, got to learn how to play!" Lee was only thirteen, and was probably the best basketball player. He was faster than all of them. He used that left hand to shoot as many hoops as Jim. Sometimes they let the girls play. The girls were as good as they were. Floyd was the funny man. He played like the Harlem Globetrotters. Jim tried to catch him, but he would throw the ball to Lee, who they called Lefty, who always scored and never missed a shot.

They had played so much ball in the yard, that they was destroying the grass. Emerson said, "Y'all gotta find somewhere else to play ball, you're messing up my yard." "You leave my children alone, Daddy." "it's my yard, too." She said it in a way that Emerson understood, that she did not like what he had said to the boys. Of course, he did not have anything else to say. However, they decided to leave the backyard, the put a basketball goal in the driveway after all.

Chapter Fifty-one
A Faithful Friend

Emerson called Mary one afternoon, and told her he was at the hospital. Mary was So upset. Her face has turned red with fear. "What's wrong with you, Daddy?" "I had an accident at work." "I'm alright, I just broke my arm." "Just don't worry, Money is here with me and he'll bring me home." Money and Emerson had a little conflict in religious beliefs. Money was a Jehovah Witness and Emerson was a Pentecostal preacher. Their beliefs did not come between them. Emerson was notable to return to work for two months. This was the second time he had been hurt on the job. The first time, he burned his hand on a hot plate bending steel.

While he was out of work, he had members from his churches sending money through the mail that kept things afloat. He had one lady, Sister Gaynell, who oftens send money wrapped in notebook paper inside an envelope, Sister Gaynell was the same woman that had said to a Missionary, Mother Weathers, who visited his church in Biloxi, Elder Weathers. "You are fat and fine, I believe you are nice and kind." Mary was so embarrassed. She took Sister Gaynell by the hand and said, "Honey, you know Sister Hodges love you, and l know you didn't mean any harm, the lady knows she's fat." "But next time don't tell her that." That very same night after church was over, Mother Weathers, Elder Weathers and his mother were killed in a car accident. After they had returned from church, they received the bad news.

Mary had dropped to her knees, saying, "Lord, why?" "Wife, don't say why, just hank God that they were in our lives." "You never know when you is seeing somebody for their last time." "I believe, they had their souls ready to meet God." "Remember, how his mother rejoiced last night?" "And when church was over, she was still rejoicing." "I ain't saying, that people rejoice like that, when it it time for them to go home and live with God." "Sometimes, people just rejoice." "Well, Daddy, God did use you and Elder Weathers." "I know Sister Gaynell probably feel bad after what she said." "When she comes to me, I jus tell her it was jus their time." The Weathers were missed.

That Monday morning, Ruthshel drove over to Mary's house, and told her Floyd had gotten a new job up north. Mary told her to follow her husband. Floyd left. He would be sending for Ruthshel soon. The night Ruthshel left, her parents took her to the train station. Mary returned home sad. Emerson didn't have much to say. They were going to miss their daughter, but they were confident that Floyd was going to take good care of her. Mary thought to herself again. That she should have left Mississippi, when her husband wanted her to go away with him. That she should not been so foolish in believing, that she had to stay close to her mother, But she was happy now, there was no more gray sunshine, but the sun was shining brightly in her life. She had a beautiful home, nice car, more clothing than she ever had. The children were doing well and no money problems. All of her bills were being paid on time. These were the good times. She and Emerson were inseparable. They went everywhere together, except work.

One day a white man came by selling Bibles. The Bibles were expensive. She knew they did not need a bill. Emerson was very interested in buying the Bible. The guy said to Emerson, "I give you a good deal." He got down on his knees and said, "Reverend I love black folks, I always loved black folks." Joy was sitting on the Sofa, she stood to her feet, opened the door, and said, "Mister, get out, you know you don't care nothing about black folks," "You, just want my Daddy to buy that Bible." Emerson said, "Girl, sit down and close your mouth." She said, "Mister, get out now." He picked up his belongings and ran out of the door. Mary said, "Daddy, somebody is going to hurt my child!" She is too mean.

"Mother, you can not say I'm mean." "I would do anything for anybody." "I don't like it when people try to make a fool out of you." "You and daddy are not very careful sometimes." "You allow people to use you." "I'm not going to let anyone use me!" "That's why I won't let Zell back in my life." "Joy, did he ever hit you?" "No, but I beat his behind." "Now, you sound like J.C." Across the street from the Hodges, was a young man who beat his wife. Whom they have known all of his life. He beat her as often as he pleased. This young woman was very much afraid of J.C. They had only been living there for a few weeks prior. As he was beating her one night, Elder Emerson Hodges knocked on his door. He said, "JC opened the door." "Waita minute, Elder Hodges, I'm getting dressed."

When he opened his front door, Mattie was crying. "Boy, stop beating that girl' "Where is your little girl?" The child was sitting on the sofa afraid to speak. "Don't you know the white folks don't want us out here already?" "Yes, sir, Elder Hodges." "I beat her because she won't do what I tell her to do." "No, sir, Eider, he's lying." "Everything I do is wrong." "Boy, do you love this girl?" "Yes, sir, I do." "Why do you beat her?" "I think he beats me, says Mattie, because his daddy beats his mother." "He says I ain't no better than she is." "JC, can sit down and talk to you?" It was taking too long for Mary. So she went over to make sure her husband was alright. Mattie was standing in the doorway. "Sister Hodges, I am so tired of being beaten, I don't know what to do." Mary talked to Mattie, as she would have spoken to her own daughter. "I know you must love him, but you don't have to stay here and be nobody's punchin bag." "He told me his daddy beats his mother." "is that true?" Mary answers, "That is what people say, she ain't never told me that." "But a real man, don't have to beat his wife." Emerson said to JC, "if you don't want your wife, let her go." "If you keep beating her like this, you might kill her." "Elder Hodges, love her." "Elder Hodges, I don't want to be like my daddy." "Most people don't like him."

"Son, God want a man to love his wife." "The Bible says, man supposed to love his wife as he loves the church." "You should love her as much as you love yourself." "Now, just stop beating that girl!" "That is all I have to say." "Elder Hodges, can you pray for me?" He said a prayer for JC, his wife and daughter and went home. "Daddy, do you think he's going to stop?" "I hopeso, wife." "If he don't, somebody is going to have him arrested." "ask Mattie, if she would come and go to church with us to on Sunday, she said she would." Mattie went to church and never stop going. JC did not stop beating her. She somehow, got him to move out. She and her child stayed alone, until he got himself together, Mary had her own way of getting people to come to church.

Emerson's fame was out. People came to church to hear him preach and sang the song, "Two Wings" and double clap his hands.

Young preachers who wanted to understand the Bible better, he took the time to teach them in a way that anyone could understand. Mary had learned much about the Bible and was able to give advice to many women. The State Mother of the Churches, asked Mary if she would become a licensed Missionary. Mary said, "My mission is at home taking care of my children and husband." She did not understand, she was already a missionary without a license. A State Mother is a woman over all the women of The Church of God in Christ in the state of Mississippi. She was always on the job, telling people to come to Christ and how to receive them in their hearts and how to live Holy. She never tried to get ahead of her husband. She was taught as a child, that the Bible says, the man is the head of the house. She knew how to stay in her place.

Mary sometimes fell asleep during the day when the children were younger and her husband was at work. Someone would say, "Madea, my go with my friend downtown" or anything they wanted to do." Being half asleep, she would say, "Yes." They knew she was not fully awake. When she woke up, and found out the child was not there, she would ask the other children, where that person was? They would say, "Madea, I don't know." Later when the child returned home, she was ready to whip he or she. They would say, "Madea, when you were lying on the floor, you said could go." "You, know I didn't know what I was saying." "Don't y'all ask me nothin when be sleepin." This would happen over and over again. Jim did not ask, he just went and stayed til late hours.

Now that most of her children had growed up and the younger ones are still in school, it was just her, Mae-Mae (Mary Elizabeth) and Little Zell. Joy was at work. Mae-Mae said to her, "Madea, me and Zell is going to tore your house down." Zell said, "Not me, I'm not going to tear this house down." "Well, do it by myself." Mary could not help herself. She laughed so hard that she had to sit at the foot of the steps. "Mae-Mae, if you tear the house down, where would you live?" "I live in my doll in your back yard." "Won't we Zell?" "No, you can't tear no house down, you just a little girl." Zell loved his little sister so much that whatever he was given, he would ask, "Do you have enough for my sister?" And she would do the same thing.

Emerson said to Mary, "You know why them two children is so close?" "No, I don't." "I guess you is gonna tell me why?" "it's 'cause that boy is crazy about their mama." "One day they would get back together." "But, I won't tell her what to do ever again." "If they get back together, it will be their own decision," "Daddy, know they will get back together." "And, you is right." "I did tell her don't want another man over my granddaughter." "Wife, we is blessed." "I pray to God that all our grandchildren will love each other as much as them two." Shay-Shay (Sharon) and Jim Jr. love each other and their oldest grandchild, Michael loves everybody.

That evening, Joy observed Mary. Her mother looked tired and weak. "Mother, are you alright?" "I'm alright." "I'm going to enroll Zell in kindergarten with Jim Jr." "Judy will keep Mae-Mae and Shay -Shay, she and Shay-Shay are best friends." "They never fight." "Shay-Shay is the boss, May-May just want to eat." "Joy, only work one day a week, I can take her wit me." "No, Mother, can take her to my mother-in-law's." "Her father is living there, I think." "I know what I do." "I will enroll them both in the HeadStart Program, while I'm working." "There is your children, do what you want." Mary said, "Daddy, l guess be by myself everyday." "NOOOO, you wont." "Your mama just wrote you this letter." "What do it say?" "It say she is comin for a visit for two weeks." "And she's bringing one of Bobby's boys wither." "Why do mama have to bring that child?" "I don't need to take care mama and a child." "Why don't she let his parents bring their own child?" What she meant was, let the parents Come with the Child.

Chapter Fifty-two

Cousin Cool

Idana and Cool came to town. Cool, as he was called, was the same age as Zell Jr. and Jim Jr. He was much shorter than the two of them. Lee did his best to help take care of Cool. Cool asked his greatuncle, Emerson to give him a dollar. "I ain't got no money, just pay bills." Cool said, "You is a lie, Emerson." Emerson picked him up and sat him on the kitchen table. "Boy, I will spank your behind" "I don't got no money now." "I pay my bills and gave the rest to your Aunt Mary." "My own grandchildren don't talk to me that way! "They know better!" "Emerson, don't spank him," says Idana. "Please, sit down, Sister Idana." "You don't need to be takin care of him." "He is your great-grandchild." "He needs to be trained." Cool did not cry as maybe another child would have done, "That boy, is too manish." "Why don't you jus let us keep him in his room." Joy and the children slept in the room with Val and Lamar, while Idana was there.

Idana and Cool slept in Joy's room. Idana understood what Emerson meant. She was too old to be taking care of a great-grandchild. After ail, she had taken care of his father, when he was a child, as well as his younger brothers and sisters. Mary went to work. Joy prepared dinner and served Idana two porkchops and vegetables. Jim was there with his children and saw her serving Idana. When Mary came home, Idana said to Mary, "I'm hungry, because that gal only gave me a little bit of food." She gave me a little piece of porkchop and jus a little vegetables." "Grandma, said Jim, why did you tell Madea that?"

"I saw your plate." "You had two porkchops with yams and vegetables." "And you ate everything." "Madea, sit down and rest." Mary picked up an envelope and tried to read what was inside. Again, Idana laughed at her. "look, at you, you can't read." "Don't laugh at my mother" " told you before, a child don't go to school on their own." "This is my last time to tell you this." "Madea, don't cry, your mama is WRONG." "All of your life, you have been letting her treat you this way." Jim stood over his grandmother. "Grandma, don't ever do this AGAN!! "Mary Lee, please forgive me." "As long as live, wont make fun of you."

Mary had never been strong enough to stand up for herself, when Idana was concerned. "I do forgive you mama." "Now can we put this behind us?' "Mary Lee, you've always been a good child, I ain't never had to beat you." "Unlike, that sister of yours." "Elder Ginn had to beat that gal's behind so much, it made me cry. "Mama, Jim was the same way Ellen was before he married Judy," "That boy could lie, slip out of church and didn't come home til after two in the morning." "Daddy would beat him, but it didn't do no good." "That boy was WILD!" "It took Judy to tame him." "They look like Muttin and Jeff together." "He knows how to stay home now." "Jim, said Idana, that is a pretty girl with them dimples and that pretty color hair." "Grandma, she must be pretty." "Everybody says so." "I think she's pretty too." Jim said, "Madea, I got so angry with Grandma, couldn't help myself." "I'm sorry, Grandma." "Mary Lee, I never thought that skinny Jim would grow up and be that big man." "Don't blame me for that." "It must be Judy's good cooking." The children were busy playing with Lamar's boxing robot, Zell had a big drum. Jim Jr. jumped through the drums. Good, that the drums were only made of stiff paper. This child could have hurt himself. Mary said, "Jim you owe your sister's child a new drum." "It's okay, Mother," Joy said. Jim was older than Joy, but they act like twins. Even after they were married to other people, they were still close. He and Ruthshel could share things with each other as well. He was a big guy and in charge. All of his siblings looked up to him. His father could always count on him.

He brought himself a new car, when he was first married and taught himself to drive. He never had a driver's license that anyone knew of. His parents were so proud of him. Out of the ten, he would be the only one not to attend college after high school. But, he was the most successful. He had a nice new house, money in the bank, and a wife that any father-in-law and mother-in-law could love. She was a church girl that loved her family. "Come, you little people, it is time to leave." Shay-Shay and May-May never wanted to part. They would be called "the spend the night kids." Because they were always sleeping over at each other houses.

Mary loved her grandchildren, but Lamar was still her baby. Tonight, he wanted grits for dinner. Mary said, Lamar, why don't you eat what already cooked?" "You can have grits in the morning for breakfast." He stuck his thumb in his mouth and sat in the chair. Lamar liked what he liked and no one could change his mind. Idana said, "May Lee, if he wants grits for Supper, give him grits," "As long as he's eatin." Idana cooked the grits for Lamar, Cool ate grits with Lamar. Cool was not a bad child. He just needed to be trained. And believe me, if you stayed with Mary Lee, you would going to be trained. The boys enjoyed running up and down the stairs. Mary had gotten used to her grandnephew. When it was time for Idana and Cool to leave, Mary said, "Mama, please stay a while longer."

Idana felt she had to leave. "May Lee, I got to go home to see about my things." "What things?" "You gave everything away." "Even the money Daddy left you." "Mama, your electricity is off a lot." "SG gives me money." SG is Sam Jr. "That ain't right, mama." "We all should be giving you something." "May Lee, you always been givin me." "You, don't owe me nothing." "I still have a little somethin." "I ain't give everythin away," "All of your brothers give me somethin now and then," "Now, I got to go home." "Bobby and his wife is staying wit me. He pay the bills, too." "Now, who is gonna take me to the Greyhound Bus Station." "Daddy, I'm glad mama come, she helped me with everything."

"She knows how to be a real mother to me." "I raised my sister and brothers." "Now, she is old and understand her much better." "I ain't been the best mother, I done things," "But I did my best and love all my children the same." "Wife, can nobody say that, you don't love your children." "Even when you have your nervous spell, you love them." "Can't you see, how much they love you." "I miss Junior and Ruthshel." "They seem to be doing good and they ain't forgot about us."

Chapter Fifty-three

Lost Faith

Life seemed to be going well. When all of a sudden, Reverend Dailey left his wife and children and his church for a whore. Mary thought he was a dear man. His wife did not know what to do with herself. Mary tried to comfort her. Sister Dailey lost her faith in God and went wild. She allowed a man to move into her house with her and her children. This man became her lover. This quiet church woman, who went to church every Sunday, had told Mary how much she loved God and her family, was now living in the wild side. Reverend Dailey was now living in California with this woman, going to nightclubs and drinking. This is where the whore killed him in that nightclub. His wife and children had to bury him. To make matters worse, she tried to take his insurance money from his wife. She took Sister Dailey to court and testified that they were married in California. Since the record showed that there was no divorce, Sister Dailey won. It was discouraging to know, that So many church people were not living the Fife they talked about. Even the Church Mother had a man living with her. She said that he was only a roomer. Until one day, two sisters went to visit her and saw both of them in their underwear. When this was told to Mary, she was hurt. It seemed to though people she trusted and cared about, was living a lie. The Church Mother later married the man. Mary and the sisters who caught them, never told anyone. They kept it to themselves, because if they had told it, it might have caused others to leave the church and their faith in God.

One thing Mary knew for Sure that God will forgive. He had forgiven she and her husband for every secretive thing in their heart and mind. She could forgive everybody, even her children. They were not going to do everything she thought they would. But one day, they are going to be judged by God, not her. She did pray that her sister, Ellen had made things right with God. So, that one day they would meet in Heaven. She told her husband the thoughts she was having about Ellen and God. "Wife, you wont know until you get there." "We is human." "I hope my papa made it." "He ain't never told me he was saved." "I don't know." "I hope we and our children will make it." "Daddy, we always took them to church and you read the Bible to them regularly." "And, if they don't do right, it ain't our fault."

Mary's father's sister Aunt Fannie was very ill. Mary asked Emerson, if he would take her to the country to visit her aunt. Aunt Fannie had a five million dollar figure and a half a penny face. All of Sam's sisters had great looking bodies and pretty faces, not Fannie. She was truly ugly, but, boy did she have a figure. On the way to Aunt Fannie's house, Mary and Emerson had to make a rest stop. The bathrooms "For Coloreds", was at the back of the gas stations. They were filthy and nasty. No one ever cleaned them. But they were allowed to come into the front of the station to buy food and water. wonder, did they put Black people's money in different cash registers, than the Whites. Black men's money must have been Black. And the white men's money must have ben White. I think not. All the money was GREEN, Emerson said, "Wife, I don't want you to have to go in them nasty restrooms." "From now on, we would just have to hold it, until we git where we're goin." "Daddy, what if I can't hold it?" "You men can go into the woods." "I think, I can do the same, as long as you are there." "No, Wife, I ain't gonna let you do that." "Your Aunt ain't that far from here." "I hope she's still alive when we get there." When they got there, Aunt Fannie was walking around the house, with her two adopted children, Aretha and Caledonia. The young teenage girl, must have had a least fifty braids in her hair. Caledonia was bare feet, wearing overalls with one strap. Aunt Fannie wore a pretty black dress, silk Stockings, earrings and a long black wig. When they saw all this, Emerson said, "Wife, think somebody done pull a trick on us." Aunt Fannie was looking good. "Aunt Fannie, we've been told that you have been sick." "I am sick." "I jus wanted to see my brother's oldest child for the last time."

"All of your brothers been down here already." "I know it costs money for you to get here." She gave Mary an envelope full of large bills. "Aunt Fannie, don't." "You keep this." "I always wanted to give you and that boy somethin." "I already done gave your mama hers and this is yours." "And, I ain't gonna take it back." "Look out yonder, Emerson in my smokehouse." "Take all the meat you want." "I want you all to spend the night." For a country house it had everything they needed. They left the next morning. That was the last time she would see her father's oldest sister. The next thing she heard, her aunt had died. The adoptive son had had a private funeral and buried her in Tylertown, Mississippi, where Grandpa Benny and her mother was buried. "Why, did that country boy do such a thing?" "It was his right, Wife." "Jus try to remember the good ol' times you had wit her." "I'll try Daddy." "When i was young, I never thought so many bad things could happen." "I guess, when was young, didn't think about a lot of things." " I shore didn't think my husband would be a preacher, and I was going to leave Comb City." "Or that I could love ten children, more than I love my brothers and sister." "I mean, love them in a different way." "Wife, you do love your children more." "That's alright." "You also care about other people."

"God put us on this earth to take care of each other." "If everybody loved and Cared about each other and did all the things God told us to do, the world will be perfect." "But, you know we ain't perfect." "That's why you See So much stuff happenin to people." "Daddy, we shore done took care of everybody we could." "Think of all the people we done kept in our house, when we didn't have enough room for ourselves." "How many times we feed people and gave from our hearts." "Wife, when you done did all you can, do some more." "Man, you say the oddest things I've ever heard." "You always know what to say, I guess that's why you is a preacher," "Even though, tell you how to handle the people in your church, you don't listen to me." "Wife, the people in the church, ain't my people, they belong to God." "He let me lead them in the right way the Bible says."

"I won't or try not to tell you how to run the church." "The people is the church", Emerson said. "Daddy, pray for you that you don't stray." "Keep the mind you got and don't let no woman pull you down." "I seen too much of that!" "I thought, all of my life would be spent in some white person's house slaving." "I told Joy so much stuff, things should have told an older woman." "She said, "Mother it is over, let it go." "Don't burden yourself with things you have no control over." "You can't go back." "Your past, is your past." "Daddy's past is his past." "Even me, Mother." "I might be young, but I have made mistakes." "I was so mean to people, I can't go back to that." "If you let your mind go back, you will kill yourself with the "what if.." "She is not only my child, she is my friend." "I know if something happen to me she would take care of my childen."

"Daddy, I worry about Lee." "He take everything to heart." "I done see how he handles himself." "Hue and David is joined at the hip." "They will always stay together." "Darnell keeps things in with a smile." "If anybody mess with his family, you will see the real Darnell." "Val is kind and sweet." "She will always be a lady." "That Lamar, can talk himself out of boiling water." "Jim is a leader." "Ruthshel is the boss." "Emerson Junior learned how to love his brothers and sisters." "I think, know my children." "So, you think you know your children, all of them," Emerson said, "We would have to wait and see." "Lee will be able to take care of himself, Wife." "I bound you that." Emerson would not use the word "bet", because he believed that if someone bet it was a sin. The words," bound you, is the same as "I bet you." Emerson was careful when how he used words. Sometimes when he was upset with one of his children, he would say "You o' monkey," when they were younger. He called someone a "monkey" in Ruthshel's presence. Ruthshel said, "You are the monkey's daddy." "Watch out, girl, watch what you say to me." Once he said to his girls, that he was good-lookin black boy, Ruthshel Said, "Daddy, you on your fourteenth leg." He had a big smile on his face. Joy said, "Daddy, she's making fun of you." "She told you that you were old." The smile was erased. He didn't say anything else, he just walked into his bedroom. "Monkey" was the only name he ever called them. After she told him, he was the "Monkey's daddy", he never used the word "monkey" anymore.

It was Christmas morning, six o'clock a.m. Mrs. Bradford picked Mary up to take her to her house to bake a turkey and make stuffing for her family. She also baked quails. Mary had made her dinner the night before. Mary brought home baked quails she had made for the Bradfords. Her children were not going to eat them. Zell Jr. ate half of one and gave the other half to May-May. May-May, who Emerson called "Lunny Starks" would eat anything. From the time she was a five month old baby, she would not eat baby food. Shay-Shay would say to her when they were together, "May-May, don't eat that." That was the only time May-May would not eat. It was one of the best Christmases the childen had ever had. For the first time, in Mary's life, someone had demanded her not to go to work. Emerson said, "Wife, don't want you to work anymore, want you to stay home and lay in bed as long as you want to." "That girl can make my breakfast" (meaning Joy). May-May said, "Make your own, my mother is not your wife." He picked her up and said, "You pretty little big eyed girl, where did you get all of that sense?"

"Daddy, children get smarter and smarter every generation." "You used to make me get up when was a teenager, and make your breakfast." "And, you know I couldn't cook." "You would eat anything." "Yeah, he will," says Mary. "Daddy, I wish you would not ask me that no more," "Please, let me keep on working." "I ain't gonna make you stop, if you don't want to." "Mother and Daddy, I want to make soup for dinner." "Why soup, Joy, "Mary asked. "Let me surprise you." She made the Soup for dinner. That soup was terrible "What was that "asked Hue. "I called it "Surprise Delight." "It was a surprise, I don't know about the delight." "Please, girl, don't make no more of that stuff." "Why, did you cook that?" "It was a way of cleaning the refrigerator out." "I used all the leftovers that no one was going to eat and put ketchup in it." "I bet the refrigerator is clean." "I washed it inside and out."

The young children didn't mind the bad soup, and did not eat it. She gave them money to go down the street and buy hamburgers. Mary made dinner for Emerson. "Wife, please tell her what to cook the next time." "No more of that whatever she calls it." "I don't know why she just can take food out of the freezer." "Mother, I made that for Zell before." "Did he eat it?" "He sure did, without complaining." "I don't think he wanted to hurt your feelings." "Zell was here again today while you were at work." "He said, his Uncle Dee was very sick." Dee was Zell's mother youngest brother. "Mother, I love his uncle and aunt." "She tells jokes about him and me." "She told me, that Zell told her that I chew tobacco, while he smoked cigarettes." "When I went to visit, she told me that same joke." "What did you say her name was?" "I said, her name was Patricia." "Oh, I remember her." "When I had Lee, she was my roommate." "She was having her first child," "Mother, it's a small world." Zell's, Uncle Dee died from cancer. He was only forty-eight years old. A very quiet man, the baby of the family. He left behind a wife and three young children. Mary could understand how it must have felt, losing a sibling. But Joy, understood why her mother always told her about Zell when he came to visit. Joy was not going to budge. Although, Mary had said, she would not push her.

But, she could see how much this young man wanted his wife and children back. And, what a hard worker he had been. She always told her daughters, you do not want a man if he doesn't have a job. If he can't take care of himself, he would not take care of you. "Mother, don't worry about me and Zell, you just go with Daddy tonight to that old broken down building."

Chapter Fifty-four
Another Child Moves Away

Emerson had rented an old clubhouse in Moss Pointe and started a new church there. He started a new church, because it was not a Church of God in Christ in Moss Point, Mississippi. Each time they went out to the old clubhouse, they went alone. Once in a while, they took Val. Emerson told the other children, "When Val went with them, she wanted to do everything." "She wanted to lead all the Songs, pass the offering pan, pray, she might've preached, if she could." "Daddy, she is only ten", said David,

"Madea, I need to speak to you." "spoke to Floyd in Baltimore, he's a foreman at his new job at Bethlehem Steel Shipyard." "David, you is going to move to Baltimore, ain't you?" "I was thinking about it." "if, that is really what you want to do, tell your Daddy, and see what he says?" Emerson was sitting at the dinning room table, reading the Bible to his children and grandchildren, as he always done. "Daddy, I want to let you know something. "He said to the children at the table, "y'all go to bed now." "I need to listen what David want to say, he got to tell me something." As the children were leaving the room, David Said, "I want them to hear this too." "Let them stay." "Daddy, I'm leaving Mississippi and moving to Baltimore." "Well, David you is a grown man, you go live your life." Mary Said, 'Daddy, everybody ain't going to stay in Mississippi." "Some people is leaving Mississippi, and Some is coming from the north to live here, and they love it here." "I guess, people who go up there, loves it there." "Everybody going to miss David when he moves to Baltimore."

This was a city where Brother and Sister Young had come from. They came to town with their two daughters and they were living in a house next door to a church. There was a bar on the Corner. Brother Young started drinking, and was no longer a member of the church. Sister Young and her daughters stayed in the church. They remained married. She later had a baby, but they both died during childbirth. Brother Young later remarried a lady from the Baptist Church. After they were married, he and she joined the Pentecostal Church, that he and his first wife were in.

His oldest daughter, Ruby became a great pianist and songwriter. She traveled all over the United Startes and abroad, and never left her faith. She remained a faithful member of The Church of God in Christ writing Gospel Songs for herself and others. Her father, stepmother, and younger sister, Kaitlynne also traveled with her. Kaitlynne did not like Gospel songs at all. She had just the right voice for opera. After graduating College, she went to New York to become an opera singer, Brother Young was somewhat disappointed in Kaitlynne, but he knew he could not stop her in pursuing her career. He returned to Pascagoula with his wife and rejoined the church. Mary liked the new wife. She almost had the same personality as the first one. She was not a very good cook. She wanted to satisfy her husband with good food. Sometimes after they left church, she would ask Mary, if she would teach her how to prepare better meals. Mary would bring a dish to the old clubhouse where they were having church.

The old clubhouse was torn down, because it was failing apart and it was too old to be repaired. Emerson was not discouraged. He preached on Street corners and later had a large tent put up in Carver Village, near where his friend Money lived. His children was teased by the other children in Carver Village. They would say, "Your father can't afford a church." "That's why y'all is in this Indian teepee. Many sick people came to have him lay his hand on their bodies and pray for them and their children. Sometimes, the tent will be filled. Other times, there was only a few. In this place, they had no music, only footstomping and hand clapping. Mary heard that Elder J.J. Harris was coming to town to run the revival for Pastor Swane. Pastor Swane was a small man, light-skinned with a dark brown-skinned wife that weighted at least four hundred pounds. Emerson, himself had laid hands on many people that were healed by God. He had the highest regard and respect for Elder J.J. Harris. There was no reason for jealousy.

Emerson knew that God used whomever he pleased. Elder J.J. Harris and his guitar player stayed with Laura and Evan. In those days, preachers who came to run the revival and the pastors who invited them, did not have enough money to put them up in hotels. Mary helped Laura out by preparing dinner for him and his guitar player. Evan, who had been a Baptist all his life, became a sanctified man in the same church with his wife and children. When Elder J.J. Harris came to town, people throughout the city of Pascagoula of all denominations, had heard of him. They brought people in wheelchairs, blind people, who were brought by others to be healed.

There was a young man with a heart condition, who was notable to play any games. After Elder Harris laid hands on him, he was able to play ball with other young men. Before Elder Harris laid hands on him, he was notable to Continue in college or have a job. But, thanks be to God, Eli's life was changed. After Elder Harris left town, a man walked into the same church, who had not walked for twenty years, to thank Pastor Swane for having this man to come to town and heal him. He also told Elder Swane, "He healed me and I know for myself there were many in a wheelchair, just like me that could not walk. Now, they are walking "Hold on brother," said Elder Swane, "it was not the man J.J. Harris that healed you, it was God!" "He prayed for you, but God healed you." "Did you believe, when you came to church that night, that you was going to get well?" "Yes sir, I did believe that." "Well, your faith had a lot to do with it." "Thank you, Reverend." You see, people of other religions called their Pastors, Reverend. But in The Church of God in Christ, they called their Pastors, Elders.

Chapter Fifty-five
The Church Tent in Carver Village

Mary, thought she and Emerson was also blessed by having a man of God sit at their table. Everyone he prayed for was not healed. Mary knew she was not healed from her high blood pressure. She, might would have been, if she would have changed her diet. She had gotten used to preparing food in a certain way, by using too much salt and fried foods. This is the way she had fed her ten children. Now, that the older ones are on their own, she was still frying chicken almost every Sunday and using too much salt for the younger ones. She was literally killing herself with this way of cooking. The food she bought was healthy, but she prepared it wrong. Hue was diagnosed with high blood pressure in his teens. He learned how to control it on his own by exercising and running. Sometimes, he would run has far as Carver Village.

They still had their tent in Carver Village, where Emerson was conducting church services. Someone was killed nearby almost every weekend. People who did not live there, thought it was a terrible place to live. Being a country woman, Mary did not know that Carver Village was "The Projects", nor has she ever heard the word, "projects", until she was a full grown woman. Mary, certainly didn't speak of any place being worse than her old house, that they had let run down after Emerson Jr. had left home. Thanks be to God those hard times are finally over. She had already been told by her daughter, "No looking back." She was looking forward. One day, all of the children will be out of the house. Her nest will be empty. "Maybe, I ought to stop working,

Daddy." "Wife, I ain't gonna talk to you about that." "But, I will ask you, if you want to go to Chicago wit me to visit my family." "Yes, Daddy, that sounds good." "We ain't gonna take nobody but ourselves." "I know, your brother, Rob will be surprised." "I can even see my baby Dieyall." "He won't know how to act, if he see his sister."

Plans were being made for the trip to Chicago, when Rob's oldest son, who had served in the Vietnam War, made it home safely. Booby was killed in a car accident. His mother, Mary Lee and Rob loved their children, as much as Emerson and Mary Lee loved their children. Stories were told to the family in Mississippi, how this really happened. The stories didn't really matter, Booby was dead. Emerson and Laura went to Chicago alone. Mary did not take the death of her nephew well.

She remembered the first time she met him. It was after the funeral of Mother Hodges, when all the family had gathered at Sam and Nora's house. Booby was quite a character. He kept everyone laughing. This was the first and last time some of his cousins had met him. Mary, Emerson and their children stayed at Idana's house. Everyone got along so well. They were all just a big melting pot of love. As many that were able to go to Chicago, Rob and Mary's life was changed drastically. Rob was never the same man. Years later, when he came to Pascagoula to visit his family, he just wasn't Rob. Chuck, Rob's youngest brother, came down on the plane with him, had served in the same Vietnam War with Booby. Chuck was only four years older than Emerson Jr. The brothers stayed at Mary and Emerson's house, hoping that Rob would come around. supposed, as time went on, he might have gotten better.

Mary never made it to Chicago. They continued having church in Moss Pointe, at Darnell's English teacher's grandparents' house, Miss Gibbs was engaged to be married. She and her fiance' had just left the church service. He pulled into the gas station to fill is tank, while she was still sitting in the car. A man walked up behind and decapitated him before her eyes. She jumped out of the car, to help him. The man looked at her, and said, "I done killed the wrong nigger," and drove away. As Emerson and Mary drove up to the same gas station, they saw the bloody body with her laying over it. This was an awful sight. Mary could not get out of the car. Emerson stayed with her until the police came. Grandpa Gibbs also came and took his granddaughter home. They went back to the Gibbs' house and stayed until morning. They, somehow got her to wash the blood from her hands and changed her bloody clothing.

After a shower, she crawled into bed. Her grandmother said, "Lizzie, I'm going to call your mother, because I don't know what to do!" Mary said, "All we can do is ask God to strengthen her and see her through this." They did not have church there, until Miss Gibbs was stronger.

The incident had made the news on television. So her children knew what had happened. Hue and Darnell said, "Madea, you have to take yourself to bed." Emerson (the strong man cried. He could not let his wife see how much he had been affected by the young man's death. He went into his bedroom, to gives words of comfort to his wife. He saw that she had already fallen asleep. He did not wake her. He laid beside her and prayed until he fell asleep.

Mary had never seen anything like this in her whole life. "Mother, I'm so sorry you and Daddy had to see that." "I feel more sorry for Miss Gibbs, they were so much in love." "I could see that." "When went with you and Daddy to their grandparents' house," said Joy. "Mother, also wrote Uncle Chuck a letter and asked him if I could come and stay with him and his wife, until I find a job." "I have enough money saved." "He never answered me." "I also wrote to Uncle Dieyall and Aunt Ree." "They said, come on." "I don't really know why I feel Uncle Chuck cared about me." "One day, I should ask him, why." "I would ask you, not to ask him, but knowing you, you is going to have your say," said Mary. "Joy, why is you going to leave?" "I want to take complete care of my own children." "I will send for them after I'm settled."

"Joy, please don't leave me!" "Will you stay with me, until after Christmas?" "Mother, that is four months away." "I know, but promise you will wait awhile." "Mother, I will wait." "When do go, think I just take Zell with me and come back for May-May, after start working." "Why will you take. Zell, Joy?" "Mother, Lamar is mean to him and I can't leave him here." "Do you think let Lamar hurt him?" "Mother, he is only five and Lamar is nine." "I know he has a way of pushing Lamar's buttons.' "Mother, I know you will take care of him and Val and Lee will protect him." "He lied to you yesterday, when he started that fire." "Joy, he did not start that fire in my front yard." "He told me that the white boys down the street, threw a match on them leaves." "Zell, come here!" "Tell your grandmother the truth about the fire yesterday." "Mamar, I lit that match and started that fire." "OH, MY GOODNESS" "That little thing, had me believing the white boys were trying to start trouble." "Mother, he is a little liar." "Mama, may go?" "Yes, you may go Zell." "Mother, you believe everything he tells you."

Lee said, “Madea, he is a DESTRUCTO TOO!” “If you see him looking at something to hard, you better MOVE IT!” “ Or he will BREAK T!” “He broke your lamp in the livingroom.” “Why did you take the blame?” “Because know my sister would have spanked his behind.” Lamar said, “I hope she does, because he was the one that put my bottle tops in the trash can.” Lamar used bottle tops as people to play games. He played with them after school every day and made hissing sounds with his mouth, as he played. Of course, he collected more soda bottle tops and kept them away from Zell.

Chapter Fifty-six

Financial Security has Arrived

It was the end of Summer, Emerson and Mary was out shopping. Buying school supplies and new clothing for the children to start school. She did not always take the children with her to buy shoes. She had her own way of buying shoes to fit, when the child was not with her. She measured their feet with a string and took it to the merchant. This is the way the merchant sized the shoe and it would be the right size everytime. She could know buy things for cash. She no longer had to charge anything. Emerson said to Mary, "You know things is better than it has been since we been married." "I know what it is to have a little money and I know what it is to have a lot of money." It didn't matter how much money they had, they were not going to keep it. Because, they were forever giving it away to the needy and sometimes to the greedy. Mary was not as willing to give as her husband, but she went along with it. Her father had allowed her mother to give in the same manner as Emerson.

Sam, Mary's father, had left houses and land for all of his children, as well as for his wife, Idana. Mr. Seals, the man with a house full of children, of whom Idana had given money to help him and his wife send their second daughter to college. Mr. Seals wanted to buy a fraction of the land next to Idana's house. Emerson said to Mary, "This fella don't need that land, he is greedy." "As much as your mama done did for him." "He ought to be ashamed to ask her." "You know how mama is, cause you is very much like her." "Ain't we always giving things away?" "Wife, that land is all of y'alls birthright." "What am gonna do?'

"Mama says she needs money." "There is coming Saturday morning for me to sign it over to him."

Idana and Mr. Seals drove down in his truck. Mary signed the papers reluctantly. She and her brother, Sam brought the land back later. Suppose, Idana needed the money at that time. Mary would do anything to keep peace between her mother and herself. Emerson never said anything to her concerning the matter. As long as the land was back in the family, as his father-in-law had intended.

Mary knew she was not going back to Comb City to live. She loved the place because her mother and two brothers, as well as Emerson's family was still living there. But sometimes, you have to move on to bigger and better. Just as her older children had moved away, she knew that it was possible they all might move away from her, except Jim. She felt that he would always be close by. The next day was Sunday, she was up at five a.m., made a cake, collard greens, Sweet potatoe pone (mashed Sweet potatoes with sugar, cinnamon, vanilla flavoring and butter), fried corn, fried chicken and potatoe Salad. "Mother, do you want me to cook anything?" "No, Joy all I want you to do is do Val's hair and git your children ready for church." Everyone went to church. Hue drove his own car, Mary and three younger children rode with Emerson. There was enough room for everybody.

After church, Darnell pulled off his shirt and wore his necktie to the dinner table. He ate a slice of cake Mary had made for dinner. "Thank you, Madea for this nice sweet bread." "It is not a cake." Emerson agreed. "Next time, let May-May make it in her EasyBake Owen." When they had finished dinner, Jim and his wife and children came in. Judy did not eat, but Jim did. Mary said to Jim, "I know Judy done fed you." "I know, Madea." "But it just that save room for your food." "You sound like your Daddy, boy." "He's always got room for more food." "Did you make it to Sunday school?" asked Hue. "You know he did," said Joy.

Jim loved Sunday school more than he loved going to school when he was younger. He ate a slice of his mother's cake. "Madea, what did you do to this cake?" "It is not like the cake you make." "Now, all y'all leave wife alone about that Sweet bread." "I ain't gonna make y'all no more cakes." "I just make pies." "Madea, you know we a were just teasing you." "Darnell is crazy," Hue replied. "Hey, Daddy, do you want to play a little basketball with us?" "Y'all know, I ain't gonna play no ball on Sunday." "Why not?" "We all were in church today," Mary said, "Jim, you know how your Daddy feels about playing ball on Sundays." "You win, Madea." "We're going to wait for Rob and Jerome." "Now that David's not here." "We need all the players we can get." This was a family affair, because there were other young men in the neighborhood that stood around and watched them as they played.

After the game, Hue took his three nephews over to the empty lot next door to the house. They was going to light fireworks. Hue accidently set the field on FIRE. The fire department was called and so was the police. Emerson asked, "Who set the fire?" They blamed it on Jim Jr. The young boy knew that it was Hue. Lamar was a talker, but not a tattle-tale and would not tell on his older brother. Mary said, "Y'all better not go over there, them white folks might call the law on us and we will have to move." "Madea, are you afraid of white people." "I want you to know that we're not slaves anymore, "We can live here, no one is going to make you move," said Joy. "You worry too much." Somebody did call the police already. They had knocked on the door. Emerson had opened it. When they saw him, one of the policeman said, "Reverend, if we knew you lived here, we would not have drove out here." "It's alright, you have to do your job.'" "Reverend, tell your children to be careful the next time." "We know you ain't gonna start no trouble." "But, you do know how some of us white people are, don't you?" "Yes, sir." "Pawpaw, don't say yes sir, say yes." "My mama said, everybody's suppose to say "yes" and "no" to white people." "Go back and watch T.V., Zell." "Who is that little person?" "That is my grandboy." "We can see he's not afraid of us." "Reverend, we're sorry, we have bothered you."

Emerson and his boys cleaned the whole lot. He planted vegetables. This kind of thing he was good at planting and growing vegetables. No one bothered to help him, because this was his project only. Planting flowers in the yard and around the house was Mary's thing. She knew the name of every flower. The yard was filled with flowers and rosebushes. Her grandchildren picked some of her flowers and gave them to her as a present. "What do you do when your grandchildren pick your own flowers and give them to you'? Mary asked her next door neighbor, Mrs. Pratt, "They are the cutest little things I've ever seen, Mrs. Hodges." "Picking flowers and giving them to their grandmother." "Now, how do get them to stop picking my flowers?" "Just tell them you don't have no place to put them and to let them grow, so that others can see them." "And let them know, they can buy you Some out of the store." "Thank you, anyway." "I can't lie." "I just have to tell them to stay away from Grandma's flowers and let the grownups pick them when they are ready to be picked."

If this had been Mary's children, when they were younger, they would have been "whipped" not "spanked." Mary's nerves were much calmer now. Mrs. Pratt had grown children and younger children, Same as Mary. Her oldest son, Phil had married an older woman, five years his senior. They were notable to have children. Gayle and Phil adopted a baby girl. Phil was having an affair. Mary and Mrs. Pratt discussed the matter. She asked Mary, if she should tell her daughter-in-law about the affair. "Mrs. Hodges, spoke to this woman about her and Phil's affair, she is crazy!' 'She told me, she would kill herself, if Phil walked out on her." "Phil said, he was going to call it off." Mary said, "Please don't tell your daughter-in-law, if he's going to quit her," "just hope the woman won't kill herself." "All we can do is pray."

Phil did call it off. The next thing, Mary heard, was the lady went to Phil's house to kill him. She killed his wife, instead. "What could she and Mrs. Pratt have done different", she thought. No one saw this coming. This young woman was mehtally ill and would spend the rest of her life in an institution for the criminally insane. Gayle, Phil's wife, was an only child. Her parents took Phil to court and they were awarded Custody of the baby girl. Phil had to live with the guilt. He sold his house where his wife was killed and started a new life in New Orleans. Mary's daughter had been in a similar situation. Everyone had walked away without any harm. This she had to be thankful for. She loved her son-in-law, as much as Mrs. Pratt had loved her daughter-in-law. Mrs. Pratt was not likely to ever forget this incident.

When there is trouble, it is good to know that it doesn't last forever. Good news is always around the Corner, Darnell will be going to College. They were happy to learn that they would not have to pay any tuition. Darnell will be playing quarterback on the football at Alcorn A&M College. This is the same College, where his great uncle Samuel, Emerson's mother's brother had attended. And they also knew the football coach, Coach McGile. They had known the family from Comb City, whose brother had been killed in the Korean War, where Mary's brother, Dieyall had served. They were happy another child would be attending college. "Daddy, ain't GOD GOOD!" "Look at us!" "Our seventh child is going to College." "Wife, GOD IS GOOD!!

Chapter Fifty-seven

She Believed in Qulity not Quantity

That Summer Mary saved every penny she could from her Avon money. She put it in a large jar for her Son. She wanted him to have everything he needed. She wasn't worried about brand names, she was concerned about the quality of the fabrics the clothing was made of. Mary tried to buy the best so that his clothes will last longer. Mary saved over five hundred dollars. That was a lot of money! The last time they had put money together for a child to go to college, she chose to get married instead. Five hundred dollars would not last forever. Mary would continue to save half of her Avon money. She seemed to be prouder for Darnell, than all the others. Something was different about Mary, she was not holding her children as close as she had in the past. She was learning to let go. She was not fussing anymore, she had a sense of calm about her.

She had heard about a rumor, concerning a preacher they knew, that was having an affair with the piano player at the church. Mary asked the preacher, if it was true. He said, "No." She was still concerned. "Don't worry, Mother, I will get to the bottom of this." "Joy, stay out of it." "Yes, mother." Of Course, she didn't. The next day after work, Joy went straight to the woman's house. She asked her, "Are you having an affair with Reverend Edwards?" She cried, like a baby. "Young lady, I am not that kind of a woman." "Me and my husband love each other." "I know, who's putting that lie out on me." "Come with me." "We're put a stop to this." Sister Randall and Joy drove to this Sister Edwards' house. Sister Edwards opened the door, they both went in. "Sister Randall said, Sister Edwards, I know who told you this lie." "It was Sister Taylor." "She also said, that the new pastor was my boyfriend." "I think, she's trying to get me killed." "I don't mean no harm, your husband is old." "And a man of God." "My mother raised me to be a lady, not a whore." "Honey, thank you for coming." "That old devil, that told me this, is always lying on people." "She's been doing this for a longtime." "Sometimes, when a person thinks they are strong, somethings like this happens." You find out, you ain't as strong as you thought you was." "Sister Edwards, my husband almost left me over that lie about me and the new pastor." "I think, should leave and go to another church." "No, honey don't leave, just stay strong." "I'm sorry, Sister Edwards, I got to leave that church." Joy and Sister Randall left Sister Edwards's house and went straight to Mary's. Sister Randall said to Mary, "I've got to leave that church." "I'll still serve God." "Me, my husband and children can go to y'alls' church, if your husband will have us." "Honey, we will be glad to have you." "I'm not the pastor."

"I say, that because, my husband is always telling me that, when I try to give him advice." "Sister Hodges, I did talk to my husband when the lies were first told on me." Sister Randall was an attractive woman, with a beautiful home and a handsome husband and the children are well-mannered. That night, Mary said to Emerson, "That daughter of yours went to Sister Randal's house and both of them went to Sister Edwards' house to confront her with the truth." "You, know Sister Taylor was the cause of all them lies being told on young Sister Randall." "She told me she wanted to join our church." "Wife, thought they were happy where they was." "They is, Daddy." "I don't mind having them as members, but I don't want no misunderstanding between me and my brother, Elder Parsons." "Daddy, the woman wants to serve God, somewhere where she can be happy." "Wife, did she talk to Elder Parsons?" "He ought to know everything." "I wouldn't want any of my members to leave me, if could do anything to have them stay."

"Daddy, you ought to know about the things being told about that young woman." "Well, wife, she needs to talk to her pastor first." "And if she really want to leave, I'll be glad to have the family as members." After Sister Randall and her husband spoke to their pastor, they decided to stay where they were. "Wife, I'm glad they stayed." "I don't want nobody to think that need to steal their members." "I wish Joy would have stayed out of it." Emerson told Joy that she needs to mind her own business. "Daddy, I did what I did."

"Because it was worrying my mother and I'm not Sorry." "If there's another time, would you please talk to me first?" "Yes, sir, fat boy." "What did you say?" "I said, Big Fat Emerson," as she ran up the stairs laughing. "Wife, I think maybe I ougttta had beat her back, when she was younger." "It would've have done you no good."

Mary looked at Emerson sadly. "You know she loves you better, than she do me." Joy had tipped down the stairs. "Mother, stop being so insecure." "You know I love you both the same." "I've always told you that." "Mother, you have to believe me, when tell you love you as much as I love Daddy." "Who am I always buying and making clothes for?" "Not Fat Emerson." He grabbed her and licked her face. Daddy, please, can't you just kiss me and not lick my face." Emerson licked his children's face just for fun.

He never licked his boy's face after they was seven. He told his boys, "Don't mess with them freehearted girls." "If you do, you would have to marry them." "If you don't want them in the light, don't mess with them in the dark." This was his way of telling them, no babies before marriage. He wished that they would not do the wrong thing before marriage. But as they say, boys will be boys. And they were BOYS. Even though, his children were called "church children", when they were young. As well as Evan and Laura's, Sam and Nora's, they were all called "church children." Although, they knew Some would stray, and some would stay.

Chapter Fifty-eight

Emerson was Respected by Others

Mary said, "All we can do is pray and hope that they would do the right thing." She hoped her daughters would not be the kind of woman, they babysit for across the street, Miss M. had different men living with her. Miss M. told Ruth and Joy, "I don't want you girls to live the life I'm living." "What I'm doing is wrong." "Please don't do this to yourselves." Miss M. had respect for Emerson, whom she called, "Preacher." She knew that he taught against women wearing shorts. If she saw him in the front yard, she would run into the house and put on a skirt.

Emerson never said anything to anyone about their clothing. But she knew what he believed in. He had a friend, Reverend Johnson. Reverend Johnson was known to use his whip, when he saw a woman in shorts. Emerson did not allow his girls to wear shorts. But if they did, the Reverend was not going to use his whip on them. He told his children, "You don't have to be afraid of anyone." "Because I'm your daddy." So when they were young girls, they was not afraid of Reverend Johnson. This was the same Reverend Johnson that was there, the day Joy was attacked from the would-be rapist. He was not of the same faith as Emerson. As a matter of fact, no one knew if he had a church at all. He traveled from city to city, preaching outside bars. Even the grown-ups were afraid of him. He wore white suits, white shoes and white hat. He had a long white beard and carried a Bible under his arm and a whip in his pocket. When he came around, the people put away their alcohol, came out of the bar and put money in his hat.

The man who owns this bar, was a nice fellow that was raising his son and daughter on his own. He also had different women living with him year after year. These women did not come between him and his children. He also had respect for Mary and Emerson. If he had a problem, he came to them for advice. He wanted his daughter to be a lady and Mary was the perfect person to ask. She had already raised two ladies. Val was a small girl, who would someday be a lady. I don't know how he did it, but the children were well-groomed and did not cause him any problems at al. Mary told Mr. Arthur, "Those children should be in church." "Yes, ma'am, Miss Mary." "I'm going to send them." Mary said, "Arthur, I want you and them children to come to our house for a visit."

On his way to Mary's house, he was shot by one of the women. He recovered. After his recovering, he visited Mary and Emerson. Mary told him, that she appreciated him being so nice when he had music too loud, when they lived behind the bar. And how grateful she was when he had turned it down. He said, "Miss Hodges, you and the preacher had been the nicest to us than anyone else." "The rest of them people treat us like we is dirt." "And won't let my children come to their houses and play." "But y'all always made them welcome."

Emerson took Arthur and his children into his garden. Arthur said to him, "Preacher, shore will like to have some of them tomatoes." "Well, boy, you can have them." "But you got a backyard, you ought to plant yourself some." "Preacher, I don't even know how to grow a flower." "All you got to have is dirt and water." He gave Arthur the tomatoes. After Arthur left, Hue said to him, "Daddy, you don't know how to do anything, but grow tomatoes and other vegetables." "Boy, don't you know who am?" Hue jumped across the chair, and said, "Daddy, bet you can't do that!" He tried and failed. Lee pulled his father up by his hand, laughing. Emerson ran after Hue and could not catch him. He knew how to have fun with his children and be the father too. He kept them in line. Whoever that was with him when he had money to spend, got what they wanted. He would say to them, as his mother, Louella would say to them, "Don't tell your sister or brother, if you tell them you start trouble for yourself." "Because I won't buy you nothing no more." "So you have to keep it to yourself." The children understood what their father meant.

Mary tried to buy for all three children at the same time. She should have done the same as her husband. It would have worked, except for Lee, who would have told the others and it would have been trouble. Lee asked his parents for money to buy Christmas presents. One Christmas, we he was seven,

Mary gave him five dollars to buy presents for his sister and brothers. Hue drove him downtown to the Five and Dime. "Lee, what are you going to buy?" "I was going to buy everyone something, but since only got five dollars, just buy something for myself." "I'll buy presents for everybody next Christmas." So he brought himself a toy truck. "Boy, I told you to stop lying to Madea and Daddy." "Hue, you don't understand." "I need much more than that five dollars they gave me." "Lee, understand, that maybe you should find a summer job." He did get a job a few years later, Hue loved his mother. When he got into trouble, or what someone might have said, "God help me," he would say, "Madea, Madea," when Mary wasn't even around. He never gave them any trouble. He loved going to church and helping his mother anyway he could. Mary noticed, that he acted as if he was still seven, following around the house and playing with his toys. He did not have any mental issues.

"Daddy, that boy is smart as he can be in his books and he's crazy about girls." "But he's still a mama's boy." "He won't let go of my coattail." "Wife, just let him be." "All children don't grow up as fast as other ones." "Don't think about him staying to close to you." "There was a time, when you wouldn't let go of him and all the rest of our children." "He will change and then you will wonder what happen to Lee." "And he will become a independent man, that his other brother and sisters will have to look up to." "He is the kind of person that you can depend on." "He's honest, and always willing to help."

It was Sunday morning, the family was getting ready for church. Emerson Cailed Hue, Lee, Val and Lamar down to pray with him and Mary. Joy and her children were visiting her mother-in-law in Carver Village. The telephone rang, while they were praying. In that house, no one answers the phone during prayer. After the prayer, the phone rang again, it was Mrs. Bradford. "Mary Lee, can you come help me today?" "I know it is Sunday and you go to church." "But you have to come and help me." "I have guests coming from out of town." "Daddy, Miss Bradford need me to come to work today." "You ain't goin." "Daddy, she wants me to cook for her." "Wife, I said, you ain't goin!" Emerson had put his foot down. "What I'm going to tell her?" "Come here, wife, give me the phone." She gave him the phone. "Hello," he said. "Who is this," said Mrs. Bradford? "This is Emerson." "Oh, yes, Emerson, have to have Mary to come today." "I have company coming." "And I need her to cook dinner," "Well, we is about to leave for church." He gave Mary the phone back. "Miss Bradford, I'm ready for church." "I can't come today."

"Mary Lee, what am going to do?" "Go to Wayne Lee's Grocery Store, somebody there will help you." "They can tell you what you need." "So, you won't have no trouble cooking yourself." But, Mary Lee do they cook for people?" "I don't know." "But they have plenty of good fresh food." "Goodbye." "Come on, wife, so we won't be late." "Wife, that lady ain't no good Catholic." "Daddy, they go to church early and stay one hour." "And we stay for hours in our church." "That was the first time in our thirty-four years of marriage, you spoke to anybody for me." Emerson asked, "Wife, is you made wit me?" "No, I'm glad." "Because I didn't know, how to say no to her." "'Cause they been so good to us." "You been good to them too." "You know it goes both ways, Wife." "You work for them and they give you stuff." "That don't mean she don't care about you, or you don't care about her." "But when it is time to go to church, then its time to go."

Mary went to work thinking Mrs. Bradford was going to be angry with her. Instead of being angry, she apologized and said, "I will not call you on Sundays." "Your place is with your husband and children." "Will you please forgive me, Mary Lee?" "Yes, ma'am." "How did everything go?" "Did you go to Wayne Lee's Store?" "No, but we all went out for dinner." "I think, we will be going out more often." "Mary Lee, do you and your husband ever take your family out to dinner?" "No, ma'am." "I ain't never been out for dinner." "I ain't gonna ask my husband nothing about taking me out to dinner." "Because he eats a lot of food and we may not have enough money to pay for it." "Mary Lee, he can't eat that much?" "Yes, he can." "Him and his whole family love food more than money." "Don't get me wrong, they love money too, but they love to eat." Mrs. Bradford said, "Mary Lee, maybe you and him can go to some cheap place." "You should try it." "My older children tell me, that they take their family out for dinner." "I won't know how to act, if me and my husband went out." "Where do Coloreds go, when they go out?" "We got places we can go, 1 never went." Mary never thought about going out. All she knew was to cook and serve dinner to her family. After Mary had finished work, Mrs. Bradford asked her if she could come to work the next day. "I guess, I can Come, because tomorrow I was going to do some things around the house." "Well, Mary Lee, come the day after." "I'll drive you home to that pretty house."

"Me and my husband is going to buy the big house on the corner, down from where we're living." "Miss Bradford, that is a pretty house, I've worked there before." "Well, we're almost at your house now." "Do you want to come in?" "Not, today," "My boys will be home soon." "I want to be there to make sure they do their homework." "Yes, ma'am." "I know how it is." Mary got out of the car and waved goodbye She walked around her house and looked at her flowers and Emerson's garden. Everything was growing beautifully.

When Mary walked in the house, everyone was looking sad. Because Van Simmons, Jim's friend, has drowned. He had jumped into the river and didn't know how to swim. They were also upset about the killing of Emmett Till. Although, Van was mentally challenged, Jim never treated him any different than his other friends. Mary just sat there and cried. She said, "Now I know I won't go to work tomorrow." "I'll just stay here and clean my house and go to the fabric store." This was Mary's way of keeping herself from dwelling on the situation.

Chapter Fifty-nine

She Asks Her Daughter to Take Care of the Children

Mary had brought blue laced fabric for Joy to make dresses for Val and May-May. For herself, she brought lilac laced fabric. Joy had finished Val and May-May's dresses. Mary crawled to the top of the stairs and sat on the floor, as she hemmed the two dresses. "joy, know you go to work, Come home and sew for people." " I don't think you going to have time to sew my dress." "Do you think you have time to sew my dress?" "I don't know if I can make it before Christmas, but I'll try. If you can't make it, just have to ask Mattie Harris and pay her twenty dollars." "You pay her twenty dollars, and just say thank you to me." "You're my mother, you can get away with it." The went downstairs at 11p.m. Mary made herself a big plate of Collard greens, corn bread, a porkchop and a quart of ice water. "Mother, it is too late to eat that, you need to stop eating, all that food and going to bed." "Joy, I can eat what I want." Emerson Hodges brought it." "Mother, one of these days, you're going to fall out and won't be able to pick you up." Mary looked at Joy and smiled, as Joy went upstairs to bed. Emerson came home late from the new church, where another pastor had been installed. Mary said, "Daddy, that daughter of yours told me, if I don't stop eating fate at night, was going to fall out and she wouldn't be able to pick me up." "You know l gained weight." "You look the same to me." "I gained two pounds." "Wife, that ain't nothin'. "You got anymore of them porkchops?" "Give me some." They both ate and went to bed.

The next morning, Emerson was getting ready for work, as Mary made his breakfast and lunch. After breakfast, he picked up his lunch, opened the door, and said to his wife, "Do you have a revelation today?" "Man, leave me alone." He kissed her on the cheek and gave her a hug, as she returned the kiss. Joy stayed home that day. "Mother, Zell is paying me to stay home with the childen, you can have the money." "No, baby, you keep it." "I know you will take care of the children, because you are like me." "I was worried, but I ain't gonna worry no more about them," "Mother, you don't have to ever worry about me and the children." "I know how much you love them all."

"Joy, look outside." "You know this is prettiest day, ever saw in my life." "Mother, it is a pretty day." The phone rang. It was Idana. Mary asked, "Who is it?" "It's your mother." She held her hand over the phone, so she could not hear. "I can't let her run my phone bill so high, she calls me every week." "Mother, go on and talk to your mother." "I'll take care of the bill." "Talk to her." After she hung the phone up, Joy says, "Mother, I'm going to clean the upstairs, and you clean the downstairs." "Mother, we will see who will finish first." "Joy, I have the worst headache, do you have any aspirin?" "No, I don't have anymore." "I'll give you some vinegar water." "I think your pressure is up." "The vinegar water will bring it down." "Here mother, drink it down." Mary dranked the vinegar water and laid on her bed. "You can go upstairs now, I'll be alright." Joy took her two children and went upstairs to clean. She heard a loud noise. "Zell, run downstairs and see what your grandmother is doing."

"Mama, you better come down." "Madea is on the bathroom floor." Joy panicked. "Mother, I'll call 911. In a faint voice, Mary said, "Don't." Joy called Hue, instead. He was working downtown. Hue must have driven a hundred miles an hour. Joy was in the bathroom, trying to revive her mother. Hue picked Mary up and laid her on the bed and called 911. "Joy, why didn't you call 911?" "I didn't know what to do." She got a towel with soap and washed her mother's feet and brushed her hair. Hue said, "What are you doing?" "I don't want anyone to see her like this," "She would have a fit, if let her go to the hospital not looking her best." They called Emerson from the shipyard. He met them at the hospital. The doctor said to Joy, "You can lose your mother, she is very sick." "She had a stroke." "God is hot going to take my mother, she said to the doctor." Emerson was standing over Mary crying. Someone called Laura's house. She was away in Florida visiting Beau.

Hue and Joy picked up the children from school. Mary had already told Joy what to buy each of the children for Christmas. Joy went back to the hospital to be with her father. Several preachers were in there praying. Emerson was sitting by her bedside. When Joy saw her mother's baby brother, Sam sitting by the window eating a hamburger. She knew her mother was dying. The family doctor was no where to be found. He was the same black doctor, who had told Joy to go to medical school and he would help her. This was a man who thought highly of Mary and knew what good care she had given to her children when they were ill.

There was a lady named Lois, that knew the family well. She sometimes went to church with Mary and Emerson. She was an employee of the Singing River Hospital. She called the house, after Joy and Hue had went back to talk to the children and explained to them, that their mother may not ever come home again. Joy assured them that she would always take care of them and her father. Miss Annie Lois, said,"Joy, come see about your father." Idana made it there, Hue and Joy made it back to the hospital to take care of their father. "Where is my mother?" said Joy. "You can't see her now." " know she's dead, I have to see her!" She pushed by the doctors and went into the room. When she saw her mother lying there, with her bottom teeth over her top lip. Joy opened her mother's mouth and placed her lips together and just stood there. Until, Emerson pulled her away. "Daddy, Daddy!" as she cried loudly, Hue could not cry. Jim and Judy came. There was no controlling Jim. He always took things hard. "I got to call my sister and brother in Baltimore and my brother in New York, who Mary hadn't seen in years, Emerson Jr. Jim said, "We don't have their phone numbers." "Do we have an address?"

Joy picked up a slip of paper, Jim let met try and call the closest police station. She called Baltimore, and spoke to someone in the police department. They were polite and said they would find them. They knew the area and address where they were living. The next time, the phone rang, Jim answered it. He spoke to Floyd and David. David said, "Ruthshel had fainted and Floyd had taken her back into the apartment." Emerson who was crying, said, "God told me he was going to take her away from us, fifteen years ago." "I asked Him not to take her." He kept saying it over and over. Everybody was crying. Lamar took his thumb out of his mouth and said, "I want to know one thing, are we going to get any money?" "Yes, Lamar, we will." "We have money to bury her," someone said. Everybody stopped crying for the moment. And said one to another, "Where is Lamar going to sleep?" Someone said, "You know how much she love her baby and she might come back and check on him." "Come on, Lamar, you can sleep with me," said Joy. Irene, Zell's mother had picked up her grandchildren, Zell and May-May She held her baby brother in her arms until the next morning. She knew Lee and Val needed her as well. It was December 17", the day Mary died. The next day was the 18", when Mary was supposed to go back to work. Hue called Mrs. Bradford and told her, Mary would not be coming back to work. Because she had died last night.

Ruthshel, David, Floyd, and Rob, their first cousin (Laura and Evan's son) arrived from Baltimore the next day. They all got together and decided to have the funeral on December 21. They wanted it done before Christmas, so that things would be as normal as possible for their younger siblings. Mrs. Mattie Harris made the dress she would have worn for Christmas. When they went to pick Darnell up, he said, "Joy must be sick or something has happened to her." Joy looked very much like her mother. When he realized it was his sister in the car, he knew it was Mary that something had happened to. The older sister went shopping and brought everything Mary had planned to buy for the children for Christmas. Ruthshel also took over the kitchen, preparing meals for everyone. She cooked as well as Mary. Joy was the baker. Val was only eleven. She helped out in every way she could. But the main focus was on Lamar. Idana was taking care of her grandchildren. Everyone was doing their part. Emerson Jr. arrived the next day alone. Everybody was happy to see him.

Chapter Sixty

After Effects

"Junior, Mother was looking forward to seeing you for Christmas." He was expected to come home for Christmas. Joy said, "Why didn't know mother was sick and that she was out of her head?" "I saw her at that morning, washing applies in dirty water." "I said, mother, you can't do that." "Your water is dirty and soapy." "You've just washed dishes in that water," "May-May wouldn't wash dishes in dirty water." Mary said, "My baby is coming home for Christmas." cleaned the sink and filled it with clean water, after washed the apples. asked her, "How is she going to fix them." She said, "I'm going to make caramel apples and cover some with chocolate." "Well, Mother, they are ready, you can finish." Of course, she never finished them.

All of the family came that night. Cleve and Marge, Sam and Nora, and Dieyall came alone from Chicago. Junior sat there softly crying to himself. Dieyall said to him, "I know how you feel." "My mama is dead too." "What do you mean, man?" "She was my mama." "Your mama is Grandma Ginn." "No, Boonie." "Mary Lee is my mama, she raised me." "She did everything for us and mama." Idana stood there loss for words. Marge said, "She treated me like a sister." "No matter what I did or said, she came to see me and she loved jig." Jig was Marge and Cleve's retarded son, as much as she did the others and treated him no different. Kitty said, "She was my sister." Joe and Cleve had little to say, as they sit in the big family room not talking to anyone.

Miss Bradford brought all the food she could find along with her husband. She told everyone Mary was her sister. "Mary Lee helped me raised my six sons." These young men, Mary helped care for. The older two had graduated from college and were married and had children of their own. The second son's wife had supplied Joy with clothing, everytime she cleaned out her closet. The other four Sons were still at home. This white family was like family to Mary. Color didn't matter. Mary's children knew that these people would be there if they needed them. But being Mary's children, they were not going to ask for anything. They rather do without, before they ask anyone for anything. Now that they were grown up, it wasn't necessary to ask Mrs. Bradford or her husband for help. They had good jobs.

Emerson was doing the best he could. But what do you do? When the love of your life is gone? The person who undertstood you better than you mother or father, sister or brother. The woman who bore your children, took care of you when you were sick and nursed you back to health. When someone told you, you couldn't succeed, she told you, you could. She shared your sadness, as well as your happiness. She calmed you down, when you were angry, and said, "It will be alright." She was beautiful inside and out. You would never feel the warmth of her body next to yours. And hear that voice say, "I love you," and you knew she meant it. She would never walk beside you again. Your lover is gone. You would have to walk alone. Her children would be all you have to remind you of her and your memories.

It was the 21st of December, the day of the funeral. All the neighbors from DuPont Circle came. Mr. Brown spoke as a neighbor. He had so many good things to say about her. If his words could have put her in Heaven, she would be there already. After the funeral, was the burial. When the grave was completely covered, Jim laid on top of it crying. His brothers pulled him away. Judy was a true sister-in-law to Jim's brothers and sisters, as Mary was to Emerson's brothers and sisters. They went back to Emerson and Mary's house for the repass. Every room was filled with people, even the kitchen. Sometime during the repass, someone stole all the money from the jar in Mary's bedroom closet, as well as her best clothing and a watch. They never found out who the thief was.

"I often wondered,"said Laura, "Why people come and sit and let you wait on them, when you are the one that's hurting." "All they do is eat and carry food with them." "I don't think they care, whether or not you eat."

"Speaking of eating," Judy said, "Joy when was the last time you ate a meal?" "Oh, my goodness, I haven't eaten since the day Mother died." "I have been drinking juices." "That's why your head is hurting, girl,.." "Sit down and eat something." Zell made her a plate of food and stood there while she ate. His brother Roy, brought the children home. He had taken them to the church, before the funeral to see their grandmother's body, Zell Jr. said, "Mammar has gone to Heaven." May-May said, "Wake up mam mar and come home."

Roy was no stranger to the family. He stayed and told jokes, which took away some of the pressure that they were feeling after the loss. Roy called Emerson, Preacher, Emerson thought of him as one of the boys. Hue, who had not shed a tear, had to be taken to the hospital. His blood pressure had gone up. Zell and Roy's mother and her husband John, had brought more food for the family. Irene said, "That boy needs to cry and let it all out," "Joy told me he has not cried since his mother died." She loved Ruthshel as well as Joy. After Ruthshel had taken the food into the kitchen, she said to Joy, "I love your sister's green eyes." "Oh, yeah." "Honey, I think she is the prettiest thing." water it, Qunie," Joy said. "Child, you ain't got nothing to worry about, you got the body and the looks." "My son don't like no ugly girl."

"Miss Irene, I'm not jealous of my sisters." "Joy, I don't know, that little sister of yours is pretty too." "Nobody's no prettier than my little sister-in-laws, Shirley and Terry." "There going to grow up to be beautiful women, like my Qunie girl." Joy could play with her mother-in-law as well as her father-in-law, John. They had that kind of relationship. Mary taught her children to never brag on themselves. Let other people do that for you. You could not say that for Emerson. Because he was always teasing his children about his pretty hair and his good looks. Out of all the children, Ruthshel looked more like her father. She was the girl version of him with her mother's complexion.

After the repass, the people and the family from out of town left and so did the food. Ruthshel and Joy had to cook dinner for the family and their husbands. The day had finally ended. There was no one there to say, "Go to bed and get some rest." This what Mary probably would have said. So they sat there and reminisced. Joy said to Ruthshel, "Do you remember the day, that you put baby powder all over my face and made me look in the mirror?" "And was too stupid to know all had to do was brush the powder off?" "Yes, Joy, you was a silly little girl." Jim said, "I also remember the day when Madea sent us to buy milk from those white people, across that big ol field and on back, we saw a baby lying on the side of the road Crying." "And we around, the baby was gone." "And we dropped the bottle of milk and ran ...ck to Grandma's house." "Nobody ever found that baby." Junior said, "You know that wasn't real."

"Daddy, do you remember the time Aunt Valma brought me that pretty pair of shoes, and you needed a new pair for church?" "You took my shoes." "That hurted me to my heart." "And you never brought me anymore." "I had to wear my old ragged ones." He started to cry. "Daddy, you know that wasn't right." "Shut up, Boonie." "You always bringing up some old mess," said Joy. David Said, " remember when Ruthshel and Floyd were dating." "Floyd had a cool car and a pink and black coat." "Man, that was the style, said Floyd. "Floyd, that was not the style, I think that was all you had to put on." "Where did you get that coat?" "Man, let's not talk about that."

Ruthshel and Floyd went shopping for food the next day to make Christmas dinner. Junior went out and got drunk, came home and went to bed. Zell would not leave Joy. She was too tired to argue with him. "Where all we all going to sleep?" said David. Hue said, "We're family, we sleep all over the house." "It's large enough." Emerson went to bed. Lamar and Lee slept with him. As Hue had said, they slept all over the house, except for the kitchen and bathrooms. They were altogether as Mary would have wanted it to be.

It was late Christmas Eve night, Ruthshel and Joy had prepared Christmas dinner. When Floyd, Emerson Jr., Zell and Roy came in from the backdoor of the kitchen, they were a little tipsy. Joy had baked a banana cake. They sat at the kitchen table. The four of them ate the whole cake. She turned around and baked another one. They knew that Christmas at the Hodges' house was a big event. Some of the family members would always come by uninvited for desert and stuffing. Emerson was in the bedroom praying. Lamar and Lee was asleep beside him. Sadness was all over the place, yet there was happiness to know that God is still with them. They had their father, who had told them all of their lives, that prayer would bring them together.

They would always miss their mother and no one would ever take her place. But there was younger ones that had to be cared for. Joy knew, she could not leave as planned. Ruthshel, Floyd and David had made their home in Baltimore. They would have to return to their jobs soon. Emerson had not asked anything from anyone. He wanted them to go back to Baltimore and be happy. Because Floyd had a good job as a Foreman at Bethlehem Steel Shipyard, where David worked also. They were earning more money than they had ever earned in Mississippi. Emerson said to Floyd and David, "One day I want to come to Baltimore and also go to Dallas, Texas."

David asked Joy, "Do you think, should come back?" "All the others wants me to come back home to help you." "David, Daddy's lost." "I hate to ask you to come back home, when you already have a good job in Baltimore." Ruthshel, Floyd and David left before New Years. Emerson Jr. went back to New York. Before Emerson Jr. left, he said to his father, "Daddy, I'm sorry for all the things I said to Madea when I was a boy." "I never told her was sorry." "I just said, Madea love you." "You didn't have to say you're sorry to your mama." "She already knowed you was." He laid his head on his father's shoulder. "Daddy, you just don't know how I feel." "We know," said Hue, Hue began to cry. Finally.

Joy took Zell back. She remembered the words spoken by her mother, "I don't want no other man over my granddaughter." "And Zell loves you." She also remembered how Mary kept saying, "Take care of the children." She now realized that Mary was not talking about her children, she was talking about Lee, Val and Lamar. "Daddy, why didn't know what she meant." "Daddy, you said, God had told you fifteen years before Mother died, that she was going to leave." "Yes, know that she was leaving us forever." What now?

We just have to remember the LOVE AND SACRIFICES she made for us and others. How beautiful and what a spiritual life she led. Everything she held dear in her heart was her husband, children, and grandchildren. Emerson said, "Wife loved everybody."